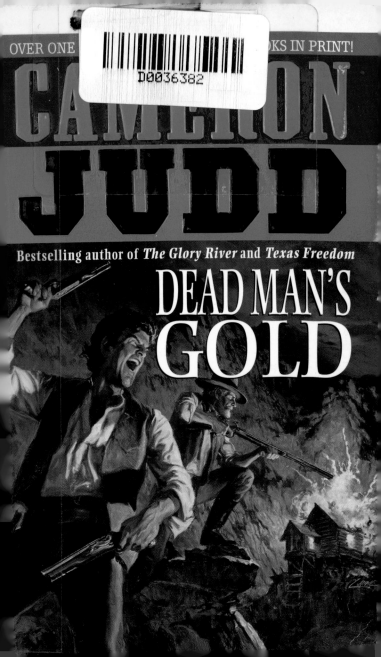

CAMERON JUDD

Bestselling author of *The Glory River* and *Texas Freedom*

DEAD MAN'S GOLD

ST. MARTIN'S
PAPERBACKS

U.S. $5.99
CAN. $7.99

Look for more epic works of
historical fiction, from Cameron Judd
and St. Martin's Paperbacks:

THE UNDERHILL SERIES
THE GLORY RIVER
TEXAS FREEDOM

SNOW SKY
CORRIGAN
TIMBER CREEK
RENEGADE LAWMEN
THE HANGING AT LEADVILLE
DEVIL WIRE

ISBN 0-312-97083-8

9 780312 970833

50599

S EAN

DEAD MAN'S GOLD

He ran as hard as he could, giving it all he had, plowing through the snow like a bull, until he was near the rifleman, separated from him by a line of boulders. He bounded atop one of the boulders, saw the reloading man look up in shock—and Sam leaped, flying though the air with the pick in his hand, swinging down as he descended.

The man had dropped his rifle and gone for a pistol stuck into his belt, but the pistol caught and never came clear. Sam descended and brought the pick down hard, intending to strike with the flat of it and knock the man cold. But the pick had turned in his hand. The sharp, rusted prong of it hit Emmett Fish in the center of the top of his head, dug through bone, and sank into his brain. . . .

ST. MARTIN'S PAPERBACKS TITLES BY CAMERON JUDD

SNOW SKY
CORRIGAN
TIMBER CREEK
RENEGADE LAWMEN
THE HANGING AT LEADVILLE
DEVIL WIRE

THE UNDERHILL SERIES

THE GLORY RIVER
TEXAS FREEDOM
DEAD MAN'S GOLD

DEAD MAN'S GOLD

CAMERON JUDD

St. Martin's Paperbacks

DEAD MAN'S GOLD

Copyright © 1999 by Cameron Judd.

ISBN: 0-312-97083-8

Printed in the United States of America

St. Martin's Paperbacks edition/August 1999

10 9 8 7 6 5 4 3 2 1

FOR JOHN ACUFF

CHAPTER ONE

By dusk the falling snow was thick, accumulating on the ground, the high stone ridges, the windswept conifers—everywhere except on the dead man who lay just below the narrow pass that led into Texas Gulch. Just enough warmth remained in his body to slowly melt the flakes that struck him.

A boy of twelve, Daniel Chase, stood rooted in the snow, staring down at this most unexpected find. He'd been headed home to the mining camp, humming to himself, his idle mind wandering. He'd almost fallen over the corpse.

The dead man was gray-haired, lightly bearded, maybe fifty years old. He looked very peaceful lying there on his back in the snow, as if he'd died swiftly and easily. But to the boy that serene appearance seemed ghastly.

Over in Texas Gulch, a dog barked. A shifting wind brought the scent of woodsmoke to Daniel's nose. A sudden desire to be indoors and away from snow, cold wind, and dead men overwhelmed the boy. Besides, somebody grown-up needed to be told about this. Daniel shivered and pulled his coat tightly around him. Then he cut a wide circle around the body and hurried along the trail and through the pass.

He trotted down the long slope toward the brown, smoke-belching, California mining camp that was home to him and a small but unusually diverse population of mining camp dwellers. The diversity was lost on the boy, who had no other experience of mining camps by which to make comparison. He did know, however, that Texas Gulch was thought to be the highest-elevated, most remote mining camp in all of California, because Crain Brown, one of the miners and residents, had told him so.

The dog Daniel had heard barking appeared. It was Arianna Winkle's dog, not a popular creature in the camp because it barked at night. Daniel liked the dog, though. Its pretty, thirteen-year-old owner he liked a lot more.

"How are you, Enoch?" he said to the canine, pausing to scratch around its ears. "There's a dead man up at the pass, you know it? You ought to run up and smell him!"

As if to obey, the dog bounded toward the pass, a natural gate that was the only known entrance into the three-mile-wide, generally circular, basinlike valley in which Texas Gulch stood. That is, if a shapeless splatter of low, rugged log buildings, which from a distance looked like scabs on the flesh of the land, could accurately be said to stand.

Daniel headed for a cabin at the northern side of the camp. Smoke was belching out its chimney into the gray sky. A fairly big cabin as mining camp cabins go, it was dwarfed, however, by another that stood in the middle of the camp, a virtual dormitory of a cabin built as a common dwelling for the original miners of this place. That had been a group from Pennsylvania who had wandered into the valley while trying to find a new route over the Sierras to the "diggings" on the other side. By accident, one of them struck color, and the group had wandered no farther. They had constructed this mining community, tried to name it Pittsburg Hill, but for reasons no one remembered, the name that actually stuck to the place was Dutch Camp.

The color hadn't lasted long and the original miners moved on. The place once called Dutch Camp was now called Texas Gulch by its newer and much smaller population of eighteen people, a population that was expected to grow swiftly come spring, when the snows were gone and word got out—as it was already beginning to do—that new gold had been found. There was still wealth to be made in the former Dutch Camp, and it was to assure that they held claim on the best of it when the gold season began again that the current Texas Gulch residents had opted to lay in food and provisions, cut massive supplies of firewood, and brave out the high Sierra winter rather than escape for the season to the warmer foothills below.

Daniel shoved the door open and walked in, bringing snow and wind with him, evoking howls of protest from four miners who were gathered around a table, playing cards. A pleasant fire roared in a big stone fireplace at one end of the cabin, though more than half the heat was going up the chimney with the smoke.

"There's a dead man up in the pass," Daniel announced from the open doorway.

"Close that door!" Sam Underhill bellowed.

Daniel obeyed. "There's a dead man up in the pass," he repeated.

"Fool boy!" one of the others, a surly man named Herbert Colfax, older than the other three miners, mumbled beneath his breath as he closed the lid on an ivory snuffbox he'd been using just as Daniel opened the door. "That wind almost blew away my snuff."

"I said that there's a dead man up in the pass," Daniel repeated yet again, a little louder.

"Oh, I'm sure there is," Colfax replied. "And what was it you said you saw back in the valley last week? A tiger, I think? And let's see . . . what work did you tell me your late father was in, before he took to mining? Vice president of the United States, you said. Yep, that was it. So I have every reason to believe you when you say there's a dead man in the pass." He winked across the table at Hiram Linfoot, another of the card players. "I'll bet it was that tiger what got the poor devil, you reckon, Hiram?"

Hiram and Ben Dillow, the fourth card player, laughed. Sam Underhill didn't.

"Daniel, this is just one of your tales, ain't it?" asked Underhill, a sandy-haired man who looked younger than his thirty-five years and was considered quite handsome by the ladies. He'd been quite proud of his looks in more youthful days, but he didn't dwell much on such things now that he was a little older.

"No," Daniel said. "There's really a dead man."

"Let's play cards," Colfax grumbled.

"Just hold on, Herbert," Sam said. "Daniel, you really do mean what you say?"

"Yes! I swear. How many times I got to say it?"

"The boy lies every time he talks, Sam," Colfax said. "He'll make a congressman before you know it. Maybe president."

"I think maybe he's telling the truth," Sam said.

"He'll get you up there, then laugh at you for having believed him," said Dillow, Sam's mining partner and fellow resident of this cabin.

"I'm not lying," Daniel said. "There's a man lying dead in the snow. It melts when it hits him."

Sam thought about that. "Then maybe that man's not dead yet." He laid down the cards and stood. "Will you show me the man, Daniel?"

"Yes."

"Underhill, are you really going out there?" Colfax asked.

"Yep. Why don't you come with me?"

"Think I'll stay."

"Come on, Herbert. In fact, all of you come. If there's really a man hurt or dead up there, I'll need help getting him down here. We can't just assume Daniel's telling a story."

"There's no dead man. The boy's a liar."

Daniel was almost in tears. "I'm not! I'm *not*! This time it's the truth!"

"It better be, Daniel," Sam said. "Come on, men. Just in case there's really somebody needing help."

Sam took his heavy bearskin coat from a wall peg, put it on, and slipped his slouch hat into place atop the thick and sandy hair of his head. He pulled a scarf-sized scrap of cloth out of his coat pocket and tied the hat in place, pulling the sides of the brim down like flaps over his ears. The other card players didn't budge.

Perturbed, Sam said, "Lead on, Daniel. You and me will go look even if nobody else will. Ben, I'm surprised that you, at least, won't come with me."

Dillow sighed and stood. "What the devil," he said, and went for his own coat and hat.

Hiram Linfoot got up and readied himself as well.

Colfax, outnumbered and facing the prospect of nothing to play but solitaire, stood with a sigh. "Hang and bury you, Sam Underhill. Hang and bury all of you. I'll come too, if for no more reason than to laugh when the little liar shows you for the fools you are."

Less than an hour later, Colfax was gazing at the corpse he'd just helped haul in, scratching his beard, and trying hard to catch his breath. Being several years older than most of the other prospectors, he tired easily. Despite his gasping, he continued to pace back and forth swiftly, unusually wrought up.

Laid out on the puncheon floor of the Underhill-Dillow cabin, the dead man looked even more placid than he had out in the weather. And more gray. His body had grown colder since Daniel had first seen him.

Dillow, whose experience raising, tending, and doctoring cattle and horses back in Kentucky as a very young man made him the closest thing the mining camp had to a physician, was examining the dead man closely, opening the shirt and studying the chest, lifting the eyelids and staring at the marbled eyes, peering inside the mouth and feeling around the back of the neck. Sam Underhill didn't know just what Dillow was looking for and wasn't sure that Dillow did, either.

"What do you reckon, Ben?" Sam asked.

Dillow reared back on his haunches and shook his head. "Don't know. I see no signs of violence. He ain't been shot or stabbed, and there's no unusual bruises to make me think he was beat."

"Natural death, then?"

"Believe so. Probably his heart gave out on him. I knew a man back when I was a boy who died climbing up a steep hill in the snow. It strains the heart something fierce."

"Why do you reckon he was coming here at this time of year, with the snows setting in?" asked Linfoot.

"Maybe he wasn't coming here," Dillow said. "Maybe he was just passing by."

Colfax, pacing back and forth very fast, snorted. "This ain't the kind of place a man passes by. We ain't located in the heart of Boston, you know."

Dillow eyed Colfax. "Why are you so nervous? Why are you pacing that way? You need to go out and drain your bladder or something?"

Sam Underhill said, "Ben, we've got a lady present." This was true; the bringing in of a dead stranger had drawn several other Texas Gulch residents to the Underhill-Dillow cabin, among them the lovely Marica Bolton, whom Ben Dillow liked quite well but was always managing to offend. It was a rarity for a mining camp to have any females—any of of the unsullied variety, anyway—but Texas Gulch had five, all of them of good repute. Sam continued, "All we'll be able to do for this man is give him a decent burial, and if we can, determine who he is and where he's from so we can notify his people."

"You search him, Sam," Dillow said, standing. "You're the man of the law here."

"That was back in Texas," Sam said. Indeed, back in the town of Underhill, founded by and named for Sam's famous father, Bushrod Underhill, the unwilling inheritor of the late Davy Crockett's mantle of peerless American frontiersman, Sam had been town marshal before he joined the rush to

California. "I don't suppose we have any *real* law in Texas Gulch."

"We don't have any real doctor, either, but I still have to do the job. Now do yours."

Given Marica Bolton's presence, Sam didn't fully undress the corpse. He did conduct a search of the dead man's clothes, but found no identification upon him. In the pockets he found a comb, a folding knife, a tinderbox, a matchblock, a snuff box, and a few scraps of paper with meaningless personal notes on them . . . but no name, nothing to indicate from whence this man had come, or why.

"Well, that's that," Sam said. "Unless somebody comes along asking after him and can identify him before he rots, we're not going to know a thing about him."

"Just a prospector looking for a new strike and a new dream, probably," said Kish Fleenor, a Texas Gulch prospector with a melancholy air, rather high voice, and philosophical bent. He wrote poetry, which he thought was a secret, though in fact everyone knew it. Colfax in particular despised him, but then, Colfax tended to despise everyone in varying measure.

Sam examined the dead man's hands. "No calluses on the hands. Soft. If he was a prospector, he hadn't gotten started yet."

"Look at the ring he's wearing," Marica said. She was the daughter of Art Bolton, a widower and Texas Gulch prospector who stood at her side. About twenty years old and quite pretty, Marica was the most idolized woman in Texas Gulch. The other females, none of whom were present at the moment, were Herbert Colfax's wife, America, and their plump and plain daughter, Letitia, whom everyone felt sorry for because she'd inherited her mother's unfortunate looks and her father's sour disposition, and the young widow Leora Winkle—whose husband had suffered a fit, fallen into a stream he was panning, and drowned the prior summer. Last and youngest of all was Arianna, Leora's thirteen-year-old daughter and the object of young Daniel Chase's undying affection.

Sam lifted the dead man's left hand and examined the ring. It was a plain, inexpensive band, widened at one point with a meaningless decorative scribble on it. Sam slipped it off and looked inside it, hoping to see a name inscribed, but there was none.

He held out the ring to Marica. "I suppose there's nothing wrong with you taking it, if you want."

She shook her head. "I'd as soon not wear a dead man's ring."

"I'd like it," Daniel Chase quickly said.

Sam handed Daniel the ring. "Here. Keep it in memory of our dead and unknown friend."

The boy slipped it on his ring finger, found it too loose, and twisted it onto his middle finger instead.

"It's sad that a man dies and is forgotten so thoroughly," said Kish Fleenor.

"It is," Sam agreed.

"Like a flower cut down in mid-blossom," Fleenor went on. "A gourd plucked too early from the vine."

"Bosh! There's men who die in the camps every day and are forgotten," said Colfax, speaking fast and restless. He was still pacing and nervous. "No reason to gush over this one. The way I figure it, he'd probably have come in and found the strike that should have gone to me. Good riddance to unwanted competition, I say. 'A gourd plucked too early from the vine.' Have mercy!"

"Colfax," Dillow said, "is talking out your backside a trick you had to teach yourself, or does it just run in your family as a gift of nature?"

"Ben, dang it," Sam scolded, "remember the lady!"

"Blast!" Colfax boomed abruptly and rather dramatically, stopping his pacing and patting about on his torso. "I've lost my pocket watch! I dropped it up there where the dead man was, I'll wager. Of all the bad luck!"

"If you dropped it up there, you may not find it until springtime," Sam said.

"Oh, I'll find it. I'll go right now and get it."

"I'll go with you," Bolton said. "It's dark now, and we'll need torches."

"Don't need any help, thank you," Colfax said sharply. He made his exit with a grand flurry and stomped off through the snow.

"What's the matter with that old goat?" Dillow asked. "He's acting even more peculiar than usual."

"I know," Sam said. "He was acting odd even when we found this body. He stayed off by himself, in the dark."

"Yeah. I noticed that."

"When will we bury this fellow, Sam?" Art Bolton asked.

"In the morning," Sam replied. "In the meantime, we'll lay him in my woodshed. It'll be good and cold there, so he'll keep."

CHAPTER TWO

THE NEXT DAY

Art Bolton, who had once preached as a lay-pastor in a Baptist church in Texas, said a few Bible verses and a prayer over the dead man, whom they buried deep in one of the empty holes left by some miner from the first days of Texas Gulch.

Such scars on the land abounded in a mining camp in its second generation. The Pennsylvanians of Dutch Camp days had damaged the land immediately around the camp very thoroughly before vacating the place.

Late the previous summer, Sam Underhill and a delegation of new prospectors from in and around the Brazos town of Underhill, had come in and taken another look at Dutch Camp, though they hadn't expected to remain. They had expected a quick and probably fruitless investigation of a site that everyone said was played out. But soon Herbert Colfax, of all people, had made a good strike right behind the abandoned log hut that now was his residence. A day later, Julius Setser had made a strike almost as good on a ridge outside town, and Joe Skinner, who traveled with his aging father in tow, had done the same yet again, at a different spot, within a week.

Dutch Camp wasn't played out after all. The first round of Forty-niners had simply been too eager, too sure they would find a better yield elsewhere, and had let impatience and the threat of severe winter weather move them out too quickly.

The new influx wouldn't be so foolish. Sam, who had helped organize the prospector group back in Texas, had counseled a cautious, patient approach.

"We'll not scratch here one day and run there the next," he'd said. "We'll work hard, and dig deep, and find gold that others have missed. We'll make our success by keeping our heads level and our noses to the grindstone. We'll keep news of our strikes to ourselves, as long as we can. We'll wait out the winter and guard our claims. We'll be wealthy before you know it."

So they'd settled into grubby little Dutch Camp and re-named the place Texas Gulch in honor of the state from which most of them had come.

When the man was buried and covered over, Colfax slapped the dirt from his hands and said, "Now you just watch. Somebody will come asking after him tomorrow and we'll have to dig him out again."

"I doubt that," Sam said. He looked up at the gray sky, which spat snow down onto his face. "There's going to be a hard winter. Before long it'll be hard for anybody to get to us, or for us to get out again."

"I hope we've laid in enough supplies to see us through the winter," Colfax grumbled. He was more his old self again, a mere grouchy old scoundrel, not pacing and nervous like the night before.

Sam said, "We've got more than enough."

Walking back down into the camp, Daniel Chase fell in beside Sam and held up his right hand. The dead man's distinctive ring was on his middle finger. "See it, Sam? Looks good, huh?"

Colfax frowned over at the ring from the other side of Daniel. "You'd best not wear a dead man's ring, Daniel," he said. "You know what happens when you do that, don't you?"

"What?"

"He comes back, that's what! Comes back looking for what was took from him."

Sam said, "Herbert, don't frighten him with nonsense."

But Colfax was having fun. He often toyed with Daniel, who had come to California from Tennessee with his older brother, Grady. The parents of the Chase brothers were dead. Grady and Daniel Chase had met and joined the Texas Gulch delegation along the way, but Grady had died of a fever shortly after, leaving Daniel alone in the world. The boy was now parented by the Texas Gulch community as a whole. He lived sometimes with Joe Skinner and his aged father, whom everyone called simply Old Man Skinner. Often he resided in the Underhill-Dillow cabin, or in the lodge house, as the big dormitorylike cabin was informally called.

"Don't believe him," Sam said. "Dead men don't come back."

"I know," Daniel said. "I'm not stupid. It's not ghosts that can hurt you. It's folks that's still alive you got to worry about."

"The boy's too smart for you, Herbert," Sam said. "Hey, did you find your watch last night?"

"I did indeed," Colfax said, and produced the watch to prove it.

"How did you manage to find it in the snow and dark?"

"Persistence," Colfax said. "With persistence, it's downright remarkable, the things a man can find." Colfax smiled, turned, and trudged away, whistling.

"He's in a remarkably good humor all at once," Sam said. "I can't imagine how he found that watch in the dark." He yanked playfully at Daniel's hat, a big flop he'd inherited from his deceased older brother. "You going to keep that ring for yourself, or give it to some pretty gal?"

"I'm thinking I might do the latter," Daniel said.

"Bet I know who she is."

"Maybe you do, maybe you don't."

"One word of advice, son: don't say where you got it. Most girls wouldn't be thrilled to know the ring a boy's given them has come off the finger of a dead man.''

"Arianna wouldn't care."

"Bet she would. Women are like that."

"I won't tell her, then."

"You think you might just up and marry Arianna one of these days?"

The boy nodded firmly. "I will. You wait and see."

Sam grinned. "Is she agreeable to the idea?"

"Not yet." Daniel paused, then looked up earnestly at Sam. "But she does want you to marry her mother."

Sam felt his face changing color. "That's just little-girl talk, that's all."

"She means it. She wants you to marry Leora. That'd make you Arianna's new father. Then, when I marry Arianna, I'll be your son-in-law. It'd be almost like being your son. That would be fine."

Sam self-consciously yanked at the brim of Daniel's hat, wondering how red his face was.

"Why haven't you ever married, Sam?"

"Never found the right woman."

"Arianna says you're handsome, and that she heard you've always had all kinds of women liking you."

"Arianna thinks she knows my life history, does she?"

"Well, is she right?"

"I was a different fellow as a younger man. A little too carefree and high-spirited. I suppose I had my share of attention."

"I wish I was handsome."

"You are."

"I'm too young to be handsome. I'll probably grow up ugly, like Grady was."

Sam laughed. "You're a character, boy. You know that?"

As they trudged along, side by side, Sam thought about what it would really be like to marry Leora Winkle. It was hard to find anything wrong in the notion.

Daniel spoke. "Sam . . . there ain't no chance of what Mr. Colfax said being true, is there?"

"What, about the dead man coming back? No, son. That man's dead and gone, and whatever he's left behind, he's left behind for good. There's nobody, living or dead, likely to be coming to Texas Gulch with this snow setting in."

The next day, Sam Underhill huddled in his big bearskin coat and wandered through the mining camp, smoking a cigar and hoping he had enough of them to see him through until spring. He trudged over to where they'd buried the dead man the day before. The snow had covered the spot and made it hard to make out. He wondered how deep the snow would become before the winter was out. He knew that at some places in the Sierras, snow would pile up ten feet or more.

Puffing and thinking, Sam stared at the grave. Who was this man? Why had he been at the pass into Texas Gulch at such an odd time, and what had made him die? He'd been gray-haired, but not particularly old. Not the age one would expect a man to be if he was going to simply fall over dead.

On the other hand, Sam realized, his perceptions about age and vitality might be a little skewed, thanks to his own unusual father. Bushrod Underhill . . . frontiersman, Indian compatriot and also Indian fighter, hunter, settler, horse dealer, and American icon. Now somewhere above seventy years old—not even Bushrod himself knew exactly how old—the man was still as strong and energetic as one twenty-five years younger. Bushrod, though definitely mature in appearance, didn't even look his full age. His skin was weathered but not particularly aged, his hair with plenty of color still amid the white. And Bush Underhill could still wear out a far younger trail partner, Sam included.

"Sam!"

Sam turned. Daniel was coming up to him, kicking through the snow.

"What you doing, Sam?"

"Just smoking and thinking."

"Can I have a cigar?"

"Wait until you're grown. I doubt they're good for a man."

"Why do you smoke them, then?"

"I like the taste. And it's something to do. Hey, your finger looks a little swole up. That ring too tight?"

Daniel held his hand up and showed it to Sam. The finger was quite puffy, but not discolored.

"It is a little tight, but I don't think enough to hurt you," Sam said. "You want me to try to file it off?"

"Would it hurt my finger?"

"I'd try not to hurt you, but I can't promise."

"Then I don't want you to do it."

"Fine, but you need to quit pulling on it so the swelling will go down."

"I will. It'll fit Arianna's finger a lot better than mine."

"When you going to give it to her?"

"First chance I get. What you thinking about out here?"

"About my father."

Daniel grinned. He was deeply impressed that a man he knew had a father as famous as Bushrod Underhill. The boy, semiliterate, had struggled through several of the _Underhill Almanac_s which printers across the country were forever putting out, to the real Bushrod's chagrin. Daniel was quite eager to be persuaded that Sam's father really had once turned an alligator inside out, and killed a grizzly by sticking his head down its throat until it choked, like the almanacs claimed. He was equally enamored of the tall tales from the exaggerated biography of Bushrod that had sparked the nonsense to begin with.

"I hope I can meet your father someday," Daniel said.

"I hope you can, too. You'd like him."

"It must be wonderful to be famous."

"Pap hates it. He wishes nobody knew who he was, and that none of those lies about him had been told, and that he could live out his old age without folks bothering him . . . not that he's really old."

"But he has to be old by now."

"He is, in years. But still he's not old. I know that don't make a lot of sense . . . but if you knew him, you'd understand. I think he'll live forever, I swear."

"Are the stories true, about the box of dirt?"

Sam smiled. "The Eden Box, you mean."

"Yes." Daniel's eyes were unblinking, fixed intently on Sam as he awaited an answer. The boy had asked plenty of questions about the legendry surrounding Bushrod Underhill, but never had he addressed Sam about the Eden Box story before.

Sam puffed his cigar and stared across the valley. "It's true in part. There is an old box of soil, very rich, pure soil, that was given to my father by a dying woman, many years ago. A very old black woman, who'd outlived all her masters, and was full of plant cures and legends and healings and superstitions. And that woman did tell him that the dirt in it was the last of the soil of Eden. And she did say that if my father would imbibe a little of that soil each year, that the passing of time would have little effect on him, that just like her he'd live on, and on . . ."[1]

"Does he really eat that dirt?"

Sam grinned. "He does. My mother puts a few grains into his cornbread at the start of every year. She thinks he doesn't know it—Pap always scoffs at the Eden Box notion, at least before other people—but the truth is, he does know she does that, and never lets on to her that he's aware of it. I think that maybe he believes in it, but doesn't want to admit it. So it's easier to go ahead and let his wife give him the soil in 'secret,' so he never has to own up." Sam puffed again, and grew thoughtful. "The odd thing is, Daniel, that my father really doesn't seem to get old as fast as other men. He never grows sick. He's as strong today as he was when I was a little boy."

"So it really is dirt from the Garden of Eden?"

[1] *The Glory River*, Book 1 in The Underhill Series

Sam laughed. "Of course not. That was just a foolish old tale from a superstitious woman."

"Then why doesn't your father get old?"

"He does get old. He just does it better than most, for some reason. He's blessed, I suppose."

Sam tossed his cigar away and listened to it sizzle out in the snow.

"I'm hungry," Daniel said.

"So am I. Ben's cooking stew. Let's go inside and see how far along it is."

CHAPTER THREE

Ten horsemen rode in the mountains, horses struggling in the snow, breath and bodies steaming.

"It's no use, Jordan!" one of the riders called to the man in front, a weathered, lean fellow with a pitted, dark countenance and black eyes. "We got to turn back!"

"Not without Dehaven!" the pitted man replied firmly. He urged his weary horse on, through the next fresh drift of snow.

"We're going to get ourselves trapped in these damned mountains!"

"We're not giving up, Remine! Not until we find Dehaven!"

In a clearing on the other side of the drift, the riders stopped, letting their horses rest. The ten horses drew close together, seeking one another's heat.

"Ross is right," said a dark-haired young man who was in many ways the image of the pitted leader, but without the pox scars. This was Searl Mahaffery, younger brother of Jordan. "He's got away from us, Jordan. We may as well admit it and go back."

"Back to where, Searl? And to what? Dehaven has took it all! The gold ... everything we've worked for! We planned it all perfectly. Performed it all perfectly. Got away perfectly. I'll not have it ruined by one man. He took everything we earned."

"Everything we *stole*, you mean," muttered one of the other riders.

"What was that, Perry?" said Jordan Mahaffery, the pitted man. "You got something to say, you say it out to be heard!"

"All I said was, we didn't earn that gold, we stole it. And Dehaven stole it from us. Sure, it makes us mad. Sure, it leaves us back where we begun. But the man, and that gold, ain't worth dying for. There's a lot of gold in California. We can steal more of it. I say forget about Dehaven. Give the man his due for outwitting us, and let's get out of these mountains before we freeze to death."

Jordan Mahaffery replied, "It's the principle of the thing. I want my gold back."

An even-featured man who appeared to possess a mix of racial bloodlines cleared his throat and spoke in a smooth, almost soothing voice. "Jordan, listen to me. You've got to consider our situation. We've come out here without being ready for this kind of weather, particularly in these mountains. The horses are worn out, and there's no trail to follow. Perry is right. Dehaven has gotten away from us."

"Besides," threw in Emmett Fish, another of the band, "Dehaven has probably froze to death by now. No reason for us to do the same." Fish had a strong Georgia drawl and teeth the color of rust.

Jordan Mahaffery appeared to be thinking very hard. At last he spoke. "You got to ask yourself: why would Dehaven have run to such a place as this, especially in the winter? Why not take that gold and go to San Francisco or some other town, where he could spend it?"

"Because he'd know that we'd search every town until we found him," replied Searl Mahaffery.

Jordan Mahaffery nodded. "That's right. So he was coming up here to huddle with the gold through the winter. Figuring that the snow and such would keep us from following. Figuring that before the springtime come, we'd forget about him and move on. Then he could take that gold at his leisure and go off and enjoy it.''

"I can't believe Dehaven would try to winter over in such a place as this,'' said Conner Broadgrass, the dark-complexioned man with the smooth and diplomatic way of speaking. He was one of the few who could counter Jordan Mahaffery and get away with it. "There's no place here for a man to live, no settlements or diggings, no shelter. And Dehaven is no mountain man. He'd never survive.''

"There *are* some diggings nearby,'' Mahaffery said. "There's Dutch Camp.''

"Never heard of it,'' Emmett Fish said, spitting into the snow.

"I have, though I admit I'd forgotten about it,'' Broadgrass said. He'd been in California since well before the start of the Gold Rush, and had robbed, gambled, and womanized his way through almost every mining camp that had sprung into being since color turned up in Sutter's millrace. "But even if there's still shelter to be had at Dutch Camp, Jordan, the camp is abandoned. There'd be no food, no company. Dehaven would never go to such a place.''

"I've heard Dutch Camp ain't empty,'' Mahaffery replied. "There's a new group who come in and started prospecting there again. Word is just beginning to get out. More rumors than anything else . . . but the talk is, there was a group of folks who bought enough food and supplies to last a full season for twenty or so folks, and hauled it up into these mountains.''

"I don't believe it,'' said Bert Mongold, the burliest of the ten. The son of a St. Louis swindler who himself was the offspring of a Natchez Trace bandit, Mongold had been criminal since he'd been able to walk. "Why would anybody prospect played-out diggings?''

"Because maybe the diggings didn't prove to be played out after all,'' Mahaffery replied. "And maybe they figure to winter over to guard their find, and to get the fastest start on the mining season come warmer weather. And maybe Dehaven heard about it, and figured that kind of place was the safest for him to be. If I heard rumors about Dutch Camp, then he could have, too. Hell, the man talked to every stranger he met, anyway, so he'd be likely to hear the latest rumors. I despise the man for what he's done to us, but even I'll admit he's got a winning way about him with people.'' Mahaffery paused. ''Maybe that's why I was fool enough to trust him.''

Broadgrass spoke again. ''Even if Dehaven is at Dutch Camp, Jordan, we still face a problem if we go after him. Look at the sky. This snow isn't going to stop. If we stay in the mountains much longer, we're likely to be snowed in. Maybe until spring. And what if Dehaven isn't there? What if we go to Dutch Camp and find the people there have abandoned it like the first group did? We could be trapped in these mountains without food or supplies.''

''We'll take the risk. I ain't giving up that gold,'' Mahaffery said firmly. ''Dehaven *is* at Dutch Camp. I can feel it. And we're going after him.'' Mahaffery looked from face to face. ''Anybody wants out of this, let him leave. But whoever doesn't stick around gives up his cut of that gold once we get it back.''

''*If* we get it back,'' muttered Emmett Fish.

''We will get it back,'' Mahaffery said. ''But we've wasted enough time jaw-flapping. This snow is piling up by the minute. We're going to Dutch Camp, gents, and we're going to peel the very hide off Dehaven when we catch him.''

The other nine cast glances at one another. There was fear in the eyes of all but Broadgrass, whose immobile countenance always hid whatever he might be feeling. But no one countered Jordan Mahaffery. It wasn't wise to do such a thing.

''Let's go, big brother,'' Searl Mahaffery said. ''Lead the way to Dutch Camp. You reckon they got any pretty little ladies there?''

"At a mining camp? Ain't likely," Mahaffery replied. "Probably just a bunch of greasy miners with beards to their bellies."

"And Dehaven with them."

"That's right. And Dehaven with them. Now let's go."

The snow fell harder, but the riders pressed on.

Arianna Winkle shivered under her heavy coat and trudged through the piling snow, thinking how much better things were back home in Texas.

Just now she didn't remember the miseries she had suffered in the height of Texas summers, when she'd fantasized about dwelling in snowy, cold mountains just like those now surrounding her. Now that she was living out that midsummer's fantasy, she found little to like about it.

"Enoch!" she yelled, her breath gusting white. "Enoch! Here, boy!"

She waited and looked around. There was no sign of Enoch, no barking or scrambling in the snow.

A dreadful thought came: might somebody have done something to Enoch because of his habit of barking at night? She instantly suspected Herbert Colfax, whom she despised. Or Crain Brown, who put on such a nice front to cover the unpleasant, harsh person he really was. Arianna was good at sensing the personalities and characters of people, despite what veneer they put over their true selves. Either Colfax or Brown were the kinds who might have shot or poisoned Enoch on the sneak.

"Here, boy! Enoch!"

Still the dog did not appear. She looked all around in the vast whiteness. What if Enoch was hurt, and buried in the snow, unable to help himself?

"Enoch!"

She continued on toward the pass. Because of the lay of the land, the snow was drifted more heavily toward the wide, notchlike opening. She never much liked going beyond the pass into the mountains; it made her feel cut off from the protection of the little society of Texas Gulch. But for Enoch's sake she went on, whistling and calling the dog's name.

Unexpectedly, she heard her own name called, from behind her. "Arianna!"

Arianna winced. That was Daniel Chase's voice, an unwelcome one. She didn't really dislike Daniel—she felt very sorry for him as an orphan, in fact—but right now she didn't really want him bothering her. Besides, she could tell that he liked her, which made her uncomfortable. He was a year younger than she, after all. And he was not the kind of boy who could appeal to her, even if he were older.

She went on, pretending not to hear, hoping she could clear the pass before he caught up with her.

"Arianna!"

He was too close now for her to pretend she hadn't heard him. Oh, well. Maybe he could help her find Enoch. She turned and saw Daniel lumbering up through the snow, stepping high and wide and kicking up white dust all around. He had his usual big grin on his face.

He reached her, out of breath, red-nosed from the cold. "Where you going, Arianna?" he panted.

"Through the pass," she said.

"He's gone again?"

"Yes. I'm worried about him. There's snow now. He could get trapped out in it."

"I saw him yesterday. When I was coming in to tell about the dead man. He was heading up toward the pass, right up through this very place, matter of fact. He goes out of the pass a lot. I've seen him chase varmints and such a long way beyond it. He'll be back."

"Not if he can't make it through the snow."

"He can do it. You know how a dog his size travels through snow, don't you? He jumps!" Daniel performed a little demonstrative hop, advancing himself another couple of feet. "Then he does it again." Another jump, and suddenly he was uncomfortably close to her, grinning more broadly. She backed away a little.

"Want me to help you look for him?" he asked.

"Well . . . yes."

"Come on, then."

They walked together through the ever-deeper snow. "Hey, Arianna, I got you something," Daniel said. He stuck out his hand.

She looked at the ring that lay on his palm.

"Where'd you get it?"

Daniel remembered Sam Underhill's advice about not telling her it was a dead man's ring. "Sam Underhill told me I could have it. I put it on and it got stuck on my finger, but a few minutes ago, I was able to get it off. I don't want it no more. So you can have it. It won't stick on your finger, your hands being smaller and all."

Given the romantic symbolism associated with the acceptance of rings, Arianna wasn't sure she should take it. But she did like baubles, and didn't own a ring just now.

"Thank you," she said, reaching out and taking the ring off his palm. She slipped it on her biggest finger and found it too large, her hands being very slender. So she tried it on her thumb, and it fit perfectly.

"Wearing a ring on your thumb!" Daniel declared, and laughed. "I never seen nobody do that before!"

She shrugged and continued walking, battling the snow, hoping he understood that there was no significance in her acceptance of his ring. "Enoch!" she called. "Here, boy!"

Daniel fell in beside her. The snow grew more obstructive as they entered the pass, but both of them managed to keep going.

CHAPTER FOUR

An hour later, well out into the craggy Sierra wilderness, a somber Daniel turned to Arianna and said, "We have to go back."

"But we haven't found Enoch."

"But the snow, Arianna. Look how deep it's getting. If we don't get back, we may not be able to."

Arianna looked around, and knew Daniel was talking sense. They'd wandered far, calling for Enoch and getting no response. The snow was deep enough now that it was hard to hold out much hope for the dog, if in fact he'd been caught out here. It broke her heart to think about it.

A noise made Arianna pause.

"Daniel, did you hear that?"

"I didn't hear nothing."

"I did. It might have been Enoch."

Daniel listened hard, but shook his head.

"It came from over that way," Arianna insisted. "I'm going to go look. Then we can start back."

"Arianna, I don't think we're going to find Enoch."

Arianna was paying no attention, already pushing through the snow in the direction from which she'd heard the noise that had drawn her ear. "Enoch!" she called. "Enoch! Can you hear me?"

Daniel started after her. "Arianna, come back."

She kept going, calling for her dog.

"Arianna!"

She clambered over a fallen tree that was piled and slick with snow. She slipped, coming down hard on the log. The snow, however, softened the impact and she got up quickly.

"Are you hurt?" Daniel reached her and put out a hand toward her.

"Leave me alone!" she declared, irritable. "Go away! If you're worried about getting home, then go home now. I'll come later, with Enoch."

"Arianna, you got to go back. It's too cold. There's too much snow."

"I'll not! Not without Enoch!"

"Enoch may be waiting for you at home right now. I think we should—" He cut off suddenly, turning his head slightly.

"Do you hear him, too?" she asked.

"I hear something. But I don't think it's . . ." His voice trailed off.

"What is it?"

"Be quiet!" he said in a sharp whisper.

"Daniel . . ."

"Look!" he said, bending slightly at the knees and pointing down a slope to their west.

Arianna saw them. Men on horses, making their way along through the snow, and having a hard time of it. They were traveling along the foot of the ridge.

Daniel and Arianna slowly knelt, letting the deep snow hide them.

"Who are they, Daniel?" Arianna whispered.

"Don't know. Odd, men traveling like that in this snow. Who in the world . . ."

"Daniel, let's go home."

Daniel nodded. When the riders had passed below, boy and girl stood and began walking as fast as they could, which was not fast at all, toward the pass. It seemed terribly far away, and Arianna felt foolish for having come this far, even for Enoch.

"Those men scare me," she said to Daniel between harsh gasps for air.

"Nothing to be afraid of," Daniel said, trying to sound manly. Arianna could tell, though, that he was scared of them, too. There was something out-of-place and disturbing about such a group, in these mountains, during a season such as this. Only some desperate reason could make men willing to plunge into this wilderness at this time of year.

Arianna and Daniel were halfway back to the pass when another sound brought them to a stop. They glanced at one another, then veered to the left, scrambling over some fallen timber that was deeply encrusted with fresh snow, forming a distorted natural sculpture. Both Arianna and Daniel fell more than once as they clambered over the timber, but in the end they made it, and were rewarded by the sight of Enoch, the straying dog, yapping at them from a recess among the logs. The dog had apparently climbed on the timber, probably chasing some woodland creature, and had slipped into the deep recess, from which he had not been able to get out again. Though the crevice had imprisoned Enoch, it had also protected him from the snow and wind.

"I'll get him," Daniel said. He flopped onto his belly, reached down, and extricated the twenty-pound mongrel.

"Here you go," Daniel said blandly, handing Enoch to Arianna, knowing he was very much the hero of the moment, but trying to be nonchalant about it. Arianna hugged the dog and planted a big kiss on the side of his snout. Daniel was instantly and obviously jealous of the dog.

He made a face. "You know, I've thought a time or two that I might like to get a kiss from you sometime. But now that I know you kiss dogs, I ain't so sure."

She was too happy at the moment to worry about insult. "Thank you, Daniel," she said sincerely. "He'd have died in there if you hadn't found him."

"It was nothing. Now we'd better keep moving. Look

yonder—it's so white you can't make out the far peaks. That means the snow's coming in even heavier."

"Do you think those riders are near?"

"I think they've moved on. Come on."

They continued, Arianna insisting on carrying her dog, even though it slowed her.

"Let him down, Arianna," Daniel said. "He'll follow us."

"No. He'll run away again."

"You're making us have to drag along, way too slow."

"Just keep going. I'll keep up."

They rounded the side of a hill, taking heed to their footing. Daniel was cheered to catch sight of the familiar pass into Texas Gulch, but the vision was quickly erased by a new sweep of falling snow, driven hard on the wind. For a frightening moment Daniel realized just how easy it would be to become hopelessly lost in such weather. He recalled campfire stories about mountain people who had frozen to death mere yards from their own homes, as lost as if they'd been a hundred miles out in the wilderness. He tried to lock in mind the exact spot where he'd seen the pass, so he wouldn't lose course.

The wind shifted again, and he saw the riders. They were riding single file, laboriously, on a diagonal path up the face of the final slope leading to the pass. Daniel stopped at once, and Arianna, having also seen them, stopped just behind him.

"Daniel, they'll get to the pass before we do," she said.

The wind swirled, and the falling snow thinned out for a few moments.

Enoch snarled in Arianna's arms, barked, and leaped free of her grasp.

"Enoch!" she said, sharply, but hardly louder than a whisper.

Her caution was pointless now. Enoch bounded through the snow, down the slope, barking loudly at the riders. The two youngsters saw the riders turn their heads, see the dog

. . . and then one pointed. Up the slope. At them.

Daniel and Arianna glanced nervously at one another, both knowing it would be futile to run.

"It's probably all right," Daniel said, watching as three of the riders turned their horses off-course and began riding up the ridge toward them. Enoch was barking and bounding, making a defiant show, but keeping well away from the advancing horses and men. "They're probably just travelers wanting shelter. Nobody to worry about."

"Yes," Arianna said. "Just men lost in the snow. They'll probably help us get in safe to Texas Gulch."

They stood there together, waiting for the advancing men to reach them.

"I'm worried, Sam," Leora Winkle said. "Arianna disappeared earlier, looking for her dog, and she hasn't come back."

Sam looked into Leora's face, pretty despite the lines of concern that tracked along it just now like thin trail marks traced on a map. "Do you think she'd have gone beyond the pass in this weather?" he asked.

"I don't know . . . I didn't think she would. That's why I let her go. Maybe I didn't think at all. I was . . . distracted today."

Distracted. Sam knew what that meant. She'd been grieving again for her lost husband. Sam felt sorry for Leora, but at the same time wished she'd find a way to put that loss behind her and take notice that there were other good and available men in the world, the most prime example he could think of being the one standing before her now.

"Might she be visiting at someone's cabin? Have you asked around for her?"

"I've been almost everywhere, every place she'd go," Leora said. "She's nowhere. And Daniel is missing, too. Mr. Colfax said he saw Daniel earlier, looking for her. I suppose they're together somewhere."

"I doubt they're far away, Leora. I'll go look for her. There's still a lot of daylight left."

"There's a place she likes to go, farther back in the valley. Where those white rocks are that the sun shines on in the evening."

"That's where we'll find her, I'll bet. Or more likely, I'll meet them already coming back. I'll find her for you. I promise."

"Thank you, Sam."

"My pleasure."

Leora left the cabin and hurried back through the snow toward the lodge house. Sam watched her go, and frowned. He'd just promised to find Arianna, a foolish pledge. His father had taught him never to make a vow he couldn't be sure of keeping. There was always the terrible chance that Arianna and Daniel had wandered too far, and had gotten lost or cut off from getting back. If so, they might not be found until the spring thaw, and maybe not even then. But Sam decided not to dwell on that possibility. He'd assume for now that he'd find both youngsters quickly.

Sam filled his water bottle from the drinking bucket, and dropped some sun-dried meat into a pocket. He considered loading himself up with his rifle and other gear, but it was hard enough to move through thick snow even without burdens. He'd forgo the weaponry in favor of unencumbrance.

If Ben Dillow was handy, he'd ask him to come too. But Ben was off somewhere else, and Sam wasn't inclined to go looking for him. He'd just make a quick hike out into the valley, round up the children, get them home, and enjoy Leora's praise.

He paused once before he set out, wondering if he was taking this all a little too lightly. Maybe he should organize a full search, take gear and weapons . . . but no. Leora was a worrier, always exaggerating things. It was possible that the youngsters were right here in the camp, just hidden away. Maybe Daniel had finally persuaded Arianna to give him a kiss, and they were off holding hands somewhere.

Probably the boy had given her that ring by now.

Tightening his hat onto his head, Sam left his cabin, paused to strap snowshoes onto his feet, and trudged out into the white.

CHAPTER FIVE

Arianna tried to hide her fear, but couldn't. She stared into the leering face of Searl Mahaffery, felt the pain of his big, rough hand around her wrist, smelled the stench of his breath in her face, and desperately wished she could run away. She was at the base of the slope, encircled by the riders. Daniel struggled in the grip of Bert Mongold, off to the side.

Enoch was up on the slope, growling, snarling, and occasionally barking at the group below, but staying far away.

"Tell me, dear thing, are all the little gals as pretty as you where you come from?" Searl asked her.

"Let me go!"

"Where do you come from? Dutch Camp?"

"Texas Gulch," she said. "Please, I want to go home!"

"Texas Gulch? Where the hell is Texas Gulch?"

Arianna tried to pull her wrist free. He tightened his grip, shoving his ugly face closer. "I asked you, where is Texas Gulch?"

"It's Dutch Camp," she said, fighting tears. "My mother is there. I want to go to her."

Searl grinned. "Your mother? Texas Gulch sounds like my kind of place. Is she as pretty as you? You don't find many mining camps with pretty gals about them, you know." He turned and winked at his companions. "Tell you what, dear thing, you give me a little kiss and maybe I'll let you go to your mama. What do you say?''

She turned her head away, sickened at the thought of kissing this man or having him kiss her. She looked at Daniel, pleading helplessly with her eyes. But Daniel was as entrapped as she was. And just as scared.

''You didn't answer my question about your mama, girl,'' Searl said, yanking her wrist. ''I asked you if she was as pretty as you.''

''Yes.''

''My, my. Lord have mercy! That's a thing to picture . . . two pretty things there together. Hey . . . in the night, do you ever see your mama and your daddy getting friendly . . . You know what I'm talking about?''

She was beginning to feel ill. ''My father's dead,'' she said. ''I want to go home.'' She looked at the faces of the men around her. No sympathy. Several very scary grins. One or two looked hungry in a way that terrified her. ''Don't hurt me.''

''Let her go!'' Daniel yelled, writhing and tugging in the grip of his own captor. ''Let us both go!''

''Shut up, boy,'' Mongold muttered at Daniel in a bored tone. Daniel might as well have been a mouse struggling in Mongold's big hands, for all the good his escape attempts were doing.

The dog up on the hill barked more intensely. One of the riders muttered a wish to shoot the cussed thing.

Daniel managed to turn and kick Mongold hard in the knee. Mongold roared, cursed, and struck Daniel in the face with a fist almost as big as the boy's head. Daniel's body jolted and he made a guttural noise. A second blow made him go limp. Mongold let him fall into the snow.

''Believe I may have hurt him,'' Mongold said. ''Ain't it a shame!'' He grinned at his partners, but grimaced as he reached down to rub the kicked knee.

Searl Mahaffery shoved his face against Arianna's, rubbing abrasive whiskers against her skin. ''Mighty pretty gal, you are," he muttered. "Pretty as a picture."

"Searl, she's hardly out of the cradle!" an outlaw named Reed Van Huss said. "Naught but a baby, that one! You're old enough to be her daddy."

"Maybe he is," said another of the band, Perry Winters.

Arianna began to cry and tried to pull away, but couldn't.

A hand gripped Searl Mahaffery's shoulder. Searl looked up at the stern face of his elder brother, the only man there, perhaps with the exception of the inscrutable Conner Broadgrass, who didn't seem to be finding this performance amusing.

"Searl," he said, and gave a little turn of his head to indicate Searl should step aside.

"You wait your own turn, Jordan," Searl said.

"There'll be no touching this girl," Mahaffery replied. "I'll not see her hurt. Let her go."

Mumbling a few obscenities, Searl freed Arianna, rose, and stomped back to his waiting horse.

Mahaffery knelt before the weeping girl. "Honey, are you afraid?"

She looked at the man. He looked at lot like the one who had just tormented her, though older, a little uglier, and with skin that bore the pitted scars of a long-past pox. But his kindly tone gave her hope. "Yes, I'm afraid."

"You don't need to be. I won't let him hurt you."

Emmett Fish said, "Hell, Jordan, you're ruining the fun." The others chuckled, except Searl Mahaffery, who was far too furious.

"You say you live where?" Mahaffery asked her.

"Texas Gulch."

Mahaffery smiled, as gentle and kindly as the friendliest schoolmaster. "Well! I didn't know until you said so that they'd changed the name from Dutch Camp. Why Texas Gulch?"

"Because most of the people there came in from Texas." She was sniffling now, not fully crying. Glancing over at

Daniel, she saw him still lying, unmoving, in the snow, and she worried about him.

"Texas, eh? What part?"

"Mostly from around Underhill."

"Underhill, Texas! Heard of it! That's where the famous Bushrod lives, ain't it? Somewhere in the Brazos country?"

"Yes."

"You from there?"

"Yes."

"Well! You know Bushrod Underhill?"

"Yes."

"He ain't in Texas Gulch, is he?"

"No. He's still in Texas." She started to mention Sam Underhill, but some cautious instinct told her to volunteer little information to these men, even to the one who seemed kind.

"I'll bet you've got lots of food, good shelter, and supplies laid in for the winter."

"Yes."

"Because, you know, I think me and my friends here might have made a mistake. We might have come into these mountains too late in the year to get out again. We might have to come live at Texas Gulch for a while."

Arianna blanched at the idea of these men infiltrating her own community. The prospect was purely dreadful.

"Tell me something, sweetheart," Mahaffery said through the most disarming of smiles. "Have there been other newcomers to Texas Gulch lately?"

"No."

"Are you sure about that?"

"Yes. It's just all the regular people."

"Then where did you get this?" He reached out and took her hand, lifting it, and pointing to the ring on her thumb.

A murmur of surprise ran through the circle of riders. "That's Dehaven's ring!" Ross Remine said.

"It was a gift to me," Arianna said, pulling her hand away.

"From a man? Gray-haired, friendly sort?"

"No. From him. From Daniel." She pointed at Daniel's still form. Tears formed in her eyes and she feared Daniel was dead.

"Really? Is he your little beau?"

"No. He's just Daniel the orphan boy."

"Mighty odd mining camp, I must say," Mahaffery commented. "Widows, pretty little girls, and orphan boys. Tell me: where did Daniel get this ring?"

"I don't know."

"Well, you know where I think he got it? I think it must have been given to him by a man named Frank Dehaven. Because Frank used to have this ring. He's an old friend of mine. I think he must be in Texas Gulch, and he must have made friends with Daniel. Now, maybe Frank ain't calling himself by his real name. He does that sometimes, uses different names. But he's a little older than I am, and with grayish hair. Fairly fine-looking figure of a man. That sound like anybody you know in Texas Gulch?"

"No. Is Daniel dead?" She was beginning to draw in her breath spasmodically, on the verge of breaking into sudden, out-of-control sobs.

"No, no. Just knocked a little silly, that's all. But you know what? I bet we do need to get him into Texas Gulch, where we can put him in a warm bed and make sure he's well. Would you like to go back to your mother?"

"Yes. But don't let him bother her." She flicked her eyes toward the sullen Searl.

"He won't bother you or her. I won't let him. He's my little brother, and I can keep him under control. Now, let's go, sweetheart. My name's Mr. Mahaffery. What's yours?"

"Arianna Winkle."

"Arianna. Pretty name to go with a pretty girl." He grinned at her in a downright heartwarming manner. "You and me can be friends, I believe."

"You promise to keep him away from my mother and

me?'' She cast another glance at Searl Mahaffery, who muttered a curse beneath his breath.

"You bet I will. He's the bad boy of the family. But I'll keep him in line." He patted her shoulder. "That your dog up there?"

"Yes."

"Barks a lot, don't he?"

"Sometimes."

"Would you like your dog back?"

"Yes."

Mahaffery stood and turned to Emmett Fish. "Emmett, go and fetch that dog for Arianna here, would you?"

"Fetch the dog? How am I supposed to fetch it?"

"Just take care of it, Emmett. You can follow our tracks in. Arianna's going to show us the way to Texas Gulch. Right, sweetheart?"

Arianna didn't want these men coming to Texas Gulch, but knew she had no choice. "Yes," she murmured.

"Bert, scoop up the boy there before he gets the chilblains. You fetch that dog, Emmett, then follow us on in. We'll lead your horse in for you."

Arianna, though intimidated, made herself ask a question: "What are you going to do when you get to Texas Gulch?"

"Well, honey, I think we're going to try to find out more about how that ring you wear came to be in Texas Gulch. When did Daniel give that ring to you, sweetheart?"

"Today." She didn't like him calling her "sweetheart," but wasn't bold enough to tell him so.

"I see. Interesting. You want to ride on my horse? You can sit in front of me and I'll pull this big coat around you. Keep you warm."

She nodded, knowing again there was no other choice.

Bert Mongold managed to get the limp Daniel Chase onto his own saddle, and swung up behind. Somehow he got a grip on the boy and managed to hold his horse's reins as well. Daniel sagged and swayed, and made groaning sounds that Arianna was relieved to hear.

The riders, all but Emmett Fish, pushed on through the almost inpenetrable snow. Fish watched them with a sour expression, and began trudging up the slope toward the dog, which barked madly at him. He muttered a few curses, and called for the dog to stay put.

Of course it didn't. When he drew nearer, Enoch turned and bounded off through the snow in big, arcing leaps. Emmett Fish swore some more and trudged on after it, taking mental note of every landmark so he wouldn't get lost.

Fish wasn't fully sure what he was supposed to do. As best he could figure it, he was putting on an act for the girl's benefit, to keep her trusting and compliant until they reached Texas Gulch. After that, it wouldn't matter. Take care of it, Jordan Mahaffery had said.

He knew how he intended to take care of it. He wasn't about to carry some barking dog across the wilderness just to please some teary-eyed little girl.

He looked after the retreating riders, who were making slow progress across the white mountain landscape. Emmett Fish despised rugged country. Give him a good, level, well-liquored town anytime. The notion of spending an entire winter in these mountains was disgusting. He hoped they had a lot of good whiskey in Texas Gulch.

He watched the horsemen for a few moments more, then checked his rifle and turned to look for the dog.

CHAPTER SIX

Sam Underhill was glad his father wasn't here to see his son make such a mockery of all the common sense and trailsmanship he'd tried to ingrain in him through the years.

Sam felt quite a fool. He'd made the twin errors of overconfidence and easy assumption. He'd assumed it would be simple to find Arianna and that he could handle the task alone. But he'd meandered over a big part of the valley and so far hadn't found a sign of her or Daniel. Not a track, not a peep of sound.

So maybe they weren't here at all. Perhaps they had gone the opposite direction, out through the pass into the mountains beyond. If so, and if they hadn't returned in Sam's absence, they were probably in severe trouble right now. Maybe dead. Dear Lord, what had he done, taking such a cavalier attitude?

Sam would have kicked himself if it would have done any good. He should have alerted all the men of Texas Gulch, had them spread out and search systematically until Arianna and Daniel were found. He should not have come out here alone and unarmed in this land of bears, mountain lions, and coyotes.

The sun was westering. Before long he'd have to end his search. He imagined facing Leora Winkle and telling her he'd failed to find her daughter, and now it was too late to do anything further because night had come.

He struggled against mounting panic. Arianna and Daniel *had* to be here. He *had* to find them.

Sam cupped his hands around his mouth. "Arianna! Daniel!"

No replies came except the echo of his own calls off the high, encircling ridges.

He drew in a deep breath and decided there was but one thing to do. He had to rush back to Texas Gulch as quickly as possible and hope that he'd find the children already there. If not, he and the men of the mining camp would have to make torches and form search teams. They'd have to position themselves at high places on both sides of the pass, and build huge bonfires both to keep them warm through the night, and to serve as guidelights for the missing youngsters. And they'd have to pray hard.

"Arianna! Daniel! Can you hear me?"

Empty echoes mocked him.

He shifted his coat, rehoisted his trousers, and put his snowshoe-clad foot out to begin the journey back to Texas Gulch. Curse the snow! It was piling faster and deeper than he'd anticipated. He'd not make it back quickly enough. Had to try, though.

A few steps later, however, he stopped. Something had caught his eye up on a bluff to his right. He stopped, put his hand across his brows, salute fashion, to shield his eyes, and studied the faint spot of color. It was too high and far away for him to be sure, but he thought it might be a small human being. Arianna or Daniel, or both huddled together. Might they have climbed the bluff, looking for shelter in a cave, and gotten stranded on the ledge?

"Daniel! Arianna! Is that you I see?"

Whoever or whatever it was, there was no answer. He prayed he wouldn't find them up there frozen to death from exposure to the cold wind.

He squinted harder, unsure whether he was seeing human

forms at all. It might be no more than a colored, eroded boulder that the wind was keeping free of snow accumulation.

But the more he looked, the more he believed that what he saw was human . . . but unmoving.

No, dear Lord, no . . . don't let me be too late. Please.

Sam began looking around for a route up the slope. He wondered how Arianna and Daniel had managed to reach such a place. Well, if they could, he could too.

He studied the area above the ledge with concern. Though the snow was still new enough not to have accumulated to dangerous levels, the slope above the ledge was of just the right angle and conditions to be favorable to snow slides. A little more accumulation, and this could become the site of small, continuing avalanches all winter long. Just one more reason to get those children away from this place . . . if that was really who he saw.

Sam rubbed his face, trying to ward off chill, blinked his eyes several times, and spotted a possible climbing route. Removing his snowshoes, he laid them aside for retrieval after he came down again. Putting hand to stone, he made the first heave. So far, so good. He found another handhold, and a crevice to accommodate his foot, and rose another half a yard.

The stone face of the bluff was cold, and the wind and stinging snow made it difficult to concentrate on where he was going. As he climbed, he glanced up repeatedly, making sure he wasn't losing his bearings and drifting away from the ledge where they were . . . *if* they were.

Keep climbing, old fellow, he urged himself. *You've got to find them and bring them home. Just keep climbing.*

Emmett Fish had thought it would be easy to shoot the dog and be through with it. But the blasted creature was running him all over creation, ever deeper into the wilderness and snow, and he was afraid that he'd lose his way back to that pass if he went any farther. Every time he tried to line up his shot, the dog would dart away.

He would have been willing to let the dog go free and freeze to death out here, but the beast had made the mistake of annoying him. Shooting the thing had become an issue of personal satisfaction.

Ah, there it was! Just ahead, up on the crest of a small rise, looking back at him as if beckoning him to follow yet another distance. Anger surged. A dog, a mere *dog*, was playing a game with him!

Fish wanted to scream at the animal, but that would be counterproductive. "Come here, fellow!" he called warmly, and whistled. "Come here just a bit closer! Old Emmett's got a little something for you!"

The dog wagged its tail, bounded toward him a couple of leaps, and eyed him with interest.

"That's right! Come on now, boy! Good doggy!"

He raised his rifle slowly, cocked it, and sighted in on the dog's midsection when he saw the beast turn its head, peer through the driving snow to its right, and begin to bark madly.

Fish lowered the rifle. The dog had smelled something, seen something.

He looked hard in the same direction as the barking dog. Images of himself being devoured by some hungry bear filled his mind. Or were bears all in their dens right now?

Fish decided to take no chances. He'd not expend a rifle ball killing a dog when there might be something dangerous nearby. He stared a little longer through the swirling snow, thinking maybe he *could* see something there, after all . . .

The dog barked in a new frenzy, and bolted off over the rise and out of sight.

Emmett Fish gazed through the snow, squinting, brows lowered.

A *man*? Was that really a man he saw out there?

"Dehaven! Is that you?"

He received no answer. The figure, barely visible, just stood there, seemingly looking back at him.

"Dehaven! It's Emmett Fish!" He paused. "Dehaven? I came to warn you that Mahaffery's come looking for you! He's mad as hell because of you taking the gold ... but don't you worry. He's gone down into that mining camp! He thinks maybe that you're there with the gold! But if you're here, and you still got the gold, you and me could take it ... we could get clean away. I'd never do a thing to betray you, Dehaven!"

The figure did not move or reply. Emmett took a few steps closer, trying to see better, but the snow was still thickly falling.

"Dehaven? Is that you? I swear, I wouldn't betray you! It'll take Jordan a while to find out you ain't at that mining camp. We could be long gone by then ... but we got to move quick, before the snow gets deeper."

No answer. Was that Dehaven he was seeing?

Maybe, maybe not. Maybe it wasn't even a man. Just a tall stump or a wind-twisted young tree.

But it surely did look like a man, just standing there. He raised his rifle again. He stepped closer yet, then cussed loudly.

It *was* a tree. Nothing but a blasted, dead tree that nature had chanced to sculpt into something roughly the shape and size of a man!

Disgusted, he lowered the rifle, and turned back to head for the pass. The devil with that dog, and everything else. He was hungry and cold and in need of shelter, ready to follow his companions into Texas Gulch.

Sam Underhill was praying hard now.

The rock he climbed was nearly sheer and cold as a block of ice. The wind was growing stronger. And he was more certain than ever that no greater fool had ever followed the gold trail to California than Sam Underhill.

"Lord," he said aloud, "if you get me out of this, I swear

I'll become a preacher. I'll give everything I got to the widows and orphans. I'll turn missionary to the heathen Chinese. I'll do anything at all, if you'll just let me get home alive. And those children. Especially those children.''

But he feared they were already dead. Up on the ledge above him, frozen to death.

Sam paused to let himself regather a little strength. At least the exertion was keeping his muscles warm. He breathed hard for half a minute, then put forth a new burst of effort. He climbed the final distance. Cutting his eyes upward, he saw the edge of the ledge within reach. He'd done it! But he dreaded what he was sure he would find when he made the final pull.

Putting a hand up, Sam gripped the rim of the ledge and pulled. No good footholds here, just smooth rock. He strained hard.

Sam's head cleared the rim of the ledge. He would have laughed at the irony of it all, if he could. There were no dead children on that ledge. No children at all.

Just colored stone. The very possibility he had considered and rejected. A mound of oddly colored stone, cropping out onto the ledge.

The discovery brought him some relief—at least the children weren't dead up here—but it was relief with a dark edge. As far as he knew, they still remained lost. And he'd just expended most of his strength, and almost the entire remaining light of day, climbing up a bluff for nothing. He'd never make it back down again, and to Texas Gulch, in time to get search teams going before dark.

He hoped that maybe Ben Dillow or somebody else' with some sense about them had become aware of what was going on, and had already started looking for the children on their own steam.

He realized that by now they might be looking for him, too.

He pulled himself up onto the ledge and crawled into a space behind the very wedge of colored stone that had deceived his eye. Here he was cut off from the wind, and when he huddled just right, could actually avoid even the driven snow.

The thought of simply staying here to wait out the night came to mind, but was dismissed. Too dangerous. A shift of wind could bring the cold and snow in right at him. If he went to sleep he might freeze to death.

He decided to stay here long enough to rest his muscles and regain his breath, then climb back down again before all the light was gone. Then he'd hurry back to Texas Gulch.

He closed his eyes, listening to the howling wind and the endless, barely audible rattle of snowflakes pelting stone. The natural world seemed a vast, dangerous, but coldly splendid place just now.

Opening his eyes when he noticed a sudden diminishing of the snowfall, he realized what a spectacular view he had from this place of the great basin that held Texas Gulch. The sun was closing on the western horizon, nearly invisible behind the clouds, but revealing its presence as a smear of gray light. Quite a piece of creation, this was! But wild and indifferent to the men who tried to exploit it for the gleaming bits of gold it had to offer. Sam remembered words his father had told him: *a man who knows his proper place in the scheme of life is a wiser man than most, but also a much more sober one.* Sam was beginning to understand what that meant.

Time to climb down again.

Leaving his place of refuge, he turned and positioned himself to edge down over the lip of the ledge. His fingers were almost numb, so he wriggled them a few moments, then got a firm grip on the stone and began to descend.

He wasn't at precisely the same spot he'd come up, and was halfway down before he realized that this was a potentially serious problem. He'd veered into an area with fewer handholds and footholds. But he went on, occasionally slipping, but not falling.

At last he reached an impasse. Nothing but smooth stone

below, and several yards yet to descend. Too far to jump. Further, it was getting darker, and he couldn't see well in any direction. Should he drift left or right? Or would he have to climb back up and try to find some new route from there?

Left, he decided. That's how it would be. The stone was rougher in that direction. More to hold on to.

Sam began edging, inch by inch, in that direction. The light was fading far too fast, and he rushed a little. It was a mistake. His foot, barely caught in a small crevice, slipped free and made his body slip to one side and turn slightly. His right hand lost its precarious grip, and with his heart leaping to his throat, he plunged, pounding down the slope into a dark, hidden area below.

CHAPTER SEVEN

In the white world beyond the pass, the tree that Emmett Fish had seen was no longer there. As soon as Fish had turned and vanished, the "tree" had moved, and become a human being.

The man had waited only long enough for Fish to gain enough of a lead that he could be followed without becoming aware of it. The man had learned a lot from that little burst of information Fish had yelled up to him when he thought he was Dehaven, whomever that might be. The implications were troubling.

He followed Fish's tracks through the falling snow, utterly silent.

While Sam Underhill had been climbing carefully up a bluff far down the valley toward what he had thought would be the two missing children, the people of Texas Gulch were slowly emerging from their cabins to encounter an unexpected and chilling sight.

Jordan Mahaffery had ended all pretenses of gentleness toward Arianna Winkle by the time the exhausted horses came through the pass and in sight of Texas Gulch. Once there, Mahaffery had remounted his horse, with Arianna directly in front of him. By the time the riders reached the edge of the mining camp, Mahaffery had his pistol out and

pressed to the temple of the girl. She was too scared even
to cry.

To Mahaffery's right, Bert Mongold had the now-semi-
conscious Daniel Chase hefted upright in the saddle before
him, with Mongold's pistol stuck up under the boy's chin,
keeping his head propped up. Mongold wore a big smile.
He loved this kind of thing.

Mahaffery, for his part, was calm and businesslike. When
a sufficient number of startled, gaping people had gathered,
he nodded in friendly style and said, "Howdy to you all.
Texas Gulch, I believe you call this place now? Well, folks,
I just want you to know that your population has just in-
creased. Your cooperation with us, your new guests, is advised, or else the population could as easily make a sudden
decline."

Ben Dillow stepped toward Mahaffery. "Lower that pistol!" he demanded. "What kind of man are you to threaten
a little girl?"

Mahaffery clicked back the lock of his pistol. "I advise
you to stop where you are, unless you'd like to see me blow
this pretty young lady's brains out through her skull. Am I
speaking with sufficient clarity?"

Dillow halted and stood glaring at Mahaffery. Mongold
chuckled. Back in the crowd, Leora Winkle, who had just
then emerged to see her daughter in such straits, let out a
scream and ran toward Mahaffery.

"Uh-uh," Mahaffery said, shaking his head. "No,
ma'am. I don't advise it."

Dillow put out his arm and caught Leora as she began to
pass him. "Hold up, Leora. He'll kill her if you don't."

"That's right," Mahaffery said. "You're an intelligent
man, sir. A veritable scholar of common sense. I will indeed
kill this young lady, and Mr. Mongold there would gladly
kill that sorry scrap of a boy, if any one of you attempt even
the slightest interference with anything we do here. Is that
understood?"

No replies were heard beyond a few subtle mutters and

growls and the pitiful sound of Leora Winkle sobbing into her hands.

"By the way, my friend," Mahaffery said to miner Julius Setser, who was creeping about the edge of the little crowd, "I do see that pistol you're trying to conceal. And that's not at all what I meant by 'cooperation.' " Mahaffery raised his pistol, sighted down it, and shot Julius Setser through the heart. Arianna jerked like a puppet with its string yanked. Setser fell, twitched, and died in the snow as screams rose from the onlookers and people reflexively backed away from the new-fallen corpse.

Mahaffery began to reload his pistol, arms still wrapped around Arianna.

"Someone take the pistol from that dead man and hand it to my brother here," Mahaffery said, indicating Searl just to his left. "That, my friends, is what I meant when I talk about quick population decline. Need I give any further demonstrations?"

"Who are you, and what do you want from us?" Dillow said.

"Who I am is Jordan Mahaffery. This man to my left is Searl Mahaffery, my younger brother. Not at all a refined young man, I have to tell you. I advise you to keep your wives and daughters away from him, if you can." Mahaffery finished his reloading, meanwhile, but kept the pistol in his hand. "To my right is Mr. Bert Mongold, a vicious sort of devil who enjoys inflicting death in slow and colorful ways. Be very, very polite to him at all times."

Mongold, beaming, nodded at the people of Texas Gulch, acknowledging his due acclaim.

"These others with me are Mr. Lennis Yeager, Mr. Ross Remine, and Mr. Conner Broadgrass, three men you don't want angry at you." He turned and looked behind him. "Ah, yes! And yonder, walking through that pass behind me to join us, is Mr. Emmett Fish. Not the smartest man, Mr. Fish, but quite good at following directions. Completely lacking in scruples. I once saw him hack an old man to death for stepping on his sore toe.

"And over there are Joe Legarde, Reed Van Huss, and Perry Winters. Not much wickedness in this world those three haven't done, and not a bit of it they wouldn't do again.

"That's who we are. As for what we are, we're thieves. Scoundrels. Murderers. The lowest breed of mankind, and quite content with our station. Only one thing disturbs our peace, and that's when what's ours is taken from us. Which, sorry to say, is what's happened. And that's why we've come here to you."

"No one here has taken anything from you," Dillow said.

Mahaffery grabbed Arianna's arm and jerked it straight up so suddenly and so hard that the girl gasped and her mother screamed.

"Look at this girl's hand," Mahaffery said. The light was fading and so was his deliberately ironic facade of friend-liness. "There's a ring on her thumb. I know that ring. There's only one ring like that. I know the man who wore it. And I want to know, right now, no delay, where that man is." He let go of Arianna's hand and turned his pistol toward Dillow. "And if I don't find out, I'll kill you, sir."

"I don't know where that ring came from," Dillow said.

"I do." The speaker was Marica Bolton. She stepped around from the rear of the clump of scared people.

"Well, ma'am!" Mahaffery said, actually smiling at the sight of this previously unnoticed pretty lady. Beside him his younger brother whistled low and muttered something. He was grinning, too. "Pleasure to meet such loveliness in a dung pit of a mining camp like this. Do tell me what you know."

"That ring came from the finger of a dead man."

"Yes . . . I remember now," Dillow said. "She's right."

Emmett Fish, cold and glum and silent, reached the clump of outlaws and swung into his saddle, from where he peered across the gathered people of the mining camp.

Behind Fish, unseen by any, a shadowy figure had also entered the pass, drawing only close enough to hear what was said, but remaining out of sight.

"Mister, I'm talking to the lady just now, so you can keep your damned mouth shut," Mahaffery said to Dillow. "Dead man, did you say, ma'am?"

"Yes. He was found dead at the pass."

"And where is he now?"

"Buried."

"And how, ma'am, did this dead man become dead?"

"He was found dead. Mr. Dillow believes the man's heart failed him."

"Mr. Dillow?"

"That's me," Ben Dillow said.

"Fine. Then you tell me, Mr. Dillow, what became of whatever baggage the dead man had with him?"

"There was no baggage."

Mahaffery raised his pistol, aimed, and sent a ball hurtling just past Dillow's head. It almost struck America Colfax behind him. She screamed and ran to her husband. Arianna, close to the pistol when it fired, squeezed her eyes tightly closed. She bit her lip so hard her teeth almost broke the skin.

Mahaffery again began reloading the pistol.

"Mr. Dillow, the next time you lie to me, I'll shoot you through the face. Do you understand?"

Marica Bolton strode to Dillow, glanced at him, then stepped boldly between him and Mahaffery. "Would you shoot a woman, sir?"

"Ma'am, I'd shoot John the Baptist, Paul the Apostle, and in the right circumstances, my own mother."

"Mr. Dillow didn't lie to you. There was no baggage with the dead man. There was only his body."

"And who found it?"

"The boy there. Daniel."

Dillow whispered to her, "I wish you hadn't told him that."

"Ah!" Mahaffery said, looking over at Daniel, who was now looking around bleary-eyed, softly groaning every now and then. "So the boy found the body, alone . . . then came into town and informed the rest of you. And Dehaven—that's the name of the dead man, by the way—was collected and buried, all but his ring. Is that it?"

"That's it."

"So we have only the boy's word that nothing else was found with the body."

Marica Bolton blanched, realizing the trouble she might have just brought upon young Daniel. "Daniel never said that nothing was found with the body. He never said anything about that at all, either way."

Dillow stepped up beside Marica. He tried a new tack, no belligerence or defiance. "Mister, we'd like to answer your questions, but maybe we could understand things better if you explained what this baggage you talk about is supposed to be."

"Gold, sir. Gold, and gold aplenty. Stolen from a bank vault many miles away from here, by myself and my partners here, at the cost of a few lives, none of them ours. Then Dehaven, one of our number, managed to take that gold for himself and flee with it. We pursued him, tracked him to these mountains . . . and now we're being told he's dead and that the gold hasn't been seen at all." Another pause. "I, for one, am skeptical about that."

"Maybe this Dehaven hid the gold himself, before he got here."

"Hid the gold, then conveniently died. I find that hard to believe."

"You can search this camp. You'll find no gold beyond what we've grubbed ourselves."

"We *will* search this camp, sir. And we'll even dig up Dehaven's grave, come morning. Capable man that you seem to be, we'll give you the honor of the task. Then we'll take a look at that corpse and see if there are any signs of violence against him." As the wind howled and the snow suddenly became a little heavier and colder, Mahaffery looked the group over and gave a final pronouncement. "It's my belief that some of you, maybe all of you, have sinned the sin of greed. I believe that Dehaven did come to this camp. And I believe that some of you, maybe all, killed him for the sake of the gold he carried. And I believe that gold is here, hidden. And I want it."

Herbert Colfax, scowling, spoke up for the first time. "It ain't true, my friend. There was no gold seen by any one of us. I helped carry the dead man down from the pass. I can tell you there was no gold on him. So if anybody found gold, it was the boy, before any of the rest of us even knew there was a dead man."

Dillow wheeled and barked at Colfax, "What the devil are you trying to do, Colfax? Get a little boy tortured or killed?"

"I'm speaking the truth, that's what I'm doing, and I'll make no apology for it! I'll not be misused, nor see my family misused, for the sake of some lying orphan child!"

"Enough of that!" Mahaffery said. "All possibilities will be examined and explored. The truth will come out quickly enough. And when my partners and I leave this place, we *will* have our gold. And it makes no difference to any of us whether we leave this camp with a living population, or a dead one." He let the dark implication sink in. "Now . . . it's dark, it's cold, and the snow is heavy. I see a long, big log building back yonder. What is that? Some kind of common dwelling you folks share?"

"Some here share it. It was built back when this place was still called Dutch Camp," Colfax volunteered. "It's been divided up with partitions and such, so a lot of folks can live in it at the same time."

"We'll go inside there, then. All of us. And if there are any others living in this camp who aren't out here, I want them brought to me—man, woman, bed-baby . . . all of them. Don't try to hide anyone or anything, for we'll be exploring every inch and every cranny of this hellhole, and there'll be no secrets kept. Any who try to hide anything from me and my companions, anything at all, will not live to see another springtime. Any questions?''

"You're very clear, sir," Colfax said.

Dillow muttered, "Why don't you just ask him to rear up a little higher in the saddle so you can kiss his rump without so much strain, Colfax?''

"Don't mock the gentleman," Mahaffery said to Dillow. "He's got the right idea. He understands how things stand. The quicker all of you do the same, the better off you'll be.''

Mahaffery spoke to his men. "Emmett, you and Lennis get a couple of these folks to help you see to the horses. I presume there's some sort of stable. Lennis, it'll be your task as long as we're here to make sure the horses stay tended and fed. For now, the rest of us will get these folks herded together in that big cabin, and we'll search this camp for guns and such. And find some food! I'm nigh starved.''

"I'd advise guarding the pass as long as we're here, Jordan," Broadgrass said. "If there's anyone hidden out here that we don't yet see, they might get out in the darkness, before we're even aware of them.''

"You're a wise man, Conner. Reed! Perry! Joe! You three get a couple of big fires blazing up in that pass. And stand guard to make sure nobody gets out. You—Dillow! Is there any other way out of this valley?''

"None," Dillow said glumly.

"Very good, then. We'll all stay here together. Reed, Joe, Perry, we'll have some food up to you soon. And we'll work out some shifts so nobody has to stay up there all night. Make those fires big, you hear? Light up that whole pass, and get yourself plenty of heat.''

Mahaffery turned back to the people. "Folks, pleased to be with you all. You behave, you cooperate, you'll be fine. You don't, and you'll wind up like that fellow there." He pointed at the body of Julius Setser. "Now let's get out of this weather, what do you say?''

CHAPTER EIGHT

The three outlaws designated by Mahaffery trudged up to the pass, taking with them wood from one of the several massive woodpiles around Texas Gulch, the fuel set aside to get an isolated mining camp through a long and cold winter. As they entered the pass, the shadowy figure that had followed Emmett Fish moved, hesitated, then moved again, slipping back toward the mountains.

Minutes later, as the flames of two bonfires rose, illuminating the gap, the unseen man watched from outside the circle of light. For a long time he waited, then at length turned and quietly moved farther into the darkness and away from the light.

Sam Underhill rolled over and did his best to groan, but the impact of his fall had temporarily paralyzed his lungs, and he couldn't draw a breath.

Sitting up, he felt the reflexive panic that comes from the inability to breathe, and struggled to suck in air. A few moments later his body cooperated and he breathed in ragged gasps. The panic subsided, but in its place came pain. He felt as if two giant fists had grabbed him like a wet rag and given him a wringing in opposing directions.

"Dear Lord," he muttered. "That was indeed a tumble."

He turned his body a little. His ribs were sore, but not

sore enough to make him think he'd broken any. That much was good. He wriggled his toes, turned his feet, drew up his knees and straightened them again. Everything worked. Nothing broken there. He checked his hands, his arms, rolled his shoulders. Everything was in operating order, though he ached all over and figured that before long he'd have enough bruises to make him look like a map.

Once he'd decided that providence had spared him any major injuries, he turned his attention to the place where he'd landed. He was in nearly total darkness, though the last lingering traces of daylight were still visible through some sort of opening above him. He saw he was inside some enclosed place, apparently a vertical cavern, or pit, at the base of the bluff.

He looked around, but the darkness spread to all sides. He stood, very slowly, still testing his body. He bumped his head, though, and stepped forward to seek more room.

Snow drifted down around him, through the opening above, but only a little. He scuffed his boot on the stony soil beneath his feet and found it relatively free of accumulation.

He dug around in the folds and pockets of his bearskin coat. The coat was a gift given him by his father and mother prior to his departure to California. Bushrod Underhill had shot the bear himself on a hunting venture into Arkansas five years earlier, and had considered it the prize bear of a long hunting career. He'd saved the skin to make a coat for himself, but when Sam had announced his intention to become a Forty-niner, he had bade his wife to make the coat to fit Sam instead. So this garment had a lot of meaning to Sam Underhill, and as he thought about it, he realized its heavy protection probably accounted in large part for how he'd managed to take such a fall without serious injury.

At last he found the matchblock he sought. Breaking a match off, he knelt, shielded it with his body, and struck fire. By the flaring light he looked around him, as far as the light would allow. Yes, he was in some sort of pit, probably another entrance to one of the many caverns running through the mountains around the Texas Gulch basin. There were plenty such caves, new entrances constantly being found by the prospectors as they poked around the landscape looking for gold.

The match burned to Sam's fingers and he shook it out. Standing partially, but keeping his head low, he crept a little farther to the center of the pit, then knelt and lit another match. By its light he studied the floor. Ah, yes. Just as he'd hoped. There were dried evergreen needles, twigs, even a few old and dried branches that had fallen or blown into this hole over the years. He shook out the match, and in blind-man fashion felt around his feet and gathered twigs and tinder. Heaping these, he struck another match and lit a fire. The dry materials caught easily, and by their flames he gathered a few of the bigger sticks and added them to the blaze. He piled on yet more fuel and soon had a small but wonderfully warm and light-generating fire, sheltered from the wind by the walls of the pit.

Remembering his notice of the angle of the slope high above him, he considered his good fortune that no snowslide had yet occurred here. If this pit had filled with snow there would be no fire to build here, nothing to do but try to struggle out some way before he froze in a crystalline pool of deep, icy white.

He tried not to think too much about the fact that the snow, if it kept falling, might pile up on that slope enough to bring on that first avalanche at almost any time. A man could die a hard death under the sudden crush of such a snow mass.

Sam sat down beside the fire, feeling like a great, weary bear in his heavy coat. He simply stared and breathed for a time, forcing himself not to worry about snowslides and other dangers he could do nothing about, and merely to take pleasure for a few moments in being alive and relatively unhurt. He must have fallen right through the opening above him, which was not much bigger than the base of a prairie schooner at its widest point. He was fortunate indeed to have avoided striking the sides of it as he went through. He said a prayer of thanks, then another for the welfare of Arianna and Daniel.

Sam added a little more fuel to the fire and stood slowly. "Well," he said aloud, "I guess I need to figure out how to get out of this hole."

He looked around, on all sides. Beneath a small, flat rock outcrop he found a crevice that led deeper into the mountainside, a small cavern opening that might go back mere yards, or might lead into some vast cave. It was large enough to accommodate a crawling man, but there was nothing to gain by plunging into the heart of a dark mountain. Other than that small cave mouth, however, there was no other evident exit from the pit except for the hole above.

He looked up at that hole, and examined the pit walls beneath it. These were not of pure stone; they also contained quite a bit of soil and imbedded, broken gravel. If he had a sharp knife, he might be able to dig himself handholds and footholds, and gradually work his way up and out again. But he'd not brought his knife. He marveled at his own foolishness. He'd never neglected carrying his knife before.

Sam studied the slope of the walls and saw exactly what he feared he would. He was effectively inside a giant bottle, the walls sloping in, narrowing toward the opening. This place seemed naturally engineered to let a man fall in easily enough, but not to get out again.

The fire, burning hot and fast and fueled by very dry materials, began to die. Sam scrounged about and found more wood. It wouldn't last long, though. Not much burnable material had chanced to find its way through that opening and into this pit.

When the blaze was going nicely again, Sam evaluated his predicament. Clearly he couldn't scale walls that sloped inward . . . but as he examined them again, he realized that one side of the "bottle" was more vertical than the others.

A man with a climbing implement might make his way out up that wall—with luck.

But he had no climbing implement. All the sticks he'd found were dried and dead, nothing worthy of crafting into a makeshift pike, nothing big enough to use as a climbing pole. Nor were there sufficient rocks about to enable him to heap up a mound high enough to take him within reach of the opening.

He began to think about how he might be in this hole for a very long time.

It was worth worrying about. He had a fire for now, but soon the fuel would be gone. Though sheltered from the direct impact of the weather, the pit still was cold. A man could freeze to death in here. Or starve. Or . . .

"Whoa, Mr. Underhill," he said to the flickering light on the cavern walls. "Hold up there right now. That kind of thinking kills a man faster than the elements. There'll be a way out. You just got to find it. This hole is no match for a determined man. Just got to look about and—"

He cut off abruptly, and held his silence for a long time. He had moved, and his own shadow had moved with him, allowing firelight to reveal something he hadn't seen earlier.

Sam drew closer and knelt before what he'd found and slowly shook his head.

"My friend, I have to tell you that it's no encouragement to find you here."

The face that stared back at him did not move nor speak. In fact it was hardly a face at all, just what was left of one after a couple of years of decay. Empty eye sockets examined him. What little flesh remained stretched across the skull of the dead man wasn't much more than yellowed, dry leather, badly eaten by rot and insects. The mouth hung open, and the clothing, what remained of it, was mere tattered rags hanging on bone.

"Two dead men found within the same week," Sam said. "One fresh dead, the other long dead. Strange times, these."

The fire was dying again, so Sam once more replenished

it, then began a closer examination of the corpse. From the clothing and situation of the fellow, he suspected he'd found an ill-fated Forty-niner, probably from back in the Dutch Camp days. Probably he, like Sam, had come into this natural trap by some accident.

But if so, why hadn't his companions noticed he was missing, and come for him?

That question bothered Sam more than he wanted to admit. From the moment he'd realized that climbing out of here wasn't going to be easy, a faint hope had held that, if nothing else, he could count on Ben Dillow or somebody else coming to look for him. He could yell, try to send up smoke, do something to get attention . . .

But wouldn't this man have done the same? Yet no one had come for him. He'd died here. And from the upright posture, Sam was sure he hadn't died immediately upon his fall into the hole. Folks don't usually tumble into a seated posture and stay there.

"You are not an encourager, my friend," he said. "Not a bit of it."

Ah, but he might be a benefactor, Sam thought. *He might have something on him I can use to get out of here.*

Sam was a little more squeamish than he liked others to know, so it wasn't easy for him to touch the dead man. But he did so, pushing the body gently to the side and examining what he found around it. There was a pistol near one of the hands. It was old and rusted, the lock snapped down, the flint still in place, the wooden grip half decayed away . . .

Dear Lord . . . A dreadful possibility came to Sam only then. He looked at the side of the skull. Sure enough, there was a rounded hole, and on the other side, a shredded exit wound.

This poor man had put a pistol ball through his own brain.

Sam pulled his hands away. Touching a dead man was bad in itself; touching one who was dead because he chose to be was worse, somehow. But a moment later, Sam resumed his examination of the man's body, feeling through the trousers and wrapping his hand around what was left of the man's legs. Hardly thicker were they now, than Sam's own forearms, and little more than bone with hide on top.

He paused when he detected a clean break in the right thighbone.

Now he understood. This poor fellow had fallen in, broken his leg, and rather than die a slow death alone, had opted to use his pistol to end things more quickly.

"Poor old soul," Sam whispered. "I'm mighty sorry for how things ended for you."

It came to mind that if this man was a Forty-niner, he might have some kind of tools. But he found none. No pan, no shovel . . . but wait! On the corpse's belt, left side, was a sheath with a knife still in it. Sam slid it free. The sheath had protected the knife from moisture and rust. He turned it, examining it in the firelight, then glanced at the vertical section of wall leading to the upper opening.

Maybe. Just maybe.

He slid the knife into one of the many pockets and pouches he'd sewn into the inside of his coat, and continued to search the corpse. He found a couple of gold nuggets, which he kept, and a picture locket, open. Whatever image had been inside had decayed away. A wife or fiancée, probably. He felt another burst of pity for this unknown man.

The knife and the rusted pistol. That was pretty much it. This man hadn't brought much with him into his final resting place. Sam still wondered why no one had ever come looking for him.

Possibly, he thought, *the reason nobody came is that nobody knew he existed. Maybe he wasn't one of the miners who founded Dutch Camp. Maybe he came across the mountains into the valley, and was prospecting in secret, fearing the people in the camp might drive him out.*

A decent theory, though he couldn't know if it was true. But it did make him wonder if there might be another route in and out of the Texas Gulch basin besides the pass.

Sam went to the far side of the pit and sat down. He dug

around in his coat until he found some of the meat he'd brought. Ben Dillow had joked before that a man could live for a month off the stray food he could find tucked away in that big coat of Sam's. He slowly ate some of it while he looked at the wall he was going to attempt to climb. Always plan your actions, his father had often advised him. A man who acts without a plan is a man soon mourned by those he left behind.

At length Sam stood. The fire was low again. One more round of searching and gathering wood, dried evergreen needles, and such. One more restoring of the blaze. As an afterthought Sam even added some of the ragged clothing of the dead man.

The light rose in the pit, and smoke billowed toward the hole through which Sam would attempt his exit. Taking several deep breaths, he went to the vertical section of wall, wriggled his arms and legs to warm the muscles, and with the knife gouged out a hole big enough to accommodate the toe of his right boot. He wedged his foot into the foothold, and hoisted himself up. Once there, Sam gouged a second hole, higher up, for his left foot. On he went, foot by precarious foot, slowly making his ascent.

CHAPTER
NINE

He was almost halfway up before he slipped and fell. It happened fast, the result of one of the gouged footholds giving way under his weight, and he barely managed to land on his feet. Standing, he brushed himself off, found the knife where he'd dropped it during the fall, and checked himself over for possible new injuries.

Nothing. Relieved, he looked over at the dead man and said, "Lucky that time. I might have busted my leg like you did." He paused, thinking how it must have been for the poor fellow. Probably the man had sat there looking at that same vertical wall Sam was now trying to climb. Probably he'd realized that he could use his knife just as Sam was using it now and gotten out of here . . . if only his leg wasn't broken.

No wonder the man had been driven to put a pistol ball through his own skull.

Sam didn't linger. He went back to the wall, began his climb anew, and this time made it even higher before falling. Once again he escaped injury, though he did abrade his left thigh badly and come down painfully hard on one heel.

The fire was almost gone now. Sam felt a mounting sense of desperation. He needed light to climb, and he'd expended almost all the meager fuel in the pit. He tried again to climb, and this time didn't fall, but still he was forced to descend again because he simply ran out of light. The fire dwindled to almost nothing.

Discouraged, Sam plopped down in the darkness and leaned back against the wall of the pit. He'd been so close to escape! But now, with the fire gone, there was nothing to do but wait for morning.

He found a comfortable space between two boulders, huddled back in his big, protective coat, and closed his eyes. His final thought before sleep came was of his friends and neighbors back in Texas Gulch. He wondered if they were safe and warm in their beds, the children having been found in his absence. He hoped so. Another part of him hoped the men of the town were out with torches, scouring the valley, searching for him.

Even if they were, they'd not find him tonight. He made himself relax and accept the situation as it stood. It wasn't long before his breathing slowed and his head sagged.

In the pit, with no company but the leathery corpse of an unknown man, Sam Underhill slept.

In Texas Gulch, no one was sleeping.

In the lodge house, home normally to several residents who had afforded themselves a touch of privacy by dividing it into chambers, with the erection of canvas screens, the entire population of Texas Gulch—minus Sam Underhill— was crowded. The canvas screens were gone, torn down with enthusiasm by Bert Mongold at the orders of Mahaffery. Mongold had ripped down the barriers with such violent destructiveness that he had seemed more animal than human to those who watched.

Now Mongold seemed eager for more meaningful violence. He paced about, mumbling and making guttural sounds, watching an interrogation now under way, with Mahaffery as questioner, young Daniel Chase as subject. Daniel was still slightly groggy and disoriented from the blow he had suffered at Mongold's hands up beyond the pass.

"I'm going to ask you again, son," Mahaffery said gently. "I want you to think hard, and tell me what you might have found at the same time you found Mr. Dehaven's body."

"I didn't find . . . nothing."

"Maybe you did. Maybe you're just a little addled right now and can't recall it. Maybe there was something lying beside Mr. Dehaven in the snow. Maybe you picked it up, and put it somewhere else."

"There was . . . there was . . ."

Mahaffery leaned forward, intent.

". . . There was nothing."

Mahaffery leaned back again. Mongold swore loudly, then said, "Let me have a try with him, Jordan. I'll make him talk."

"Stay out of this, Bert. We'll do it my way."

"He's lying to you!"

Mahaffery said, "I don't think he is."

Mongold snorted disdainfully.

Leora Winkle let out a screech on the other side of the room. Mahaffery looked just in time to see his younger brother take a hard slap across the face from the woman.

Leora was drawing back for another slap, when Searl Mahaffery grabbed her arm and stopped the blow. He doubled up a big fist and pulled it back . . .

"Searl!"

Searl stopped his fist in mid-swing. His elder brother had risen and was striding toward him.

"She slapped me, Jordan! The shrew slapped me!"

"He insulted my daughter," Leora said, her face even redder than the handprint clearly visible across Searl Mahaffery's stinging face. "What he said to her no mother should have to hear spoken to her child!"

"All I said was that the little gal's pretty enough to—"

"Searl, shut up. Now," Mahaffery said. He hadn't raised his voice, yet the command bore the authority of a shout. "There'll be no more of this kind of behavior."

Searl gaped. "Jordan, you shot a man to death before

these people! And you're telling *me* I should act the high-stocking gentleman?''

"I shot a man to make a point that had to be made. You'll stay away from this lady, and her daughter, or you'll deal with me. You understand me, Searl?''

Searl glowered. Turning away, he swaggered off to a corner and plopped down on a stool.

Mahaffery turned to Leora. "I beg your pardon for my brother's behavior, ma'am. He's not a couth man.''

"You, sir, and your brother, may both go to hell,'' Leora said, eyes unblinkingly staring into his.

Mahaffery arched his brows, flaring his nostrils in anger, then paused and chuckled. "You are a high-spirited woman as well as a lovely one,'' he said. "Two fine qualities, those.'' He turned and headed back over to resume his interrogation of Daniel Chase.

"High-spirited, he says,'' Texas Gulch prospector Copp Nolen muttered to Ben Dillow, who sat beside him. They were across the so-called lodge house from the place where the little drama had just played out. "So she does seem to be. That ain't the humble, meek little Leora Winkle I've known before.''

"She's protecting her child. That brings out a new aspect in a woman,'' Dillow replied.

"She surely did slap the fire out of Little Brother over there.''

"Refreshing sight, I thought.''

"Tell me something, Ben. What do you think's going to happen come morning?''

"Mahaffery's already said he'll have the dead man dug up. He'll look over the corpse and see that the man wasn't shot or stabbed. Then he'll know we weren't lying to him, that we haven't killed the man and taken his gold for ourselves.''

"There ain't wounds on the body . . . right?''

"None. I looked him over close. Whatever killed him, killed him from the inside."

"What if they *did* come to believe, for some reason, that any of us killed the man?"

"I don't want to think about that."

"There'd be threatening and torturing, trying to make somebody talk . . . you reckon?" Copp suggested.

"I'd say so."

"You *sure* there was no mark of violence on that corpse?"

"I'm sure. But I don't know that it will matter in the end. These devils are going to end up killing us all, anyway."

A pause. "You don't mean that, do you, Ben?"

"I do. These are desperate and wicked men. They've already murdered one man in cold blood, right before our eyes. Once we become useless, they'll not leave us alive to cause them trouble later. This protect-the-ladies, play-the-gentleman act that Mahaffery's putting on will vanish fast once he has nothing more to gain from us, I'll bet."

"How do you know so much about it?"

"Because I know Mahaffery's type." Dillow paused. "I was a constable once, back in Kentucky. I had to deal with a lot of such folk. The frontier always draws that kind."

"You were a constable? Then why did you let them make Sam Underhill the marshal here, instead of you?"

"I've been a man of the law once. That's enough. Besides, in truth there is no real law here, not even Sam. He was just willing to take the title. I doubt he ever anticipated anything like this coming up."

"Speaking of Sam . . . Ben, he ain't here."

"I know."

"So where is he?"

"I don't know . . . but the fact he ain't here is the one thing that gives me some hope. If Sam is out there, and they don't know it, then that's an edge we've got on Mahaffery. Our one and only edge."

"Not much of one. One man, alone. And all the rest of us under the gun."

"Don't underestimate Sam Underhill. He's got more gravel in his craw than a dozen average men. There's a lot of his daddy in that old boy. I just hope he knows what's going on. Otherwise he might just stumble into the midst of it and be caught along with the rest of us."

The door opened, and Emmett Fish and Ross Remine entered, bearing armloads of weapons. Dillow shook his head.

"There's my rifle. And my pistols, too. And every other durn weapon in this mining camp, judging from the size of the load they're carrying."

"We're helpless, then. No weapons at all, and all of us hostages."

A few moments of silence followed this somber evaluation.

Nolen broke the silence. "So we'll dig up the body, and they'll see that the dead man wasn't killed by us. What then?"

"I think they'll turn to the idea that the man either dropped or hid the gold out in the mountains on his way here. Most likely they'll go to where his body was found, and dig about in the snow. Or have us do it for them."

"Maybe there really is gold up there."

"There could be. But I hope we don't find it."

"Why? They'd go away then."

"They'll go away, and leave us moldering as corpses."

"You believe they'll kill us even if they get their gold?"

"Like I said: they'll never leave folks alive who've witnessed them commit murder."

On the other side of Dillow, Herbert Colfax grunted. He'd been sitting there, listening, silent until now. "That's nonsense, Ben Dillow. You don't know what they'll do."

Nolen looked around Dillow at Colfax. "Ben may be right, Colfax. We did witness them murdering Julius. That makes any one of us a potential witness against them."

"Julius was sneaking about with a gun. He brought it on himself."

"Just whose side are you on, anyhow?" Nolen asked.

"My side. Me and my family's side. And I'm not giving up and declaring myself doomed just yet, no matter what Dillow here believes."

"I hope you're right and I'm wrong," Dillow said. "But I see little grounds to be optimistic about these scoundrels."

Copp Nolen abruptly asked Colfax, "Herbert, what time is it?"

Colfax pulled his pocket watch from under his vest. "Three in the morning."

"Found that pocket watch, I see. Remarkable that you could find it out in that snow, in the dark."

"What are you trying to say, Copp?"

"Nothing. Just commenting that it was remarkable that you could go out in the snow, in the dark, and find that pocket watch."

"I was lucky."

"Yeah. Tell me. Did you find anything else while you were poking about in the snow up there last night, all by yourself?"

Colfax rose and faced Nolen. "I don't like what you're implying, Copp."

Dillow said, "Herbert, sit down. And Copp, keep your mouth shut. You're attracting some unwanted attention our way."

Colfax turned to see Searl Mahaffery striding toward him. The red mark left by Leora Winkle's hand was still clearly visible on Searl's face.

"Set your fat backside down again, old man," Searl commanded.

"Show some respect for your elders, boy," Colfax replied.

Searl Mahaffery's fist rocked Colfax's jaw. The older man staggered and made a deep, guttural noise, but did not fall. America Colfax cried out on the other side of the room, where she had been seated, weeping and scared, beside Marica Bolton, receiving comfort and reassurances from the kindhearted younger woman.

"Sit down, Searl!" This came from Jordan Mahaffery. "You too, old-timer."

Colfax, hand gingerly on jaw, glanced down at Nolen, and softly said, "You'd best be careful, throwing around allegations at a time like this."

"In your seat, old man!" Jordan Mahaffery commanded again, more harshly.

Colfax strode across the room and sat down beside his wife. She wept and laid her head on his shoulder, her broad shoulders heaving.

"Herbert's right," Dillow said. "You ought not have said what you did, Copp. You were hinting pretty strong that he might have found that gold last night."

"If a man can find a missing pocket watch in the dark, he might find something else, too. Or more likely, he never had lost that pocket watch at all. Maybe he stubbed his toe on that cache of gold while we were fetching the body, and went back up to claim it later. Remember how he was staying back in the dark while we were up there? Remember how nervous he was after we brought back the body? Remember how he refused to let anyone go back with him to look for his watch?"

Dillow whispered, "If speculation like that got to the ears of our new friends, you could get Colfax killed really fast."

"I don't trust Colfax. Never have."

"You've also never liked him, and he's never liked you. But don't let that get us off track. If there's any hope of making it through this, we have to work together. And trust each other."

"I'll never trust Colfax. I don't have it in me. And as far as dangerous speculations go, you heard how Colfax was trying so hard before to persuade Mahaffery that poor little Daniel yonder had probably found the gold. Did you see anybody else trying to throw off blame that way? Old Colfax was mighty quick with his *own* accusations, it seems to me.''

Dillow sighed and leaned back. Maybe Nolen had a point, though he hoped not. He'd hate to think that even sour old Herbert Colfax would be willing to betray and endanger his friends and fellow miners for the sake of a cache of stolen gold.

A desperate desire to find some way out of this predicament overwhelmed Dillow, but all he could do was sit there, helpless. With all the weapons in the hands of the outlaws, and every resident of Texas Gulch held hostage, he could do nothing.

No, he reminded himself, there was one resident yet who wasn't hostage.

''Sam,'' he murmured toward the underside of the roof, ''I hope you're out there, and that you've figured out what's going on, and that you've got some way in mind to get us out of this. Because for the life of me, I surely don't.''

''What'd you say, Ben?'' Copp Nolen asked.

''Nothing, Copp,'' Dillow replied. ''Just talking to myself.''

CHAPTER
TEN

Slowly and warily, Sam Underhill picked himself up one more time from the rocky floor of the pit. Sore now . . . no, beyond sore. Since the first welcome morning light had spilled into the hole, he'd tried three times to climb his way out. Three times he'd fallen. And three times, he was thankful to discover, he'd managed to break no bones.

The bruises, though, were going to be a sight worth seeing.

He stood and looked sadly up at the sky beyond the hole. Would he never find a way out of here?

"The devil with this!" Sam muttered. "I'm not going to die down here in this hole!"

He'd dropped his knife again, so he looked for it. There it was, on the floor, the blade cleanly snapped off at the hilt.

He gazed at it, fighting despair. *Now* what would he do?

His eye turned to the dead man. Walking over, he eyed the fellow. "Friend, is there a chance at all you've got anything for me that I haven't found yet?" He nudged the corpse to one side with his toe.

What was revealed had been previously covered by the dead man's corpse. Sam stared down at it thankfully, and picked it up.

It was a small rock pick, typical of the sort prospectors carried. The handle was made of hardwood and had a thick

varnish finish, and was not at all rotted, even for having
been nestled up against a dead man for Lord knew how long.
The head of the pick, though badly rusted, was still sharp
and strong.

"Thank you, my friend," Sam said with honest emotion.
"Thank you. What you've given me here very well may
save my life. I'm only sorry it wasn't able to save yours."

The ground had begun to freeze, so the dirt, gravel, and
rubble that filled the makeshift grave of the dead outlaw was
much more difficult to dig out than it had been to put in.
Further, none of the laborers had slept the night before,
which made exhaustion loom all the closer. Still they
worked hard, under the constant threat of the guns of Mahaffery's men.

Dillow slowly stood up in the hole, letting his straining
back relax as he leaned on his shovel. Mahaffery paced back
and forth in the snow with a cigar in his hand. Dillow said,
"We just got down to the body."

"Haul him out, then."

Dillow was thinking about how satisfying it would be to
ram his shovel suddenly into Mahaffery's belly and give it
a hard twist. Just a pleasant fantasy, that was all. To really
try it would get him killed. "We've got a little more dirt
and rock to clear before we can get him out."

"Then why are you standing there working your jaws
instead of your shovel?"

In the hole with Dillow was Fleenor, the would-be poet
and philosopher. The pair of them went back to their labors,
and within three minutes had the body exposed. Thanks to
the cold weather, decay and stench were minimal.

With effort, and help from Crain Brown and Joe Skinner,
they managed to haul the stiffened dead man out of the hole,
where he was dumped without ceremony in the snow, land-
ing facedown. Fleenor and Dillow climbed out. Emmett Fish
came over and knelt by the body. He'd always found the

dead fascinating. Searl came near, too, and stood beside Fish.

"Roll him over," Mahaffery ordered. Emmett Fish obeyed, revealing the face to the outlaws.

Searl Mahaffery leaned over and spat tobacco juice into the dead man's face. "Howdy, Dehaven," he said, and cackled with laughter. "You're looking kind of sickly."

"Searl, don't dirty him up more than he is. I want to be able to examine that body for wounds. Get down there and strip the clothes off him."

"I ain't stripping the clothes off no dead man!"

"Then get out of the way. If you won't be useful, at least don't be underfoot for those who are."

Emmett Fish did the job instead. When the gray, mottled, and late Frank Dehaven lay naked in the snow, Mahaffery knelt and began examining him thoroughly, even looking through the hair for hidden entrance wounds from a bullet or blade. Eventually he stood.

"What'd you find?" Searl asked his older brother.

Mahaffery's answer was to shove the corpse back into the hole with a single hard push of his booted foot.

"No bullet holes or nothing, huh?"

"Not a one. It appears we've been told the truth. Dehaven wasn't killed. The old thief up and died on his own."

"Maybe they strangled him, or beat him to death."

"It would show."

"Maybe they smothered him."

"Why would they smother him instead of just shooting him and being done with it?" Mahaffery was beginning to sound irritable. "It isn't like they knew we were going to be showing up to look him over."

Searl spat into the hole on the dead man again.

"Cover him up," Mahaffery ordered Fleenor and Dillow.

"So where do you reckon the gold is, if these folks didn't take it from him?" Remine asked.

"Either he hid it or dropped it. If he hid it, we may never

find it. If he dropped it, that probably happened somewhere near where he died."

"Up in the snow?"

"That's right." Mahaffery turned and called to Conner Broadgrass. "Broadgrass! Gather up the menfolk and herd them up to the pass." Mahaffery looked over the glum assembly of his hostages. "It's going to be a day of pleasure for you folks. You're going to dig in the snow, just like children."

Arianna Winkle, standing beside her mother, did not hear a word Mahaffery said. She was too distracted by a sight that only she had noticed: Hiram Linfoot was sneaking away from the group of hostages, unnoticed by Mahaffery or his distracted guards. Arianna dared not breathe. She inwardly cheered for him. *Run, Mr. Linfoot! Get away from them! And find help for us.*

She didn't know how he could find help by running back into the enclosed, unpopulated valley instead of toward the pass, but she didn't dwell on that. It was satisfying merely to see someone getting away.

"What are you looking at, girly?"

Arianna snapped her head around to look at the bulky Bert Mongold. "Nothing."

Mongold turned in the direction she had been staring, but Linfoot dropped to the ground just as Mongold looked his way. Arianna thought he'd dropped too late, but Mongold didn't seem to have seen him. She noticed that Mongold was squinting badly. Bad eyes. *Good thing for Mr. Linfoot*, she thought.

Mongold turned back to Arianna. "Did I see something move out yonder?"

"I don't know what you saw."

"You speak up, girly! Tell me if there was somebody out there! My eyes ain't the best."

"I saw my dog running across," Arianna lied.

"That was all? Your dog?"

"Yes."

"I don't want you talking to my daughter," Leora said, putting her arm around Arianna's shoulder. "Speak to me, if you have anything to say to either of us."

"I'll talk to the girly if I want," Mongold said. He stepped forward and looked down at Arianna. "You sure it was just a dog?"

"Yes, sir."

Mongold stared at her a few moments. "My, my, but ain't you a pretty little thing. There's a few lessons I could teach you, little gal, if you was just a year or two older."

Leora stepped between Arianna and Mongold, which placed her uncomfortably close to the stinking, ugly man. But she did not flinch back from him. "I told you: I don't want you talking to my daughter. Especially not that kind of talk."

Mongold grinned at her; his teeth were brown as dirt. "That kind of talk, eh? What kind of talk do you mean? This kind, maybe?" He leaned forward and whispered in Leora's ear.

Leora's knee came up fast and hard, and caught the big man in the groin with a force scarcely less than that of a sledgehammer. Mongold sucked in two lungfuls of breath in record time, made a strange, high sound, and backed away, doubling over and growing brilliant red in the face, gripping himself in a most indiscreet fashion.

"Was that the kind of attention you were talking about, sir?" Leora asked him.

The other outlaws howled with laughter. Even Mahaffery seemed amused, and an uncharacteristic smile crossed the usually inscrutable face of brooding, deep-thinking Conner Broadgrass.

Mongold slowly raised his crimson, bleary-eyed face to look up at the hard-as-iron, coldly beautiful visage of Leora Winkle. "I'll kill you for that," he said in a very tight and pain-wracked voice.

Daniel Chase had been in a daze through most of the

night, even while being questioned by Mahaffery, but the coming of morning had restored him. He ran over to Mongold, stopped just outside the bent-over man's reach, and said, "You wouldn't dare threaten her if Mr. Underhill was here!"

Over by the hole, Dillow closed his eyes and thought, *Oh, no.* He'd hoped that word of the existence of Sam Underhill wouldn't reach the ears of the outlaws.

Mongold tried to kick at Daniel with the side of his foot, but the effort was rather pitiful and drew more laughter from the other outlaws. The residents of Texas Gulch were enjoying it, too, though they dared not show it.

"Mr. Underhill wouldn't be afraid of you! He'd tie you up into a ball and roll you down the mountain!"

Shut up, boy! Dillow was thinking. *Just keep your mouth shut!*

"Get away from me, boy," Mongold said, slowly trying to straighten. His face was still very red and he was breathing strangely.

Arianna shifted her eyes leftward. Hiram Linfoot was on the move again, darting through the snow and back into the valley. Just a little farther and he'd be over a rise and out of sight. She prayed for him, silently.

Mahaffery said, "Who's this Underhill the boy speaks of?"

Dillow had a sudden inspiration. "He's talking about Bushrod Underhill," he said quickly, hoping no one would counter him.

"Bushrod Underhill?"

"That's right," Dillow said. "Bushrod Underhill, who ropes the moon and rides tornadoes like they were horses and drinks the Great Lakes dry when he's thirsty. I tell the boy tales to entertain him, and he takes them a bit too seriously at times."

Dillow glanced around at the faces of the other people of Texas Gulch, and saw a lot of confusion, but also some dawning understanding of what he was doing. For the first time some of those people seemed to be realizing that Sam wasn't with them, and that with one of their number, especially one so capable and intelligent as Sam, free and able to act in the background, there might be hope.

"Is that right, boy?" Mahaffery asked Daniel.

Daniel glanced at Dillow, confused, but read the message in Dillow's eyes and obediently said, "Yes."

"Bushrod Underhill, eh?" Mahaffery said. "I've read some of them almanacs. Old Bushrod's quite a character, eh, son? A bigger wildman than even old Davy Crockett was in his day."

"That's right," Daniel said, beginning to rise to the occasion. "And if he was here, he'd whup you all!"

"So he might, but he ain't here."

"Mahaffery." The speaker was Conner Broadgrass, and he was pointing back into the valley.

Arianna felt her heart sink as she saw that Broadgrass had spotted Hiram Linfoot just as he topped the rise. Now Mahaffery saw him too, and snapped his fingers twice.

"Emmett Fish! And you, Mongold! Go after him!"

Mongold twisted his head, watched Linfoot scramble away, then looked back at his chief, perplexed. "Jordan, I can't hardly walk, much less chase a man through the snow!"

"You got enough energy to be talking filth to decent women and little girls, you got enough to make yourself useful. Get your rifle and go after him, now! And when you catch him, don't feel inclined to mercy. Let's make a good lesson out of that man, hmmm?"

Fish and Mongold set out through the snow, pursuing Hiram Linfoot toward the heart of the valley, Fish moving much more quickly than Mongold and soon leaving him behind.

CHAPTER ELEVEN

Sam Underhill sat at the edge of the hole at the top of the pit, legs dangling into the space below. He was sore, out of breath, and cold, but very happy. Out at last! If not for finding that pick, he might never have gotten free.

He bowed his head and said a prayer. Then, with head still bowed, he looked into the hole again, and spoke his silent gratitude to the silent dead man now unseen down there. Before commencing his climb out of the pit, he'd taken time to move the corpse into the small cavern beneath the stone outcrop, and laid him there on his back, arms folded across his chest. It was a final gesture of respect for an unknown man long passed on, and his thanks for the life-saving gift of the little rock pick.

Sam rose, looking around the bright landscape. Time to head home. He marveled to think that what had started as a simple hike to bring in two straying children had turned into an all-night ordeal. He wondered if his peers were out searching for him.

Most of all he wondered what had happened to Daniel and Arianna.

He paused to eat a few bites of jerked meat from one of the pockets of his bulky coat, then rose and began looking for the snowshoes he'd left at the base of the slope the day before. He couldn't find them; snow had covered them thoroughly.

He sighed and made the best of it. The snow wasn't so deep yet that he couldn't make it even without snowshoes.

Sam began hiking through the white valley back in the direction of Texas Gulch.

Progress was slow, and an hour passed before Sam topped a small rise and saw that he was nearing the final stretch to the mining camp. He also saw something else, which confused and dismayed him.

A man was running, scrambling wildly, through the snow, coming roughly in Sam's direction at first, then veering to the south. The way he moved, the wild manner in which he looked over his shoulder and then ran harder, made Sam wonder what kind of demon was on the fellow's trail.

Sam looked harder, squinting, and recognized the man as Hiram Linfoot.

He started to shout at Hiram but didn't. Something unusual obviously was happening here. He realized he needed to understand it before he threw himself into the middle of it.

A second figure came over the hill, racing after Hiram. A man with a rifle. And behind him, a long way back, a second man, much bigger and quite a bit slower, but also armed. The second man had an odd gait, as if he was injured.

Both the pursuers were strangers, as best Sam could see from this distance. Strangers in Texas Gulch? With the snow piled high in the pass and the mountains virtually impassable?

How did they get here? And when? And why were they chasing Hiram Linfoot?

The first pursuer stopped and dropped to one knee in the snow, raising his rifle. Linfoot kept running, hard. Sam opened his mouth to shout a warning, but Linfoot went out of range and the man with the rifle didn't fire. Sam watched him rise and continue chasing Linfoot, who was making for the rugged country at the northern side of the basin. *Good move, Hiram. You can lose them if you make it into the rocks.*

The second pursuer was still coming on, but even slower than before. A big man, he looked like he might drop exhausted at any moment. At his speed it would take him five minutes at best just to catch up with his companion.

So Sam decided not to worry about that second pursuer yet. The smaller one at the lead of the chase was the most dangerous one to Linfoot. Hefting up the pick, wishing he had his rifle, Sam began running across the uneven country, trying to close in on the man from the side, and if possible, to do so without revealing his presence too quickly.

The most worrisome possibility was that the second pursuer would draw close enough to see him and yell a warning to the first, but a glance revealed the second pursuer was not to be seen. Sam figured the man had dropped, probably exhausted. Good.

There was Hiram, running up a slope and not doing too well at it. He fell twice, mired in drifting snow. The man after him dropped to his knee again, raised the rifle, aimed carefully, and this time did fire.

The rifle's crack was thin and empty in the vast open space of the valley. Sam glanced at Hiram, and grimaced when he saw his friend throw his arms out and up, and fall in the snow.

The rifleman hurriedly engaged himself in reloading, giving Sam, who was now driven by fury, the best opportunity he was going to find. He ran as hard as he could, giving it all he had, plowing through the snow like a bull, until he was near the rifleman, separated from him by only a small line of boulders. He bounded atop one of the boulders, saw the reloading man look up in shock—and Sam leaped, flying through the air with the pick in his hand, swinging down as he descended.

The man had dropped his rifle and gone for a pistol stuck

into his belt, but the pistol caught and never came clear. Sam descended and brought the pick down hard, intending to strike with the flat of it and knock the man cold. But the pick had turned in his hand. The sharp, rusted prong of it hit Emmett Fish in the center of the top of his head, dug through bone, and sank into his brain.

Fish shuddered and died before he hit the snow, his weight pulling the pick out of Sam's hand and taking it down with him.

Sam landed atop the corpse, rolled off, and came to his feet. He stared at the dead man with the pick buried in his head, and felt a numb horror. He'd just killed a man!

All at once he was back in Texas, about a decade and a half back, with his father and brothers, fighting a band of ruffians who believed the Underhills bore ransom. That night Sam Underhill, then a much different, less settled kind of fellow, had killed another human being for the first time. He'd tried to hide the horror of it behind bravado back then—that was his way in those days—but the feeling was one he'd never forgotten.[2]

He felt it again now.

Remembering that the slower, second pursuer might reappear at any moment, Sam went for the dead man's weapons. He took the rifle, finished the reloading job, and commandeered the dead man's shot and powder as well. He stuck the pistol into his own belt.

It felt good to be armed again . . . though even now he didn't know what in the devil was going on, why Hiram Linfoot had been chased down and shot, or who this fellow was he'd just pickaxed to death.

Sam ran toward the hillside where Hiram lay in snow that was swiftly turning red around him. Hiram was alive, but his wound was bad. Blood was flowing frighteningly fast.

"Hiram . . . it's me, Sam!" He dropped to Hiram's side. The man had managed to roll himself over onto his back.

[2] *Texas Freedom,* Book 2 in The Underhill Series

He blinked up numbly, almost stupidly, at Sam's face.

"Sam . . . Sam, they've shot me."

"I know, Hiram. But the man who did it is dead. I killed him. Just now. Who was he?"

"Bad men . . . they're in the camp. Several of them . . . come looking for gold . . . that the dead man had stole from them."

"The dead man Daniel found in the pass?"

"Yes . . . Dehaven, they called him. Dehaven."

Sam glanced back. Still no sign of the slower-running pursuer. Perhaps the man had given up.

He looked at Hiram's pallid face and saw that death was coming. "Tell me what's happened, Hiram."

"They came in . . . they already had Arianna, Daniel . . . guns to their heads. They took everyone in the camp hostage . . . searched the houses, took all the weapons. The dead man . . . he'd been one of them . . . he'd taken gold from them that they'd all stolen somewhere . . . they chased him into the mountains, all the way to Texas Gulch . . . he died, trying to reach the mining camp . . . now no one knows where the gold is . . . they'll kill us in the end, Sam. They'll kill everyone."

"Hiram, are you sure of all this?"

"Yes . . . they've already killed Julius . . . now they've killed me, too."

Sam wanted to assure Linfoot that he'd be fine, but it would be a lie, and he and Linfoot would both know it.

"You say they had the children. So Daniel and Arianna are alive."

"Yes . . . they'd found them out beyond the pass. Took them prisoner."

Sam was glad to know the children hadn't frozen to death, though it appeared their predicament at the moment was not much better. "You're sure all the weapons in the camp are taken?"

"All of them. And all the people . . . kept under guard every minute. I was the first to . . . try to escape . . ." He actually laughed a little, bitterly, and blood came to his lips. "Didn't do ... too well, I guess. I don't even know ... where I was running to. I just had to try."

"I know, Hiram. And I'm sorry it went bad for you."

"They don't know ... about you, Sam. The bad ones don't know that you even exist ... it's up to you, Sam, if our people ... are going to be saved."

Something changed in Hiram's face, very suddenly. A moment before, his body had been animated. Now it was empty. He was gone.

Sam stood slowly and stared down at the corpse of his friend. All this was too much to take in. Texas Gulch taken by outlaws. People murdered. A dead man's lost gold endangering the entire camp. It seemed very unreal.

Sam felt the twin weights of responsibility and terror descend upon him. He had to help his people ... but what could one man do, alone, minimally armed with weapons that weren't his own, against an entire band of armed desperadoes?

The only edge he had was that they didn't know he existed. He needed to keep it that way.

He had to make the outlaws believe that it was Linfoot who had killed the rifleman. And that Linfoot was still alive. That might draw some of them out, hunting for Linfoot. Maybe, a few at a time, Sam could deal with them.

Sam slung his newfound weapons and gear across his shoulder, reached down, and picked up the body of Hiram Linfoot. Carrying Hiram in his arms like an oversized baby, he staggered back down the slope, trying his best to stay in the tracks already made. He reached the ridge of boulders near the place where Emmett Fish lay with a pick through his brain, and worked his way behind them. No way to avoid leaving tracks, but his father had always told him not to worry about that which couldn't be helped. With any luck, that second pursuer wouldn't be a clever man, and wouldn't realize there had been a third man here besides Linfoot and the first pursuer.

*   *   *

With Hiram Linfoot's body lying nearby, Sam peered over the snow-covered rim of the boulders before him and watched the slower pursuer finally appear. The man must have taken a long rest. He walked slowly even now, and kept rubbing his groin as if it pained him.

Sam listened to the man curse in astonishment as he found the body of the man with the pick in his head. The bigger fellow knelt and looked at the appalling sight, making a face of disgust. He looked at the tracks that went on up the hill, but did not study or follow them.

The man muttered something, picked up the body of the pickaxed man, turned, and made his way back in the direction he'd come, heading for Texas Gulch. Burdened, he was especially slow now. Sam watched him a long time; the fellow had to dump the corpse and rest several times even before he was out of sight.

When the man was finally gone, Sam rose, wondering if he should have simply shot the fellow while he had the chance. It would have given him one less enemy to face later.

He picked up Hiram's corpse again, took a deep breath, and began making his way slowly back into the valley again, where he'd hide Hiram's body somewhere. He'd find a hole, or a hollow log, or a crevice in some bluff. He'd like to do better by Hiram, but for now any resting place would have to do. He was sure Hiram would have understood, and under the circumstances, agreed.

As Sam traveled, he watched new, gray clouds coagulating in the sky. Good. More snow would cover tracks and blood and any other sign back at the death scene.

And maybe give him a little more time to figure out what the devil he was going to do.

CHAPTER TWELVE

Mongold's voice still had a tight, pained sound, and he continually shifted from one foot to another while he stood, talking intently to Mahaffery. It would be a good while before he'd be back to his old self again, thanks to Leora Winkle's sledgehammer knee. He'd never made it all the way in with Fish's corpse, but had dropped it out in the valley.

"The man had to have had that pick on him, hid somewhere," Mongold said. "Either that, or he found it while he was running, somehow. Because he gouged it clean through Emmett's head. An ugly sight. You'll see, when you see his corpse. I got it within a quarter mile of here before I had to leave it. We'll need to fetch Emmett in soon, or we'll not be able to find him. It's snowing hard again."

"And Emmett's guns . . ."

"Gone. I reckon the running man took them."

Mahaffery swore softly. "So one's gotten away from us . . . and now he's armed. There's no chance that Emmett wounded him before the fellow pickaxed him?"

"I don't know. There were some bad tore-up tracks, heading up a hillside . . ."

"And you didn't follow them?"

"No."

"Why the hell not?"

"Because . . . because Emmett was lying there, dead, with his head split open. I figured you'd want to know. And because the guns was gone, so I knowed this other man was armed now. I was afraid he might be lying in wait for me. And besides . . . I was hurting from what that woman did to me. She hurt me bad, Jordan. It still hurts."

"You're useless, you know it, Mongold? I should never have sent you with Emmett. I should have sent Broadgrass, or Remine, or somebody else with sense and a little courage. That running man should have been tracked down while we had the chance. Now, with the new snow coming in, there'll be no way to track him."

Mongold looked at his chief for a long time before speaking. "I don't take well to being treated as a coward, Jordan."

"Then don't act like one. Thanks to you letting up your chase we now have an armed man roaming around the valley. A source of trouble for us . . . one you allowed to come about, Mongold."

"What does it matter, Jordan? We'll find that gold wherever Dehaven dropped it. We can leave here, then, and that fellow can roam the valley forever, if he wants."

Mahaffery drew close and spoke quietly. "Nobody's going to be roaming any part of this valley when we leave here. They know our faces, our names, and what we've done. Do you understand me?"

Mongold thought it over, then nodded when the implication set in. "I should have gone after him, Jordan. I'm sorry."

Mahaffery lost some of his anger. "What's done is done. We'll catch him again. He's got no food, and the people here say there's no way out of this valley except the front pass." Mahaffery paused. "Just don't make any more mistakes, Mongold. We can't afford them."

"I won't."

"Good. Good." Abruptly, Mahaffery passed into a better frame of mind. "You know, Bert, I'm hungry. Let's get

some of the women here to fix us up some food. We'll eat
. . . then we'll leave Emmett's corpse where you dropped it.
I don't want our hostages knowing about him being dead.
Might give them notions that we can be overcome.

"Meanwhile, once we've eaten, we'll get some digging
started up in that pass and see if we can't put our hands on
that gold, and get all this over with as soon as possible."

Mahaffery paced back and forth in a gully beaten through
the snow at the pass, nibbling on bread and meat and glowering as the captive men of Texas Gulch dug in the snow.
A vain search, so far. Though they had begun digging right
at the place the body had been found, widening the circle
as they went, no gold had turned up.

Mahaffery chewed his beef and hated the late Dehaven.
He hated him for having taken the gold for himself, for
having lost or hidden it, and most of all, for dying and
taking with him the secret of where the gold now was.

One of the digging men tripped on something in the snow,
and fell. Mahaffery instantly became interested. "What did
you find?"

Kish Fleenor climbed back up on his feet, brushed himself
off, and looked at what he'd stumbled on. "I tripped over
a rock."

Mahaffery swore at him. "Next time you fall over something, it'd best be that gold."

"I'm so starved I can hardly work," Fleenor said, em-
boldened by anger, hunger, and lack of sleep. "When are
you going to let us eat?"

"When you find that gold, there'll be food," Mahaffery
said, and took a big bite of his bread, chewing slowly while
Fleenor watched.

Joe Skinner moved closer to Dillow as work began again.
"Ben," he said, softly and without looking at him, "I want
to ask you something."

"What's that?"

"I been thinking . . . if we find that gold, what's to keep them from just killing us?"

"Nothing that I can see."

"Do you think they would? Kill us, I mean?"

"I don't really know what would happen. My strong suspicion is that they'd kill us all. But I think that's going to happen, eventually, even if we don't find the gold."

"You really think that?"

"The moment we cease to be useful to them, either by finding the gold, or by failing to find it for so long that they cease to believe the gold *can* be found, then I think they're going to be ready to rid themselves of us. We're one of two things to them: tools or threats. So the key for now is to remain useful for as long as we can, and pray for the chance to make something happen." He paused, thinking of Sam Underhill. "Or for a miracle to come."

"So the best thing we can do right now . . ."

Dillow finished for him. "Is to keep on digging, and to find nothing. But we have to keep them believing that we're just a hair away from finding the gold . . . yet never actually find it."

"Because we want all the time we can get."

"That's right."

"For us to make something happen . . . or for a miracle."

"That's right. So, Joe, spread the word among the others, quietly, without being heard. Look for the gold, but don't find it . . . even if you *do* find it. Do you understand what I mean?"

Mahaffery yelled, "You two hush the talking. Get to work!"

"I'd like to ram this shovel through his neck," Dillow muttered.

Skinner moved off to the right a few paces and began to dig in a fresh patch of snow. The sky, grayed over and heavy, was spitting flakes again, already beginning to refill the snowy chasm the searchers had created. Dillow was glad. More snow meant a slower and less certain search.

More time to remain useful to the outlaws . . . more time to remain alive.

He wondered again what had become of Sam Underhill, and whether Sam had any notion of what was going on in Texas Gulch.

Back in the sprawling, so-called lodge house, Daniel Chase was restless in body and mind. And he was already very tired of being imprisoned, tired of these harsh, stinking outlaws pacing around with their guns, eating in front of hungry people, insulting the ladies, threatening the men, displaying their weaponry like strutting cocks showing off plumage . . .

Daniel had endured all he could stand. Time to change the scenario a little.

There were advantages to being a boy, being small, being sneaky. A boy could do things a man could not. And boys always knew secrets. Sitting there among the women, listening to the snoring of Old Man Skinner, father of Joe Skinner and the only truly old person in the camp, Daniel had remembered a secret of his own. Something that maybe could make a difference.

Lennis Yeager of the outlaw band paced back and forth in the lodge house, bearing his rifle and wearing two pistols. He seemed irritable and bored. His hostages were bored, too, all of them ignoring him and brooding in private worlds. Every now and then Yeager would pause to kick at the boot of Old Man Skinner, stopping his snoring for a few seconds. And occasionally Yeager would go to the door, open it, and look out almost wistfully toward the pass, where most of his companions were standing guard over the men of the mining camp as they prospected the snow for that lost gold. At least there was something going on up at the pass.

There was a second guard in the lodge house, too, the evil-tempered Searl. But he was sleeping in his chair in the corner, hat tilted over his eyes and rifle lying crossways on his big chest. He seemed to be sleeping, anyway; Daniel had been eyeing him and wasn't really sure. Maybe Searl was faking, just waiting for someone to make a wrong move so he could have reason to shoot them and break the boredom. If he was faking, though, he was doing it well. His chest moved up and down, slowly and consistently, with the breathing rhythm of a true sleeper. Daniel decided that Searl really was asleep.

Yeager went back to the door again and opened it. Cold air and snow blew in as he stared up at the pass, his profile visible to Daniel. But suddenly he stepped forward half a pace, putting the door between Daniel and himself, and at that moment Daniel moved.

He'd always been a fast and silent boy. His motion was so sudden and unexpected that only a couple of people in the place noticed he had moved at all, and they did not react. The people here were quickly learning not to react to anything, because that tended to draw the attention of their captors.

A big, homemade wardrobe stood beside one of the shuttered windows. Daniel darted behind it, got the shutter open without a sound, and was out the window in exactly five seconds. From the outside, he pushed the shutter closed again just as Yeager eased the door shut and began pacing once more. Yeager passed the empty place Daniel had been moments before, and did not even notice the boy's absence.

Arianna, one of the two who had noticed what Daniel had done, for the next five minutes held her breath every time Yeager passed the place Daniel had been. At last she realized the man was hardly aware of those around him, and ceased to worry so much. Whatever Daniel was up to, he'd gotten away with it so far.

Her dog, Enoch, had returned to the mining camp the day before, and now slept at her feet. She scratched at his ears with her shoe.

Outside, Daniel was bounding through the snow like a rabbit, keeping cover between himself and the pass up above, where men who looked like black, moving spots in the snow labored under armed guard. Daniel slipped down to the rear,

lower section of the camp, near the place they had buried Dehaven, and reached a nearby crumbled old cabin, one of the
first ever built here, a relic of the first days of the Gold Rush.
Too shabby and broken-down for use as a residence, the
cabin was simply left alone by most of the people of Texas
Gulch, or occasionally scavenged for a log or shingle to make
a repair on one of the better dwellings. But for Daniel it had
been a place of play, refuge . . . and treasure-stashing.

He entered the cabin through its broken door. There was
no floor but the earth itself, hard-packed, cold, and dusted
with snow that managed to infiltrate the very inefficient roof.
Daniel paused a moment just to enjoy being here, in a hidden place, for now out of reach of outlaws and danger. He
thought about and hated the men who terrorized this camp.
Texas Gulch and its people were all Daniel Chase had in
the world. He loved them. The murder of Julius Setser had
shocked and infuriated him. He'd decided even then, while
he'd been lost in a fog of stupor and horror, that he would
do something, somehow, to stop these men.

He still didn't know exactly what that would be, but sitting there in the lodge house, watching that cursed guard
pace back and forth, he'd remembered a certain item that
would make a very handy tool just now.

Daniel moved a log that seemed to have simply fallen out
of the crumbling wall to its current spot by chance, but
which in fact was strategically placed to cover a well-
wrapped item behind it. Daniel pulled that item out, a bundle
of oiled cloth tied up with string.

Squatting on his haunches, Daniel untied the string and
unrolled the cloth. Examining his little treasure, he found
everything in good condition. Nodding with satisfaction, he
put what he'd recovered in the pocket of his coat.

Daniel went back to the door of the cabin, looked right
and left, and headed out into the snow. Climbing back up
the slope and ready to turn left back toward the lodge house
along the same path he'd come, he glanced up at the pass
again, expecting to see the distant laborers just as before.

Instead, they were much closer, and heading in his direction, coming back down from the pass toward the lodge house.

Daniel dropped into the snow, sucking in his breath.

He was almost sure that the big one, Mongold, had looked right at him.

CHAPTER THIRTEEN

Food had never tasted so good.

Ben Dillow ate his meal of fatty meat, bread, and water as if he were a king at his banquet rather than an endangered, trapped miner reluctantly allowed a few bites by his captor. The others ate with similar relish.

Mahaffery, meanwhile, paced back and forth in the crowded lodge house, looking quite unhappy. No gold had been found, and this delay bothered him. But even the doomed must eat if they are expected to have the strength to work.

When Dillow had gotten down the last of his food and literally licked the juices and crumbs off his fingers, he stood and approached Mahaffery, who turned a glaring eye on the upstart.

"What do you want?"

"We need sleep. You've got us all working out there, and none of us slept last night."

"You could have slept. No one stopped you."

"It's difficult to sleep when you've just been overrun by men with guns."

"Not my problem, friend. You'll sleep once the gold is found."

Dillow could believe that. A long sleep indeed would follow the finding of that gold. An endless sleep. He'd reached the point of hoping that Colfax indeed did have the gold, and would keep its location secret as long as possible. Buying time, that was the key to survival.

"Sir, these men are exhausted. Even your own men are tired."

"Go sit down, Mr. . . ."

"Dillow. Ben Dillow."

"Whoever. Sit down, shut up, and give an ear to me." Mahaffery raised his voice and spoke to the group in general. "In fact, all of you give me an ear. I got a few things to say."

Silence fell. Mahaffery walked back and forth a few times, gathering his thoughts. He cleared his throat and spoke.

"You think me a hard man, I'm sure. You think right. I am a hard man, but fair. You're tired and afraid, I know, but you'll have your rest. Tonight you'll get your sleep. Or if you find that gold before then, you'll have your chance to rest even earlier."

Copp Nolen and Ben Dillow, the latter having now returned to his seat, exchanged a glance. Mahaffery was following a simple but sensible strategy: throw the enticement of coming rest to weary men to make them work harder. Then, when their labor bears its fruit, line them up and shoot them down.

Mahaffery went on, his voice booming loud in the wide, low cabin. "The thing for you to do, all of you, is to cooperate completely. Don't complain, don't try to run. One of your number did that earlier. I sent two men after him, and your friend paid the price. He's lying dead out there in the valley."

Arianna lowered her head, sadly remembering how she'd inwardly cheered for Hiram Linfoot when she saw him slipping away.

"Let this man's death be a warning to you," Mahaffery said. "Don't think you can outwit, outrun, or out-think us. You can't. Just cooperate, and you'll stay alive. Cross us, and you'll pay the same price as your man out there some-where in the snow ... what was his name?" Mahaffery turned to Ben Dillow as he asked this, and Dillow knew that the outlaw chief had come to perceive him, at least in some measure, as a leader and spokesman for the people of Texas Gulch.

"I believe that would be Mr. Hiram Linfoot," Dillow said quietly.

"Hiram Linfoot," Mahaffery repeated. "Well, Hiram Linfoot is now a dead man because he was foolish enough to think he could run away. Don't anybody else be foolish, all right?" He looked from face to face, like a schoolmaster making sure his lesson had sunk in.

"I'd like to ask the right to go fetch Hiram's body so he can be given a decent burial," Dillow said.

"Mr. Hiram Linfoot can lie where he fell, and feed the scavengers," Mahaffery said.

Dillow looked around the group. "You're missing a man. The one you call Emmett."

"Emmett Fish is in another cabin, sleeping," Mahaffery said. "His reward for work well done in taking care of the runaway Linfoot."

Mahaffery paced about a little more, ranting about the need for cooperation. He was tired, too, and it showed.

Mahaffery suddenly cut off in midsentence. "Some-body's missing," he said. "Where's the boy?"

Dillow looked around. Sure enough, Daniel Chase wasn't to be seen.

Mongold said, "Jordan, I thought I seen him outside while we were coming in from the pass."

"Why didn't you speak up?"

"Because I looked closer and decided it was just a shadow on the snow. The sun was in my eyes."

"You and your bad eyes ... you can't see fifty feet past the end of your nose on your best day. Hell, I want that boy found! Even a little runt like him, running around free, could be dangerous."

Dillow had a sudden realization: *Maybe Mahaffery's not as sure of himself as he likes to put on, if he worries that much about no more than a child getting loose.*

"Broadgrass, Remine, I want you two to go out and find that boy. Find him fast, before he gets away. Bring him directly to me when you do, and—"

"I'm right here," Daniel stepped out from behind the wardrobe. "I ain't been nowhere. I'd just fell asleep back there, that's all."

Mahaffery stared at him, silent, then suddenly seemed to lose all interest. He turned his back on Daniel, and said, "Back up to the pass, gentlemen. We've got much more digging to do."

Trudging wearily back up toward the pass for what promised to be more hours of digging in snow, Dillow managed to get close to Copp Nolen.

"Tell me, Copp," he whispered, "did something strike you odd about the way Mahaffery talked about Hiram being killed, and this Emmett fellow being somewhere taking a nap, and all that?"

"Indeed it did. That man's covering up something. Telling us what he wants us to hear."

"My feeling is precisely the same. I'm even wondering if it's this Emmett fellow who got himself killed instead of Hiram. Or maybe they killed each other."

"Hard to imagine Hiram having the brass about him to kill anyone. And how would he do it, with no weapons?"

Dillow thought about that one for a while. "Maybe it wasn't Hiram who did it. Maybe Sam did it."

"I hadn't considered that. It is the kind of thing Sam would do."

"Yep. I can tell you one thing: if Sam Underhill's alive, and if he knows what's happened in Texas Gulch, he's already trying to do something about it. Let's just hope Sam has some kind of plan."

*   *   *

Sam Underhill had no plan at all.

He sat in a deep niche on a rocky ridge, staring out across the valley and at the gray sky overarching it, watching yet another round of snowfall come down. There was little wind at the moment, though, and the snow fell slowly and peacefully. All in all it was a beautiful, placid scene, quite different in mood from the way Sam felt just now.

He looked down at the weapons he'd taken from the man he'd hit with the pick, and wondered what a lone man could do against an armed gang so desperate it would gun down a fine fellow like Hiram Linfoot, just for running away. He figured that the more stalwart men of the community, such as Ben Dillow, probably were doing what they could, or at least trying to . . . but if Hiram's story was right and the outlaws had all the weapons, what could Dillow or anyone else on the inside do?

Sam had built a small fire, situated perfectly in the rock niche to hide the smoke until it had time to disperse and become invisible in the falling snow. Heat reflected off the rocks and back onto him. He'd nibbled a little more of his food and pondered that before long he'd have to do a bit of hunting or snaring.

Sam sighed, stood, and walked toward the outer part of the niche. There he examined the high, encircling mountains, and tried to think logically, instead of emotionally, about his situation and that of his friends. The honest fact was, he wasn't likely to be able to do much for them alone. A gang of outlaws against a group of unarmed men, women, and children didn't add up to odds likely to be improved much by the addition of one mere camp marshal armed with commandeered weapons. No, Sam decided, he'd have to find help.

The only way to do that, though, would be to make it out of this valley, through the nearly impassable snows of the Sierras, then down to the lower diggings and towns. Once there, he'd have the hard task of persuading others that his wild tale of an outlaw gang, holding a group of people hostage in a mining camp that most still believed was deserted, was not a delusion. Even if he could do that, he wasn't sure he could convince anyone to go back into the dangerous mountains with him, all the way back—if possible—to Texas Gulch, and into likely battle with armed outlaws. And by that time, how might the scenario have changed? The outlaws might have killed off the entire population by then.

Not much of a plan, to be sure, but all he had. Sam, discouraged and deeply worried, again eyed the mountains. The first step in trying to find help was to get out of the valley. He couldn't do this by way of the pass, considering that he'd have to travel right through Texas Gulch to reach it. Besides, the outlaws probably had the pass guarded.

The only way out would be to find another way over the mountains. Another pass. The general consensus at Texas Gulch was that no such alternative pass existed. And if this proved accurate, Sam faced some serious mountain climbing, burdened with weapons, lacking ropes or equipment, and without sufficient food to see him through.

He lifted his eyes to the sky and prayed again. *Lord, I need help. I don't know what to do, and I need help.*

But when he looked at the mountains again, no new pass had miraculously appeared, and no fresh ideas had sprung into his mind.

More discouraged than ever, he returned to his fire, sat down again, and lowered his head for a few minutes of sleep and, he hoped, mental refreshment that might give rise to a plan.

CHAPTER
FOURTEEN

The few minutes became an hour. Sam slept deeply, but awakened fast—his usual pattern at times of tension. He moved stiff, cold muscles, rose, and added more fuel to the fire. He noticed that the snow had, for now, stopped. Hoping he had literally dreamed up some inspired plan, he searched his brain and found . . . nothing.

Discouraged and depressed despite his hour of sleep, Sam wandered again to the opening of the niche and gazed over the valley. Such beauty! But he couldn't appreciate the splendor while his own people were in danger of losing their lives. And Julius Setser and Hiram Linfoot were already dead.

Sam traced the outlines of the peaks against the sky and despaired of finding another route out of this huge, ragged-edged basin. He slowly followed the lines of the mountains as they circled around, until his vision caught something on the side of one of the nearer slopes. Not really close, but close enough that he was almost sure what he saw was a man.

He stared as hard as he could, wishing he had a spyglass. It *was* a man, alone, moving across the snow. But who? And why?

Most of all, how?

Judging from the man's direction of travel, Sam was

nearly sure the fellow had come into the valley from the side opposite the pass at Texas Gulch.

Another way in . . . another way out.

Sam settled down to watch the distant figure creep across the snowy landscape, very steadily, making good progress considering the snow. An experienced wilderness traveler, obviously.

Before long, Sam realized that the man was about to move out of his sight. Couldn't have that. He needed to meet this man and find out from him how he'd entered the valley. Maybe this newcomer would even be a source of help.

Sam kicked snow over his fire, gathered his weaponry, and began to descend to the lower part of the valley. He tried to anticipate where the man would go, hoping he could keep him in sight or at least stand a reasonable chance of relocating him if he did lose him. He wondered if the man was aware of him, maybe watching him even as he watched.

Sam did lose sight of the man. It was inevitable, given the rugged land, and when Sam came out an hour later onto a broad, sloping meadow where he had anticipated the man might emerge from the foothills, he saw no sign of him. This bothered Sam to a degree that surprised him; he actually struggled against tears.

The newcomer, coming when he had, had given Sam hope. The thought that there might be something approaching the supernatural in this unexpected appearance had whispered across Sam's mind, barely acknowledged, but definitely there. An answer to his prayer for help, maybe. Now he wondered if he was just foolish.

Had he not watched the man for so long, it would be easy to believe that he'd simply imagined him.

Sam looked at the area from which the man had been traveling. Somewhere beyond those ridges, there was surely a route out of the valley. In theory, he might find it. In reality, he was more likely to starve or freeze to death trying.

He found another place to make a camp, and built himself a lean-to shelter of the sort his father had taught him to make years ago. He made a fire and settled down to pass the night. Come morning he would make a decision. Either he would go on and try to get out of this valley, and down the mountains for help, or he would walk back to Texas Gulch, reveal himself to the outlaws there, and try to persuade them to spare the lives of his people.

Odd, he thought, managing to smile. He'd never taken seriously the idea that he was the law in Texas Gulch. It had seemed a pointless, silly idea before. Now it didn't feel that way. He felt a real sense of responsibility.

Sam slept soundly again. The night was deep and cold and long, but Sam was comfortable throughout. Strangely, when he awakened at the first glimmer of dawn, the fire still burned high. It had been replenished by a man who sat nearby, huddled in a big bearskin coat, similar to Sam's, and topped by a heavy woolen blanket. An identical blanket had been laid across Sam while he slept.

The man stood and grinned. He had a ragged beard now, mostly white, but other than that, looked the same as he had when Sam had last seen him in Texas.

Sam stared, disbelieving, then rubbed at his eyes. Rising, he went to the man and wrapped his arms around him, embracing him with the deepest affection.

"Hello, Pap," he said. "You don't know how fine it is to see you again."

"Fine to see you, too, son," Bushrod Underhill replied. "Though I'm sorry for the trouble that's come on your mining camp."

"How do you know of that?"

"I came along at the right time to witness it . . . enough of it, anyway. And I'm glad I've found you safe, Sam. Because you and me together have some work ahead of us."

"I can't believe you're here, Pap."

"Well, I am here. I had it in mind for a long time to make this journey and see you."

"But in the winter? The mountains and the snow . . ."

Bushrod's lips parted, but for some reason he hesitated a

moment before he spoke. "You know me, son. That kind of thing makes little difference to me."

Sam was struggling with emotion. "What work are you talking about?"

"We've got to save your mining camp, son. You and me, against a small army of armed outlaws. How do those odds strike you?"

"Mighty uneven," Sam said.

Bushrod's own eyes were glistening. "That's right. With you and me both here, they don't stand a chance."

Weary and scared, facing a new morning under the gun, the people of Texas Gulch ate glumly of the meager food prepared for them by the women. Over it all the intimidating Jordan Mahaffery stood watch, far more somber and intense today than the day before. He walked back and forth, speaking to no one, every glance full of threat and fury.

"Look at him!" Copp Nolen said to Dillow as he bit off a hunk of hard biscuit. "All pompous and huffy, like he's making a great sacrifice just allowing us to eat!"

"Pompous and huffy isn't how I'd term his manner today."

"What, then?"

"Dangerous. There's more anger in him. He's beginning to face the possibility that he may not ever find his gold."

Mahaffery pulled out his pocket watch, glanced at it. Less than a minute later he did it again.

"Eager to get us digging in the snow again," Nolen said.

"Yep."

"Know what I believe? I believe Colfax already has the gold."

"So do I."

"How long before Mahaffery gives up and decides there'll be no gold found?"

"Don't know. Not too soon, I hope."

A sudden burst of activity on the far end of the lodge house startled everyone in the place. Art Bolton had come to his feet, dumping his plate on the floor, and was lunging at Searl Mahaffery, who'd been standing close and closer yet to Art's daughter Marica as she served sausages from a griddle. He'd been speaking to her softly, grinning, hiding his words from the others. She'd gradually reddened and looked more upset . . . and just now, Searl had touched her. On the shoulder at first, but then his hand had trailed down . . .

"Get your hands off my daughter!" Art Bolton yelled as he threw himself at Searl Mahaffery. Marica screamed and jumped back. Art's body bumped the griddle and sent it falling, sausages dumping out across the puncheon floor. Searl went down, Bolton atop him, the latter's fists flying, pounding the younger man's face and head.

Some of the outlaws hooted and whooped, enjoying the moment at Searl's expense. But Searl was at a disadvantage only a few moments. Younger, stronger, and meaner than Art Bolton, he quickly threw the man off him, came up, and went for his pistol. Marica screamed again, and for a moment all believed that the younger Mahaffery was about to shoot the man. Instead he pistol-whipped him, laying open a small but ugly cut across the side of Bolton's face.

Cursing through clenched teeth, Searl was about to pound Bolton a second time, but Jordan Mahaffery got to him and pulled him away.

"Don't kill him, Searl," Jordan said. "We need every digger we got."

"He attacked me, Jordan. Came right at me! Knocked me down!"

"I saw what happened. A father will do that kind of thing when somebody goes to bothering his daughter."

"I'll kill the bastard, Jordan! You ain't stopping me!"

"I *will* stop you. We need the labor, Searl. Unless you want to dig out that whole mountainside yourself."

Nolen and Dillow shared a glance. What Mahaffery had just said was, oddly, a relief to hear. Dig out that whole mountainside . . . though they didn't take that literally, it did give hope that Mahaffery wasn't going to give up the search quickly.

"Let me make an example of him for the others!" Searl pleaded. "There's enough here to dig without him. Let me put a hole through his head!"

"No!" Marica yelled, and threw herself down, wrapping her arms around her father's shoulders and covering him protectively.

"You'll kill no one," Jordan said.

Searl and his older brother stared at one another from a distance of six inches. Jordan's stare held the longest.

"I'll bide my time," Searl said. "But not forever."

"If you hurt my father," Marica said, "I'll kill you myself."

Jordan Mahaffery suddenly seemed to lose interest in all this. "That's enough," he said, turning away from Searl and back to the hostages. "Finish that food, and head out to the pass, every damned one of you men! You women, you stay here and clean this mess up. And somebody bandage this fool on the floor." He shoved at Art Bolton with his foot. "Ross, you stay here and guard these folks. You too, Mongold. And when this one gets over being addled, bring him up so he can dig, too."

"I'm staying down here . . . with her," Searl said, pointing at Marica.

"Afraid not, Searl. I want you to help keep watch up at the pass."

"Hell! I was up there three hours last night!" Indeed, Mahaffery's men had been guarding the pass in pairs all night, keeping two huge bonfires blazing, making sure no resident of Texas Gulch managed to escape . . . or tried to come up and do any grubbing for lost gold in the snow on their own behalf rather than Mahaffery's. Given the huge amount of firewood that the Texas Gulch people had laid in to see them through the winter, there was no lack of fuel for the bonfires, and the guards used the wood freely to fight off the cold.

"You'll be up there for more hours than that today. This afternoon, maybe we'll let you come down here and sleep a bit . . . if you'll keep your hands off the women."

Searl muttered a curse and wheeled, stomping away from his brother in very little-boy style. Jordan Mahaffery looked disgusted and shook his head.

"Come on," he said. "We've got a lot of snow to sift."

Four hours later, the forced laborers had cleared much more snow, but still no gold had been found. Art Bolton had showed up after an hour, still dizzy and disoriented. He did his best to work, but it was difficult for him.

For his part, Dillow worked hard, not talking to anyone. He kept his eye on Jordan Mahaffery and didn't like what he saw. Mahaffery was glowering, impatient, edgy. Worse, he'd produced a flask from his coat and had been taking pulls on it all morning.

Mahaffery, though heartless and cruel, was at least somewhat sensible in how he dealt with his hostages. He sought to keep them alive and functioning as long as he needed their slave labors. But drunken men were often different men than when they were sober.

Dillow hoped that Mahaffery would put the flask away for good. But it kept coming out, again and again.

CHAPTER
FIFTEEN

Dillow was clearing a snowdrift, working near Kish Fleenor, when the latter stumbled over something in the snow and fell backward. Fleenor tried to use his shovel to catch himself, jamming it not into the ground, but into the ankle of Dillow.

Dillow howled in pain and collapsed, gripping his injured extremity.

"What'd you stumble over?" Mahaffery said, running to the spot. The obviously injured Dillow was of no concern to him at all.

"Don't know," Fleenor said. "Ben, I'm sorry. I didn't mean to—"

"Hell with him!" Mahaffery said. "Find whatever you tripped over!"

Fleenor felt about in the snow, put his hand on something, and rolled it out.

Just an old piece of dropped firewood.

Mahaffery let out a long string of vile words and produced his flask again. "Keep digging!" he yelled to the laborers, who had stopped work to watch the commotion. "Move that snow and find that gold. Hell, find it in the next hour, or I'll kill you all!"

Work resumed at a nearly frantic pace.

"My ankle's hurt," Dillow said. "Let me go back to the lodge house and wrap it up in something."

Mahaffery cursed him thoroughly and drank from his flask again, then waved Dillow dismissively in the direction of the lodge house.

"I'll guard him on down," Searl said quickly.

"I don't care what you do," Mahaffery muttered.

Searl seemed surprised, but delighted, to hear this. He grinned slyly, behind his brother's back, and to Dillow said, "Come on, you. Let's go."

Dillow didn't want to go, now that Mahaffery had ceased to concern himself with keeping Searl away from Marica. But when he expressed his change of mind to Searl, the latter began to kick and curse him. Dillow managed to get himself upright, even to put a little weight on the injured ankle. He began hobbling toward the lodge house, Searl prodding him on.

Daniel had been put to helping the women with the food and dishes, and so was present when Dillow and Searl Mahaffery reappeared at the cabin.

"You hurt, Mr. Ben?" Daniel asked when he saw how Dillow was limping.

"Took a knock on the ankle. I don't believe it's bad, but I need to wrap it up."

Searl was already beelining for Marica Bolton, whose face blanched as soon as she saw him.

"Hello, sweetheart," Searl said, drawing near. She was washing dishes in a big kettle, and backed away from it, hands dripping.

"Get away from me."

"No! No! You're taking everything all wrong, honey. I don't want nothing but your help. In fact, I'm mighty sorry I offended you earlier. I swear on my mother's grave, we came back only because we got a hurt man here. Dillow there needs some cloth wrapped around his hurt foot. You can do that for him, can't you?"

Marica looked distrustful, but eyed Dillow a moment, saw he was really hurt, and nodded quickly.

"I can do that."

"Yeah, I knew you could. I'll bet there's all kinds of things she could do to benefit a man. Eh, Mongold?" Searl winked at the big outlaw guard.

"That's right, Searl." Mongold's grin was big. With Jordan not present to keep things under control, there was no telling what might happen here, and that suited Mongold.

Remine, more loyal to the cause than either Searl or Mongold, did his duty and said, "You'd best watch out, Searl. I don't believe Jordan would like you bothering that woman."

"Bothering? Who's bothering?" Searl's ugly grin beamed toward Marica, who had just sat down to tear a rag into binding strips for Dillow's ankle. "I could show you 'bothering.' And maybe I will." He winked at Marica and sat down beside her. She scooted away. He laughed and scooted after her, until she was on the end of the puncheon bench.

"Leave me alone," she said, and rose with the torn strips to go to Dillow.

The ankle looked a bit swollen, and the shovel had made a significant abrasion on the skin, but Marica quickly made it look better by washing it clean and applying the cloth strips. As she knelt, working, Searl came and knelt beside her, putting his arm over her shoulder and winking at Mongold.

"Mighty pretty lady, you are. Got you a husband?"

"No."

"Want one?"

"Get away from me."

"I'd make a good husband. I could do all the things a husband does. One thing most of all. Let me show you. Bet you'd like that, huh?"

She violently pulled out of his clutches. "Get away from me!"

Old Man Skinner rose from his seat and tottered over toward Searl. Too old to labor at the pass, he wasn't too old to understand what kind of men these were or what was going on before his eyes.

"You leave that woman be!" he demanded, lifting his walking stick as if to use it for a club.

Searl came to his feet and spun, grabbing the stick and clouting the man on the side of the head. Old Man Skinner fell. Daniel yelled in alarm and ran to the elderly man's side.

"Don't hit him!" Daniel begged, placing himself protectively over the old fellow just as Marica had protected her fallen father earlier.

"Well, the little hero! I'll hit him if he don't keep out of my way! Never had no use for meddlesome old fools . . . or young ones." Searl glanced at Marica. "Of course, maybe I'd be nicer to him, and to everybody, if somebody in particular would be a little nicer to *me*."

Marica rose. "You make me sick. I hate the look of you, the way of you, the smell of you." She paused, lip trembling, and there was in her manner a visible change, a line crossed only with the greatest effort of self-sacrificing will. In a weakened voice, she went on, "But if you'll leave these others alone, if you'll stop your threats and your cruel ways . . . then—"

"No, Marica!" Dillow said. "Don't say it. Don't . . . don't."

But Searl already knew what she'd been about to say, and was grinning again. He tossed the walking stick to the floor, went to Marica, and gave her a long kiss on the mouth before the entire population of the lodge house. He was obviously enjoying shocking his watchers as much as he enjoyed the kiss itself. Remine, meanwhile, grinned and looked nervous. Mongold chuckled loudly.

The kiss went on endlessly, Marica stiff and struggling against it, Searl lewd in his manner, his hands moving freely upon her. Across the cabin, America Colfax wept quietly, and someone murmured, "God help us."

Marica pulled away enough to speak. "Please, not here . . . not before these people."

"Why not?" Searl said, closing his mouth upon hers again. "We'll give that little boy there some lessons in manhood. And remind that old man of things he's forgot."

Old Man Skinner began to sing a mournful hymn about the end of the world. America Colfax wept more loudly. And Ben Dillow began to rise, determined to get his hands on Searl Mahaffery's neck and break it if at all possible, no matter what they did to him in turn.

Daniel was faster than the limping Dillow. He grabbed the walking stick and began to pound Searl with it. Searl roared, let go of Marica, and grabbed the stick away. He swung it at Daniel, but Daniel dodged it and ran back to the corner. Searl flung the stick to Mongold's feet.

"Keep that thing away from these people, and I'll let you have a turn with her."

Mongold nodded eagerly and put his heavy foot atop the stick.

In Old Man Skinner's song, Judgment Day had come and the unsaved wicked were being banished to the lake of fire.

Searl advanced, got his hands on Marica again. He kissed her harder and began tugging at her dress. Dillow started to rise, but his hurt ankle turned on him and forced him back down.

At that point, Marica vomited, a violent, forceful heaving. Searl cursed and backed away, foul matter on his chin, down his front. He spat and swiped at his tongue and swore.

She knew she was in trouble. "I'm . . . sorry . . . I tried not to . . ."

Searl drew back his arm to backhand her, but suddenly Daniel was there, at Searl's side, arms extended up and hands gripping a small pistol. This was the treasure he had taken from the ramshackle cabin: an old flintlock with a damaged grip, but still functional. A small, secret inheritance from his late brother. He'd had only three pistol balls for it, and only three charges of powder, but he'd loaded it carefully and knew it would fire, if he could find the courage to pull the trigger.

It had been his plan to slip this pistol to some reliable adult, such as Ben Dillow, but the opportunity for that hadn't come.

"I'll kill you!" Daniel yelled.

"Why you little cuss, where'd you get that pistol? Huh? Speak up, boy!"

Remine was frozen, too stunned by this odd development to move. Mongold began to advance, but the walking stick under his foot rolled beneath him and made him stumble. He went down on one knee, out of balance.

Searl tried to grab the pistol, but Daniel darted back, evading him. He cocked the pistol.

"I'll kill you!" Daniel repeated.

"You ain't got the courage, boy." Searl groped for the pistol again.

Daniel shot him between the eyes.

For maybe three seconds, utter silence held in the lodge house. Mongold rose, staring at the dead body of Searl Mahaffery, and the paralyzed Remine looked like a man about to wet his trousers.

Without a word, Daniel darted toward the same window through which he'd escaped earlier, grabbing his coat and hat from off a peg on the wall as he went. He was out of the lodge house before either Remine or Mongold could react, and running through the snow back toward the big valley.

More silence. Then Old Man Skinner started his song again.

Up in the pass, Jordan Mahaffery turned his head toward the lodge house.

"Did you hear that?" he asked Conner Broadgrass. "Sounded like a shot."

"I did hear."

"What the hell's going on down there?"

"I'll go find out for you, if you want, Jordan."

"I'll come, too. Most likely Searl's involved if there's some kind of trouble. He always is."

CHAPTER SIXTEEN

Dillow watched closely as Jordan Mahaffery stood staring at the dead body of his younger brother. Little emotion beyond surprise showed in the outlaw's face, and soon even that faded . . . but Dillow was sure that an emotional and possibly violent explosion was imminent. The killing of Searl Mahaffery might prove to be the spark of judgment day for the people of Texas Gulch.

"Who did this?" Mahaffery asked at last. His voice was soft, ominous-sounding.

Dillow was about to step forward and manfully shoulder the blame, but the realization came that he had no pistol and therefore could hardly claim to be the shooter. In that moment of hesitation on his part, America Colfax made all valiant intentions moot by chiming in, "It was the boy! Daniel Chase! He had a little pistol in his coat pocket!"

Dillow thought drolly what a wonderful family the Colfaxes were. Always ready to make sure their own hides were safe, and the devil take the rest.

"The *boy*, you say?"

"That's right, sir. No one else had anything to do with it. Oh, please, sir, don't hurt any of the rest of us for a thing we never done!" America Colfax whined like a cur. Just then Dillow despised her as much as he often despised her husband.

"My brother . . . shot to death by a boy." Mahaffery stood absorbing that. Dillow braced for that emotional explosion. "Twenty-three years of life . . . and he's shot between the eyes by some cussed little boy."

Mahaffery chuckled. Dillow couldn't believe it. The chuckle grew into a deep, spastic laugh.

"Wouldn't you know it'd be something like that!" Mahaffery turned to Conner Broadgrass. "Don't it just seem to fit, somehow, Searl having his sorry life brought to an end by a snot-nose boy?"

Broadgrass replied, "It does indeed, Jordan. Tragic. Just tragic."

"A *boy*!" Mahaffery laughed until his eyes watered. Pulling out a handkerchief, he dabbed the tears as mirth gradually subsided. "Oh, well. So it goes. No loss to the world, eh, Conner? In fact, the world's probably a better place with Searl gone."

Broadgrass again agreed.

Mahaffery took a swig from his flask and wiped his mouth with the handkerchief, which he then unfolded. Stooping, he laid it over his brother's face.

"Still, I have to respond to this. Can't let this go unpunished." He stood and looked around. "Where's the boy?"

America Colfax was again more than glad to provide information. "He went out the window, sir. He's probably running back into the valley to hide."

"Still got his pistol?"

"Yes, sir."

"We'll have to assume he's also got powder and shot, then," Mahaffery said. "I wonder how that boy managed to hide that pistol from us? Anyway, Conner, you take Remine there and head out after him. He should be easy enough to track in the snow. Bring him back alive, unless he forces you to kill him. I'll decide what to do with him then."

Dillow had to speak up. "He's just a boy, Mahaffery. And he only shot your brother because he was trying to protect the honor of a woman your brother would have raped right here before the eyes of all these people.''

''My brother was a sorry piece of dung, and that I won't deny,'' Mahaffery said. ''I'll not miss him, and won't pretend otherwise. Don't worry, friend. I probably won't kill the boy. But I do have to bring him in.''

Mahaffery took a final look at his brother's covered face, then turned to Mongold: ''Get him outside, Bert. We'll bury him right away.''

Mongold nodded and quickly got to the task.

Mahaffery drained another swallow of whiskey, left the lodge house, and trudged back up the beaten, snowy path to the pass, returning his attention to more important matters.

As Dillow anticipated, the actual burying job wasn't given to the outlaws. Dillow and Nolen were assigned the task. As they had with Dehaven, they opted to bury the dead man in a pre-existing hole left from the old Dutch Camp days. This was fine by Mahaffery, who seemed to desire no particular ceremony or special treatment for one more dead man, even if that dead man happened to be his own brother.

The hole, however, was filled with rocks and trash, and there was cleaning out to be done before it could accommodate its unmourned new occupant. Mahaffery seemed impatient to have it all done as quickly as possible.

As they worked, Dillow and Nolen talked quietly to one another, momentarily out of earshot of Mahaffery and his men.

''Think they'll catch Daniel?'' Nolen asked.

''Maybe. But Daniel's slippery. He just might get away.''

''He'll freeze to death if he does. Better to be caught than to freeze.''

''Don't take Daniel lightly. The boy is a survivor. He's explored this valley more than anyone else in the camp, and Sam Underhill has told me more than once that Daniel knows more caves and nooks and crannies and hiding places than you could count on five hands. He could give them the slip easier than you or me. And if he can find shelter—a cave, maybe—he might make it."

"I hope so. Hey, maybe he'll find what's become of Sam."

"You never know. I'm beginning to grow concerned about that, by the way. You'd think Sam would have shown himself by now . . . done *something*."

"Maybe something bad happened to him."

"I hate to consider it."

"Or maybe there's just nothing he can do, one man against a small army of outlaws."

"Sam's unarmed out there, I think."

"What? How would you know that?"

"When they brought in the weapons they'd rounded up the first night, I saw Sam's rifle and pistol both among it all. I only thought about that earlier today, though."

"Why was he out there to start with?"

"I had a chance this morning to talk quietly to Leora. It seems she'd asked him to go out and find Arianna and Daniel, who'd gone missing at the time. We know now they'd gone out of the pass, but Sam went back into the valley to search. Took his snowshoes, but apparently no weapons."

"So even if he does know what's happening here, there's probably nothing he can do."

"With no weapons, there's not a thing I can think of he could do for us. For that matter, against so many, and them as mean as they are, I don't know what he could do if he had a dozen rifles."

Mahaffery walked up to the hole, suddenly out of patience. "Hell, Searl's not worth this much trouble!" he said, looking at the amount of rubble still awaiting removal. "You two get out of there. Forget about it. Searl doesn't have to have a grave."

"You don't want to bury your own brother?" Dillow asked.

"Nope. Not when we can haul him out in the valley

somewhere and dump him. Let the varmints and the buzzards eat him, if they can stand him."

"Not a close and sentimental family, you Mahafferys," Dillow muttered.

Mahaffery heard, but took no offense. "My brother wasn't even a human being, friend. He had not a trace of goodness in him, nor loyalty. He'd have betrayed me in half a breath if it would have benefited him. I'm not sure why I even let him stay around . . . I suppose I'm made of more loyal stuff than he was. But loyal or not, I'll not waste my time burying trash when I need to be digging for treasure. Come on up out of there. And get back up to that pass and find me that gold."

"He's a clever little devil, I'll say that for him," Broadgrass said, referring to Daniel Chase. "And a lucky one, too . . . unless this isn't luck. Maybe the boy knows this valley well."

"He came to the right place, no doubt of that," said Remine.

The trail through the snow had been quite clear, all the way from the lodge house and far back into the valley. Remine and Broadgrass had followed it with ease, anticipating an equally easy capture, unless the young fellow laid some kind of ambush with that pistol he had.

They'd found no ambush—not yet, anyway—but it did appear that Daniel Chase had found a way to present them with an interesting puzzle.

He'd run more than a mile, straight to a stream that splashed through a short and rocky course at the base of a jagged knoll in the midst of the valley. The stream ran out of one hillside cavern, went on for no more than a hundred feet, then vanished again into the earth, swallowed by another cavern after having made only the briefest of appearances in the sunlit world.

Either cavern opening was big enough to accommodate a man. Daniel had obviously stepped into the stream, following it into one of the openings . . . but which? He might have entered either place; a stream revealed no tracks.

"We'll have to split up," Broadgrass said to Remine. "You go in that cave, I'll go in that one."

"But the boy has a pistol, Conner. He could be lying in wait for either one of us."

"It's a chance we'll have to take. We have our orders."

"Forget our orders. We can tell Mahaffery the boy tried to hide in a cave and fell in a hole too deep to get him out. He'll never know the difference. And the boy'll just freeze or starve out here, so he won't be a problem either way. He's just a boy."

"A boy who just killed a grown man by shooting him between the eyes," Broadgrass reminded Remine. "Don't take him lightly. As for him surviving: these mountains, I'd wager, are full of caves. In a cave, if it's deep enough, the temperature will stay mostly the same all year round. And a boy as clever as that one could set rabbit snares, snag trout from streams . . . he'll not die."

"I don't want to go in these caves. He could shoot either one of us."

"Maybe you want us to go back to Mahaffery and tell him you decided to disobey him."

Remine glared at the other. "Very well, then, we'll look in these caves. But I don't think it's worth the risk, just for a damned kid. I'll take that entrance there."

"No. That'll be mine. It's smaller, and I'm smaller than you. You go in that bigger one there, where the water flows out. Look at it this way: he's most likely in the cave I'm going into. He'd have chosen it because he'd figure a grown man would be less likely to follow him into the smaller cave."

Remine thought about it, nodded, and stepped into the creek. "That's hellacious cold water," he said.

"You won't be in it long," Broadgrass said.

"Ain't you going in the other cave? Because I'm not

going to bear all the risk here, Broadgrass. We go in, we go in at the same time. Equal risk.''

"I agree. It's the only fair way. I'll see you in a few minutes. One of us should have the boy by then.''

Remine advanced against the cold, rushing water, stooped, and entered the cave from which water emerged. Broadgrass made a show of going into the other entrance at the same time, but quickly ducked to the side, just inside the cave mouth, and hid in the shadows. There he waited.

A minute later he heard a muffled shot echo out of the cavern Remine had entered. It sounded like a pistol shot. Broadgrass stepped out of his cave and onto the bank. He'd had a feeling, for some reason, that the other cave was the one Daniel Chase had selected.

A few moments passed before a pink tinge began to appear in the water running out of the other cave. Broadgrass shook his head. Poor, gullible Remine. Well, at least Broadgrass had managed to verify which cave the boy had entered without taking a bullet himself.

A half-minute later, Remine's body came washing down the creek, out of the cave, floating on its back. He'd been shot in the chest, and his eyes were dead marbles, staring up at the sky without blinking. He floated down the icy creek, and hung up at the mouth of the opposite cave entrance. The water passed around him, making him move and bob. Slowly he rolled over, turned by the water. More color spread in the creek, then was swallowed by the receptacle cavern.

Broadgrass surmised that Daniel must have positioned himself just deep enough in the cavern, and in just the right position, to let him see the limned outline of any other person who entered the cave after him. A simple shot to the mid-chest area was enough to do the job. A more perfect trap could hardly have been made. Remine, like Broadgrass, had anticipated it, but he'd been foolish and subservient enough to let Broadgrass talk him into making himself the first potential target.

Broadgrass had to admire the boy. A devilishly clever lad, this one. He'd managed to do in two grown men in one day, and Broadgrass was hanged if he was going to see the boy punished after showing that kind of ingenuity.

"I take my hat off to you, son," Broadgrass called into the cave that had belched forth Remine. "Just such a scheme is the very kind I would have come up with. I admire you, my friend, and now I'm going back to report that you've killed Mr. Remine, but not, unfortunately, before he killed you, too. They'll not look for you if they believe you're dead." Broadgrass paused, then reached beneath his coat and pulled out a packet of pemmican.

"I'm laying some food here by the cave mouth. You can get it later, when you've satisfied yourself that I'm really gone, and that this is no trap. You take that food, make it last as long as you can. Find yourself a shelter somewhere. Trap yourself some rabbits, catch some fish. If you're as clever as I think you are, you can survive until the spring. And by then, all this will long be over, one way or the other." He paused. "You'll probably be the only one of your people left by then. But you deserve to survive. You proved yourself worthy here today."

Broadgrass waited for an answer, but none came. He hadn't really thought one would. But he knew Daniel was in there, listening.

"I salute you, young man. Take care of yourself. I'm going back now, and if you'll keep yourself hidden, you should have no more trouble from any of us."

He looked over to where Remine floated and bobbed at the mouth of the other cave. He muttered, "Good-bye, my friend. One less with which to divide that gold . . . if ever it's found. Ten of us before . . . now only seven. Life truly is but a shadow. Well, good-bye."

Broadgrass trudged away, through the snow, back toward Texas Gulch.

CHAPTER
SEVENTEEN

Sam Underhill ate slowly of the rabbit meat his father provided perfectly roasted on a spit, and listened to Bushrod recount his long journey from Texas to California, a journey made, the aging frontiersman said, just to see a son he missed, and to walk through some country he hadn't yet explored.

Sam listened, but it was a bill of goods he wasn't buying.

"Pap," he said at last, laying aside a bone gnawed clean. "Tell me the *real* reason you came."

"What are you talking about?"

"Pap, it's winter. You've come all the way from Texas, trudged up mountains in heavy snow, and so far all I hear from you is that you just hankered to see me. But there's more to it than that. There has to be."

Bushrod Underhill looked quite offended. "You had a mystic vision, did you, that tells you I lie to my own son?"

"It doesn't require a mystic vision to see that it would take more than a desire for a family visit to draw you this far, this time of year. Besides, I can tell there's something on your mind."

"Of course there's something on my mind. You've got a mining camp full of innocent people, overrun by a horde of outlaws and murderers. You're probably facing a mass execution of men, women, and children before this finishes.

And to counter all that, there's just me and you."

"But you didn't know any of that when you left Texas. It's not why you came."

"I don't know why you find it so hard to believe that I'd come see you just because you're my son."

"In the dead of winter? In the mountains?"

"Like I said, Sam: you know me. Inconvenience never stopped me from doing anything I wanted to do. Besides, it took me a mite longer to track you down than I thought it would. There's not many below who know there's anybody at Dutch Camp."

"It ain't Dutch Camp now. We call it Texas Gulch."

"Hallelujah. I'm all for honoring the great state where thrive the Underhills."

"Something's wrong back home, Pap, and you're not telling me."

"Boy, the something that's wrong lies across this valley in that mining camp. I suggest we concentrate our minds and efforts on that."

Sam studied his father's face. Bushrod was hard to read when he wanted to be, but some pains even he couldn't hide. Despite Bush's protestations, Sam saw veiled things buried deep in the frontiersman's familiar eyes, things that hurt.

"Pap, just tell me one thing, and I'll leave it be for now: is it Ma?"

There might have been the quick glint of a tear in the old frontiersman's eye, but Sam couldn't be sure. "No, son. It ain't your mother."

"But there is something."

"I told you, Sam. I just wanted to see you. We'll leave it there, all right?"

A hundred dreadful possibilities were playing through Sam's mind, but he knew it would be futile to pursue them right now. "Whatever you want, Pap."

Bushrod nodded. "What I want is for us to rid your little community of the vermin that's infested it."

"I want the same. But I ain't been able to figure out how."

Bushrod was somber. They'd joked before about how the odds had swung in their favor, now that two Underhills were together, but the grim truth of what faced them hung heavy as a stormcloud about them. Two lone men, minimally armed, bore the duty of rescuing an entire community of endangered innocents.

"Tell me what you know, Pap, and how you came to know it."

"What I've learned I've learned by chance, Sam, or by some design bigger than our own. It happened that as I neared the final stretch up to this valley, heading for the entrance pass, I saw the riders, struggling up through the snow. I watched them—they didn't see me—and witnessed them taking two children hostage. One of them was Arianna Winkle, from back home, though she's growed considerable since I last saw her, and I didn't know her at once. The other was a boy, a stranger to me."

"Daniel Chase," Sam cut in. "He's an orphan, sort of a child of the whole mining camp. He came to us with his older brother, and then the brother died and left him alone."

Bushrod paused after hearing that, a look of concern on his face. Sam understood. Bushrod's own childhood had placed in him a deep sense of affection for and protectiveness toward orphans.

Bush went on. "I was too far away to do aught about the taking of the children, and I'd counted ten of them scoundrels. Wasn't much I could do.

"But I was able to hear enough to begin to get a notion of what was going on, and when I determined they were going to ride in to your camp, I followed. But one of them broke off from the rest—for some reason, he was chasing a dog, Arianna's dog, I think—probably just trying to keep the poor girl trusting them until they could reach the camp. But of course this fellow ends up ready to shoot the dog instead. He saw me, though, through the snowfall. I stood still as a stone, hoping that my clothing, the blurring of the snow, all that, would camouflage me. But he spoke to me. Called me 'Dehaven.' The name mean anything to you?''

"Dehaven . . .'' Sam recalled what Hiram Linfoot had told him before he died. "That was the name of a man we found dead in the snow just outside the pass, the evening before the outlaws came in.''

"This fellow, apart from the rest of his group, was making me an offer—or making this Dehaven an offer, from his point of view—to divide and take some gold, and to run off and leave the rest of the group without. I made no answer, just stood there. Eventually he wandered off, figuring that his eyes were playing tricks on him in the snow, I suppose.

"When he'd gone on a distance, I followed, wanting to see what this gang was up to. I came up into the pass after dark, and hid there, and listened. And I heard it all.

"Your camp is hostage, Sam, all of them. This Dehaven fellow had taken stolen gold from the others and tried to keep it all for himself.'' Bushrod told the story as he'd been able to piece it together from what he'd heard. "The leader of the gang, a man named Mahaffery, killed one of your people that first night, Sam. Shot him dead, before the others, because the man was sneaking a gun on his person. And I knew right then just how serious a danger all the people there are in.''

Sam said, "All you're telling me confirms what I was told by a man who managed to get away from the camp . . . though he was mortally wounded at the time he told me.''

"So there's *two* Texas Gulch people dead?''

"Yes. You remember Hiram Linfoot? Came to Texas about six months before we headed for California?''

"I do remember him.''

"He's the second who was killed. He'd gotten away, and told me, without all the details, the same things you just did. But, Pap, if you were in the pass that first night, why didn't you just sneak on in the rest of the way, instead of coming all the way around and over the mountains?''

"Because this Mahaffery put watchmen at the pass," Bushrod said. "I was driven out by their approach before I could get all the way in. But I knew I had to get in somehow. I'd looked for you among the people, and hadn't been able to spot you. I thought maybe I'd just overlooked you. I had to find out. I circled and explored all through the mountains the next day, until finally I found a new way into the valley."

"I've always heard there is no other way in besides the pass," Sam said.

"The general wisdom is wrong. There is one. High and narrow, hard to reach, but it's there. And I found it."

"How?"

"I've got a nose for these things. Like Dan Boone used to say, 'The land can tell you a lot when you know how to read it.' "

"So you came all the way around, and into the valley, just to look for me?"

"Mostly. And to help the others, too. They're my people, too, after all." Bush smiled at his son. "I'm mighty relieved I've found you alive, Sam. I was afraid, when I didn't see you amongst the people, that something bad had befallen you since last I'd heard from you."

"I'm still among the living . . . for now."

"Yes, thank God. Well, I've told you my tale. Now let me hear yours."

Sam took a deep breath and started at the beginning. He told Bush, briefly, the history of Texas Gulch, and of those who prospected its environs. Most of the people Bush already knew. He was particularly saddened to hear of the death of Leora Winkle's husband, a man he'd always thought of very highly.

Sam described, with some shame, his own ill-advised, inadequately prepared-for jaunt into the snowy wilderness for what he'd thought would be a quick find of two missing children. But if his father judged him harshly for having ventured out without weapons and adequate planning, he said nothing of it. Sam figured that lecture would probably come later.

Sam also told how his search for the children had been providentially timed. It had gotten him away from Texas Gulch just in time to avoid being taken as one of the hostages of the Mahaffery gang.

Sam described his fall into the pit and the finding of the rock pick, which he'd used not only to get himself out of a quite literal hole, but to kill the rifleman who'd mortally wounded Hiram Linfoot.

"I hid Hiram's body, and the second man who'd been chasing him never saw me, nor did he see Hiram dead. I can only suppose the outlaws must believe that Hiram's still alive out here, alone, and that it must have been Hiram who pickaxed that fellow to death. Hiram himself told me, before he died, that the Mahaffery gang doesn't even know I exist . . . unless, of course, someone has told them since."

"Either way," Bush said, thinking, "it's a good thing you played that hand as you did. Whether or not they know about you, they do believe that Linfoot is still alive and roaming around . . . and likely they'll try to search him down at some point. Maybe we'll get a chance at them, a few at a time, that way."

Sam felt daunted. "It frightens me to consider that there's only two of us, and so many of them."

Bushrod's eyes twinkled. "But we're Underhills, remember? And an Underhill can shoot a hole in the moon and spit through it. An Underhill can light his pipe from the flames of the sun. And an Underhill can belch and knock down a grove of California redwoods. Says so right in the almanacs."

"As I hear it, there's only one Underhill who could do such wonders, and I'm looking at him. But don't tell me you've taken to believing all those tales you profess to despise so," Sam said.

"Son, in the situation we're in, we'd both best start believing them. For what we're going to have to pull off is nothing less than a miracle."

CHAPTER
EIGHTEEN

Conner Broadgrass reported the death of Ross Remine in his usual impassive style. And he told his lie about the supposed death of young Daniel Chase in such a bland and convincing manner that tears came to almost all the Texas Gulch residents who heard it and had no cause to disbelieve it.

Ben Dillow didn't weep. The news about Daniel filled him with sorrow, but even more with fury, and he decided on the spot that he would, somehow, get this camp and these people out of this horrific situation, or sacrifice his life trying.

America Colfax did shed tears—despite the fact she'd been more than ready to feed Daniel Chase to Mahaffery for the sake of her own sagging and sallow hide. Herbert Colfax did not cry. He seemed lost in his own deep brooding, his thick brows descending low across the bridge of a hawklike nose, deepening the crease that ran along its top and the furrows in his forehead.

Broadgrass had returned at a time when the work at the pass was at a temporary stop so the exhausted men could rest. So hard had they been pushed, and in such a mentally and physically draining manner, that even Mahaffery had been forced to see that efforts had to slow down a little, or they'd stop of their own accord.

Mahaffery didn't seem concerned about Daniel's fate, but Dillow noticed that the outlaw blanched a little to hear that one more of his men, Ross Remine, was dead.

That makes three gone, Dillow thought, for he'd decided already that Mahaffery's claim that the one named Fish was off somewhere, resting, was a lie. The man was dead. Hiram Linfoot, or an accident—or maybe even Sam Underhill—must have gotten Fish. *Ten outlaws to begin with, now down to only seven. They've got the weapons, and therefore the odds are still theirs . . . but not quite as heavily as before.*

That two of the outlaws had died at the hand of a mere boy inspired and humbled Dillow. If Daniel Chase had the wherewithal to take one of his enemies with him to the grave, shouldn't a group of grown men be able to do as well?

Dillow had accepted the fact that any or all of them might die before this was done, but he pledged to himself not to die without taking a member or two of the Mahaffery gang along for the same ride. He'd not let young Daniel outdo him. He'd honor the orphan boy's memory with the blood of the same outlaws who had killed him.

Mahaffery was obviously troubled and trying to think, but his drinking wasn't helping him. He paced back and forth in the lodge house, staggering slightly this way and that, so that the hostages seated around him were careful to keep their feet out of his way so as to avoid tripping him and maybe getting shot for it.

Mahaffery was red-faced, red-eyed, and swearing with every breath. Ben Dillow could hardly blame him. Mahaffery had come here to recover lost gold, only to find it elusive. And three of his men, including his own brother, were dead.

Dillow took some satisfaction in Mahaffery's unhappiness, but it also worried him. Mahaffery might decide to give up his gold quest early. If so, the people of Texas Gulch would probably not live to see another setting of the sun.

But Mahaffery wasn't through quite yet. He barked an

order, and under guard, the weary men of Texas Gulch trudged up the slope to the pass, to spend more long hours prospecting the snow for stolen gold.

Through the white valley, Sam and Bushrod Underhill walked together, father and son, heading toward Texas Gulch.

It was a terrible burden to carry the fate of an entire group of people in one's hands, Sam thought. But an easier burden, now that his father was here. Maybe Bushrod Underhill really couldn't shoot holes through the moon or drink the Great Lakes dry, like the almanacs claimed, but he still was Bushrod Underhill, frontiersman, survivor, companion. Most of all, father. Sam needed that right now.

"There it is," Sam said, when the mining camp at last came into view. It was, from their vantage point, nothing more than a few squares and rectangles of dull brown against a backdrop of white. He watched the plume of smoke rise from the twin chimneys of the big lodge house. "Looks remarkably peaceful, considering."

The pair of them stood there, watching the camp. Sam lifted his eyes to the pass and could barely make out the forms of men up there, digging in the snow, widening the search area ever more. Men under the gun. Good men, working like slaves because their lives, and the lives of their neighbors, and in a few cases, their families, depended on it.

Suddenly it was all overwhelming, impossible . . . and Sam turned his head away.

"I don't know what we'll do, Pap," he said. "We've talked, figured . . . and we still have no answer."

"Maybe we've got part of one," Bush said. He touched Sam's shoulder. "Take a look, son. Then back up, slow, and let's you and me drift into these rocks over here."

Sam looked. Coming toward them, out of Texas Gulch, were two men bearing a burden. They struggled slowly through the snow, heavily laden.

Bushrod reached beneath his coat and brought out a familiar spyglass, one Sam had seen him use all his life. Pressing it to his eye, adjusting it, Bushrod looked for a few
moments and said, "Sam, they're carrying a corpse."

Sam winced.

"Take a look."

Reluctantly, Sam took the spyglass, found the image, and
brought it into focus. He didn't recognize the men who carried the body. Two of the outlaws. The body was wrapped,
the face hidden. Judging from the size of the dead man, Sam
figured it could be Ben Dillow, maybe Jack Gray, Leora's
brother.

He lowered the glass slowly. He and his father drifted to
the side, hiding themselves behind a conglomeration of
boulders as the corpse-bearers slowly advanced in their direction.

"Let's get them, Pap," Sam said. "Let's eliminate two
pieces of the problem right now."

"Let's do."

Reed Van Huss and Lennis Yeager were not happy men,
and expressed their displeasure to one another as they stumbled and staggered through the snow, bearing the wrapped
corpse of Searl Mahaffery. Who did Jordan Mahaffery think
they were, anyway? Why did two of the best thieves on the
continent—in their own estimation, anyway—have to serve
as mere guards and corpse-carriers for Jordan Mahaffery?
Though both had always admired Mahaffery's skill as a
criminal organizer, schemer, and technician—it was he who
had conceived and carried out the brilliant robbery that had
netted them the gold Dehaven had taken—just now they saw
nothing to like in the man. Just a sorry drunk, throwing his
weight around, making everyone around him labor while he
stood swigging from his flask like some minor king.

"I've got half a mind to dump old Searl right here on the
ground and forget about it," Van Huss said. "Why should

we go trekking any farther through this snow? This is far enough.''

Yeager, though agreeing with the emotion of Van Huss's statement, was a more practical man. ''We dump him here, and we'll just be sent back to redo the job. Let's put up with the headache and carry him back a little farther. We'll find someplace among the rocks to lay him. Or we'll hide him beneath a snow drift if we have to.''

''Hell, it isn't going to matter,'' Van Huss said. ''We'll be out of here before long anyway.''

''You think we're getting out of here before spring? You think we could get down that mountain in this kind of snow?''

''I could. Just find that gold, give me my share, and I'll be gone.''

''You'd never make it. Hey, see those rocks yonder? Let's go dump him there.''

The other was agreeable. They struggled with the body toward the place they'd chosen, and were almost there when two unfamiliar men rose before them, rifles leveled. One was young, the other white-haired.

''Hold just as still as your dead friend there,'' the old one said. ''Or you'll find yourself in the same unhappy condition he's in.''

Van Huss and Yeager glanced at one another. They'd always been able to read each other well, and did so now.

''Let us lay down this body,'' Yeager said.

''Let him drop,'' the white-haired man replied.

But they didn't drop Searl; they squatted slowly and laid him gently on the snow, as if he had been the dearest friend they'd ever had. They moved as one, abruptly, pulling pistols from beneath their coats and throwing themselves in opposite directions, finding the nearest cover as they cocked their weapons.

The two outlaws didn't know who these strangers were, but they'd be hanged before they'd let themselves be taken without a fight.

*   *   *

In the lodge house, Jordan Mahaffery snapped up his head.

"You hear that?"

"Gunshots," Mongold said.

"What the hell . . . ?" Mahaffery grabbed his rifle from the corner and headed out the door and around the lodge house. Another shot sounded from out in the valley, a high, cracking sound at this distance.

Mongold came to Mahaffery's side. "Reed and Lennis must have run across trouble. But who? The one who me and Emmett chased?"

"Has to be. Who else could it be?"

"But there were more shots than I'd expect from them finding one unarmed man."

"Maybe that runaway got his hands on a weapon, somehow. He managed to find a pick to kill Emmett with, didn't he?"

Another shot, then another, closer this time.

"Hey!" Mahaffery exclaimed. "There they come!"

Mongold didn't see Van Huss and Yeager nearly as quickly as Mahaffery had. But soon even his piggish, myopic eyes spotted them. Both were running as hard as the snow would allow, back toward Texas Gulch. They leaped snow drifts and bounded over the rugged terrain with the kind of grace and athletic prowess often inspired by mortally dangerous encounters.

They were breathless by the time they reached Mahaffery and Mongold, and leaned over with legs bent, hands on knees, gasping out white clouds of steam.

"Two men . . . tried to take us," Yeager managed to get out.

"*Two* men?" Mahaffery said.

"Yes . . . Never seen them before."

Van Huss found his voice and added, "One of them was young . . . the other an old fellow."

"Almost had us, too," Yeager said. "But we moved . . .

quicker than they'd anticipated. Did you hear . . . the shots?''

"I did. Did you hit them?''

"No. And they didn't hit us. We were lucky. They had rifles, us just our pistols.''

"Two men . . . how in the devil? And where did they come from?''

"No idea, Jordan. No idea.''

"The younger one . . . might he have been our running man, the one Mongold and poor old Emmett chased?''

"We'd have known him. It wasn't him. I swear, these two were strangers.''

Mahaffery let out a slow breath. "Get back inside. Let's go have a word with the good people of this sorry camp. I have a feeling some of them might know who this pair is. If there's somebody living elsewhere in this valley, somebody here's bound to know about it.''

CHAPTER NINETEEN

The gunshots had been heard up in the pass, too. The men laboring there were brought down, at Mahaffery's orders, and stood up in the trampled snow outside the lodge house. The other hostages were lined up alongside them. The sky had cleared momentarily, though new clouds were thickening on the horizon, and the sun was bright on the snow, making them all squint and wince.

Mahaffery paced before his hostages like a commander before troops with whom he is not pleased.

"I want to know one thing: who are they, and which of you knew of them?"

No one replied.

Mahaffery stopped pacing and stared into individual faces. "Why am I getting no answer? Two of my men were nigh killed today in that valley, attacked by a pair of men they'd never seen before. Now, if there's others living in this valley, some one of you is going to know it."

When no one answered again, Ben Dillow cleared his throat and tried to find something to say, just to keep Mahaffery's steam from rising any further.

"What did they look like?" he asked.

"What kind of question is that?" Mahaffery shot back. "Is there a whole damned population of folks living back in that valley so that you have to get a description to know which ones we're talking about?''

Dillow wasn't going to spar with this man. He said no more.

Mahaffery said to Van Huss, ''Tell them what they looked like.''

Van Huss gave a remarkably thorough description, considering the tense situation in which he and Yeager had encountered the pair.

Letitia Colfax sniffled and whimpered, ''Oh, it sounds like Mr. Sam and Mr. Bush!''

Dillow sighed. There'd be no more keeping secret the existence of Sam Underhill.

Dillow himself had to wonder who the older man could be. The description sounded like Bushrod Underhill, of all people, but that was impossible. Bushrod was still in Texas.

Mahaffery's nose was three inches from Letitia's broad face almost as soon as she spoke. ''What'd you say, girl?''

''I said, it sounds like Mr. Sam and Mr. Bush.''

''And who might they be?''

''Sam and Bushrod Underhill. But it isn't possible that it's really—''

Mahaffery slapped her, evoking a screech. ''What are you talking about, heifer? Are you trying to mock me? Bushrod Underhill? Hell, I thought maybe it was Father Christmas!'' He slapped her again.

Herbert Colfax, going crimson, stepped out of the line and pointed into Mahaffery's face. ''Don't you hit her again!''

Mahaffery did hit her again, harder, staring at Colfax while he did so. ''What do you aim to do about that, old man? Get your fat rump back where it was, or I'll turn your two cows here over to Mongold and let him do what he wants with them.''

Colfax's breath was coming hard. He tried to speak but couldn't. For a moment he hesitated, overwhelmed by fury, then, with effort, he made himself step back into place. Letitia stood with her face buried in her hands, crying. America Colfax looked like she could faint where she stood, her face as white as snow.

It was the first time in Dillow's memory that he'd actually felt sorry for Herbert Colfax. Just now he'd have killed to protect the man and his family.

The time had come to speak up. Dillow cleared his throat and said, "Mahaffery."

The outlaw turned. "Speak up."

"The young lady wasn't mocking you. There is a Sam Underhill who lives among us. You might consider him the closest thing we've had to a community leader, if you want."

Mahaffery strode over and faced Dillow. "Go on."

"The people of this mining camp came from Texas, for the most part. The town of Underhill stands on land that was given by Sam Houston to Bushrod Underhill for his part in putting down the Tripplerite Conspiracy that would have given the Mexicans a foothold in Texas."[3]

"Pass over the history lesson and get to the point," Mahaffery said.

"Sam Underhill is the son of Bushrod. The real Bushrod, not the make-believe almanac version of the man. Sam led this band of Forty-niners here, and has been a leader among us ever since."

"So why wasn't he among you when we took over this sorry place?"

"He was out searching for two lost children, that's why. The same pair you came riding in with, pistols to their heads, being the brave and fearless man you are." The sarcasm had been irresistible.

Mahaffery ignored it. "You're telling me that the younger of the pair who attacked my men is Sam Underhill. Son of the great Bushrod himself. So who was the older man?"

"I can't tell you, Mahaffery. But Letitia was right. From

[3]*Texas Freedom*, Book 2 in The Underhill Series

the description, I'd have to say it sounds like Bushrod Underhill.''

"So Bushrod Underhill came to Texas Gulch, too?"

"He did not. Which is why it can't really be him. Yet the description of him matches, right down to the last detail.''

Mahaffery pondered matters a few moments. "So Sam Underhill has found himself a mysterious partner who looks like his pap in Texas. Interesting situation. But it won't matter. We'll kill them both all the same, no matter what their names are or how famous their pappies might be.''

Just then, farther down the line, Herbert Colfax said, "Mr. Mahaffery . . . sir . . . there's something I need to say."

Dillow frowned. There was something odd and strained in Colfax's speech. It sounded like it had taken an excruciating effort to get the words out.

"Speak up, then.''

Colfax frowned and tilted his head, putting one hand on the side of his head. "I want to tell . . . you . . . that . . . uh, that there's . . . the gold, you see . . . I'm sorry, I'm sorry . . . I don't feel very well right now.''

He made an odd, gurgling moan, twisted his face strangely, and collapsed slowly to the ground.

High in the rocks of one of the many ridges that made up the great stone circle enclosing the valley holding Texas Gulch, Sam Underhill sat listlessly, staring at the ground before him as his father silently paced back and forth.

Sam spoke first. "We didn't handle that particular battle too well, eh, Pap?''

Bushrod mumbled something Sam couldn't make out. Sam didn't ask him to repeat it because it really didn't matter. Nothing said now could alter the fact that they'd underestimated the two they'd tried to capture. Though they themselves had escaped unharmed, they'd also failed to so much as nick either of the outlaws.

And the only edge they had, the element of surprise, now was lost. By now Mahaffery had heard those two outlaws' entire tale, no doubt, and probably was making plans to defend against, or maybe even hunt down, the troublesome pair out in the valley.

"We're fools, Sam," Bushrod said at length. "A pair of fools not up to the task that's been given us. But you're a young man. You've got an excuse. I'm old and experienced. I should have handled it better."

"I was just getting ready to say that *I'm* the one who has no excuse."

"The truth is, neither one of us do," Bushrod said. "But there's no point in chasing water that's already flowed away, as old Tuckaseh used to tell me back in Coldwater Town. We've got to move on from here. Maybe, if we look long enough, we can find some advantage we gained from what happened, even if we don't see it yet."

It was a positive suggestion, and a good one to hear, but as Sam reviewed the fiasco of the failed attack, he could find nothing, and admitted this to his father.

Bush looked stoic. "I reckon I just proved that old Bushrod can't shoot a hole through the moon after all."

"Neither one of us is anything more than a man," Sam said. "We're facing a situation that there truly may be no way to get out of."

"Don't say that," Bush said sharply. "The moment you decide there's no way out, you've lost. And we mustn't lose."

"No." Sam paused. "We mustn't. Because there are good people down there. And children. For the sake of the children alone, we have to find a way."

Something odd occurred right then. Bushrod's look changed, and his eyes reddened. He turned his back on his son very quickly, but his shoulders heaved and he could not hide it.

Sam watched in amazement as his father wept. Bushrod

Underhill was shaken, deeply so, and Sam was sure it was not merely because of one failed gun battle.

"Pap, you're going to have to tell me sometime."

Bush drew in a deep breath, and straightened his shoulders. The quaking subsided. With his back still turned, he said, "Tell you what?"

"Whatever it is you haven't told me yet. Whatever it is that really brought you all the way here from Texas."

There was a long silence, then Bushrod said, "We'll be talking a lot, you and me, once we're through all this. Once we have your people free."

"You can tell me now, if you want."

But Bushrod had nothing to say.

They laid Herbert Colfax on a pallet inside the lodge house, but he would not lie still. He kept rocking, moving, as if trying to roll himself over, but he couldn't make it. The left side of his face drooped stiffly, as if the corner of his mouth was being pulled down by an unseen finger. His left arm lay motionless at his side, hand twisted oddly, fingers curling up.

"Oh, Herbert, please, please lie still!" America Colfax pleaded through tears. Her daughter, already shaken and never strong even in good times, huddled in a corner, knees drawn up, face hidden—to all appearances a young woman making a strong attempt to become a fetus again.

Dillow was at America's side, watching Colfax's odd motions. Any hostility he'd felt toward this fellow couldn't survive now. The man was pitiful and wretched, and Dillow felt sorry for him.

"It's apoplexy, America," he said to the crying woman. "I've seen it before. He can't really help what he's doing . . . it's just that his body won't obey him anymore."

She cried, refusing to look at her husband. Mahaffery stood behind America and Dillow, a few feet back, looking on silently. To Dillow's surprise, the outlaw was actually being relatively humane in this situation. He'd allowed Colfax to be brought inside, his family with him, and when he learned that Dillow served as a doctor substitute in Texas Gulch, allowed him to enter, too.

"I think he's trying to say something," Mahaffery said.

Dillow looked into Colfax's eyes, watched his struggling attempts to move his face. He saw at once that Mahaffery was right.

"Herbert . . . are you trying to talk?"

More strain, more twisting of the one side of the face that would still move. And this time, a bit of noise, but no words.

"Herbert, don't try. I'll get you something to write with."

Colfax relaxed then, lying back, but his body still seemed strained and awkward. The stroke had hurt him badly, and Dillow felt no optimism about Colfax's survival.

Dillow rose and looked back at Mahaffery, who nodded his permission for Dillow to search out writing materials. All Dillow could find was a slate and bit of chalk that Arianna Winkle used when her mother gave her schooling. Dillow held up the slate and let Colfax take the chalk in his right hand. Colfax, however, was left-handed by nature, and it was difficult for him to write on the slate, which Dillow held up for him. Letters kept showing a tendency to come out turned backward, but still the apoplectic man managed to produce scratchings that could be read.

He wrote slowly and laboriously, his breath catching and face reddening. Then he lay back, still gripping the chalk.

Dillow turned the slate and looked at it. America ceased hiding her face and read, too, and Mahaffery stepped over and looked down as well.

"What the devil . . . ?" the outlaw muttered.

Colfax had written: HID THE GOLD.

CHAPTER
TWENTY

"What's he mean by that?" Mahaffery said, intense all at once. "What gold? *My* gold?"

Whether it was good or bad that Colfax was revealing this now, Dillow could not say. But the dam was broken and whatever flowed over now would simply have to come.

Dillow leaned over and spoke into Colfax's face. "Herbert, I'll take the chalk from your hand and put my finger in its place. When I ask you a question, you squeeze once for yes, twice for no."

It seemed that Colfax tried to nod.

Dillow did as he had said. "Herbert, is the gold you wrote about gold you've mined?"

Two squeezes.

"Is it the gold that Mahaffery and his men have been searching for?"

A pause, then a single squeeze. Mahaffery saw it and cursed.

"Are you saying, Herbert, that you have Mahaffery's missing gold?"

Again, a single squeeze.

Mahaffery dropped to his knees, shoving Dillow aside. He put his own finger into Colfax's hand. "You saying you got my gold, old man?"

Colfax, looking as scared as his facial paralysis would

allow, gazed into the outlaw's face and squeezed his yes.

"Why, you sorry old thief! All this time, you've had my gold, and you said nothing?"

Another single squeeze.

"Well, you devil, before you die and go to hell, you're going to tell me where it is . . . ain't you!"

Another squeeze. A yes.

"Give him the chalk and the slate," Mahaffery directed Dillow.

Dillow went to Colfax's opposite side and picked up the slate as before, first dusting off the prior words with the heel of his hand. He put the chalk into Colfax's hand, then helped him lift his arm, propping it to let him write.

Colfax wrote: NO.

Mahaffery cursed thoroughly. "Old man, you don't cooperate, and I'll let you watch me cut your wife's throat, then your fat daughter's."

"Wait a minute," Dillow said, forcefully. "He wants to write more."

Dillow cleaned the slate; Colfax wrote again.

PEOPLE FREE.

"He wants you to let the people here go," Dillow said. "Then he'll tell you where the gold is." *Good for you, Colfax,* Dillow thought. *Maybe you're a better man than I ever thought. What you're trying to do might not work, but at least you're trying.*

"Does this old fool think he can lie there and tell me what to do?" Mahaffery glared down at Colfax. "You're dying, old man. But your wife and daughter ain't. Keep in mind that the situation could change."

A tear streamed down Colfax's face. Dillow fought emotion himself: a pure, righteous anger that made him want to take Mahaffery's throat in his own hands and squeeze the life from the man. For a few moments he seriously thought of doing so, but gave it up. Mahaffery was armed, and he wasn't. He'd never succeed.

But if Mahaffery threatened the lives of the Colfax

women, he decided, he'd attack him right there, and die with
Mahaffery's throat in his teeth.

Mahaffery put his face inches from Colfax's. "Old man,
you're going to write out where that gold is. No games from
you, no promises from me . . . except one. If you'll tell me
where that gold is, I'll see your family treated well. I'll see
that, no matter what, they survive this."

Colfax was listening. Dillow couldn't blame him. What
man wouldn't care about the safety of his family more than
about any other matter? But he hoped Colfax had the sense
not to believe Mahaffery. The outlaw would have no reason
to keep his pledge once he had what he wanted.

"You going to help me out, old man? You going to make
sure your women are safe and sound after you're gone?"

Colfax blinked his wet eyes rapidly. The meaning was
obvious.

Mahaffery grinned and put the chalk into Colfax's hand.
Colfax began to scratch the chalk over the slate.

Dillow closed his eyes. It was almost over now. Mahaffery was about to be handed his gold, and what would happen after that he could not say, but he wasn't optimistic.

Dillow heard something clack against the puncheon floor.
He opened his eyes.

America Colfax was sobbing all at once. Dillow looked
at Colfax's face and saw why.

Herbert Colfax was dead. A second stroke, probably, silent and quick. The chalk, falling from his fingers, was what
had made the clacking noise on the floor.

Mahaffery, a little slow to comprehend what had just happened, finally did a moment or so later. He turned the slate
he'd been holding and cursed loudly.

Colfax, though he had tried hard, had managed to produce
nothing more than a few indecipherable, childish scribbles.

Mahaffery rose and smashed the slate against the wall.
America Colfax sobbed louder and went to her dead hus-

band, while Letitia made whimpering animal sounds that
were quite pitiful.

Dillow perceived this moment as the most precarious he
and his fellows had faced from the moment all this began.
The one man who knew where the gold was hidden was
dead. It would take Mahaffery only a few moments to come
around to the possibility that Colfax might have told his wife
or daughter where the gold was, which would lead to interrogation, maybe torture. Dillow knew Colfax well enough
to believe that he'd probably kept the matter of the gold
secret even from his own family. All the ugliness would
lead nowhere but to more frustration and anger on Mahaffery's part . . . and probably to a mad search of the camp,
and a mass killing at the end of it all.

In such moments inspiration often comes, and it came to
Dillow right then.

He turned to the rampaging Mahaffery and said, "That's
it, Mahaffery. I reckon there's no point in me holding out
any more."

Mahaffery turned his frown on him. "What are you talking about?"

"It's just that I know what'll come next. You'll want to
hurt these women on the chance that he told them where he
hid that gold. But please don't do that, for I know he didn't
tell them. He told me instead. Colfax and I were in this thing
together . . . and we hid the gold together. He didn't let on
just now, trying to protect me, I guess. But I'll not hide the
truth anymore."

Mahaffery drew his pistol. "Tell me where the gold is,
right now."

"I can't describe the location to you. Too complicated to
explain . . . you'd never find it that way. I'll have to lead
you to it."

Mahaffery studied him silently, then said, "You're
damned right you will. And if you're lying to me, I'll make
you die a hundred deaths."

"You're mighty rude to those who offer to help you, you know it, Mahaffery?"

"Watch your mouth, my friend. I'm not a man who abides insult."

"You'll abide mine. Because right now I'm the only hope you have of ever putting your hands on that gold."

Mahaffery stared coldly at him, but it was obvious that Dillow's disrespectfulness was, paradoxically, gaining Dillow some respect from the outlaw. That daredevil defiance was the very kind of attitude Mahaffery himself would have had if the roles in this scenario were reversed. Dillow had anticipated just this reaction, and it gave him a certain sense of power to see that he'd correctly gauged his foe's mental processes. These outlaws might be bold and cruel, but there was a shallowness about them, too, that a clever man might be able to manipulate to his advantage.

"Very well, Dillow," Mahaffery said. "I have no desire for your respect. All I want is my gold. And I want it now. Take me to it. But tell me first how I can be sure you really know where it is."

"You can't. All I can tell you is that Herbert Colfax and me found that gold alongside the corpse of Dehaven, even before young Daniel found the body. We hauled that gold out and hid it well, planning to get it in the spring, divide it, and go our way." Dillow glanced at America Colfax and her daughter. Both were still silently crying, but listening intently. He wondered if they believed what he'd told Mahaffery, or saw the design behind his lie.

Mahaffery said, "So all this time you've known where that gold is, and you've said nothing."

"It's a lot of gold. Colfax and I were banking on the hope that you'd give up eventually, vacate this place, and leave the gold to us."

"So you let your own people work under our guns, and let men die, and still you kept your mouths closed."

"Like I said, it's a lot of gold. And if we'd told you

where it is, you'd have killed us all as soon as you got your hands on it.''

Mahaffery's lip twitched, and he smiled, just a little, just for a moment. ''And once I get it now . . . what do you think I'll do?''

''I'm going to ask that you spare us. There's not a thing I can do to make you do that, but I can tell you that I'm a man with influence among these people. I'll keep them quiet. No one will ever tell about what you and your men have done here. You have my promise.''

''So that's what I'm to rely on: your promise.''

''It's all I can give you. But I'm in the same situation. I have nothing but your word to go on. So let's exchange our pledges, so to speak. I promise to put that gold into your hands, and to keep all these people quiet, if you'll promise to spare our lives in the end.''

Mahaffery gave Dillow a smile worthy of Old Scratch himself striking a bargain for a human soul. ''You have yourself an agreement, Dillow. I'm a reasonable man, after all. The way you said it is the way it will be. I get my gold . . . and you get your lives.''

CHAPTER TWENTY-ONE

Dillow limped out of the lodge house, trying to remember if there was ever before a time he'd felt this tired, body and soul. This ongoing ordeal had drained from him something vital that he wasn't sure could be restored with any amount of future rest. But he had to hold on a little longer. He had a plan, a desperate one, but one that might work.

The guarded people of the mining camp stood in a cold cluster, watching him approach. He addressed Perry Winters. "Mahaffery wants you to bring everyone back inside. And he wants to talk to you, Van Huss, and Legarde."

"It wouldn't hurt you none to use the word 'Mister' every now and again," Winters said.

"Please accept my apology, Mr. Winters." Dillow struggled not to let too much sarcasm come through, knowing it wouldn't pay.

The people were eager to get inside. It was cold and the clouds had moved from the horizon to cover the entire sky. Dillow turned to the group. "Herbert Colfax is dead," he said. "A natural death. Apoplexy."

There were no strong responses to the news. A few lifted brows and a few shaking heads with sorrowful faces. That was all. These people were simply too weary, and had already seen too much dying, to react much to news of one more passing. They walked toward the lodge house, from which Mahaffery himself now emerged. He pulled out his flask and took a sip as he watched the people file past him to go inside and find places to sit, or more or less collapse. Dillow came in last, glancing at Mahaffery as he went inside. He limped across the room and sat down on an empty spot at the end of a bench, near Art and Marica Bolton.

Bert Mongold closed the door and leaned against the wall with rifle in hand, picking at his teeth with a splinter and eyeing Marica Bolton and Leora Winkle alternately. Lennis Yeager held his post at the opposite end of the room, and Conner Broadgrass, leaning in a corner, looked typically mysterious, brooding, and confident.

Outside, Legarde, Van Huss, and Winters gathered around Mahaffery, who gave them an uncharacteristically warm grin and, even more uncharacteristically, offered them his flask. "Take yourselves a good swallow," he said jovially. "It's mighty cold out here."

"Thank you, Jordan," Van Huss said, taking the flask, draining away a mouthful, then passing it on to Winters. Strange, Mahaffery being generous with his liquor. The man seemed to be in a revived and optimistic mood.

"I guess you heard the old man died," Mahaffery announced as the flask finished its round and came back to him. He pocketed it. "Apoplexy. But forget about him for now. I have something for you to do. I want you to go hunting for me. Manhunting."

Van Huss, who had already had one encounter with the men he was sure Mahaffery wanted hunted, looked quite unhappy, but Winters and Legarde, both of whom loved a chase dearly, perked up considerably. Better to be doing something, anything, than this endless standing guard over a bunch of snow-digging gold searchers who seemed unlikely to turn up anything more valuable than rocks and frozen dog dung.

Mahaffery went on, "I want you to put an end to these men in the valley, this Sam Underhill fellow, and the old man with him. The old man must be some stray hermit prospector, maybe some holdover from the old Dutch Camp days. And then there's the possibility of a third man, that being the runaway who Emmett and Bert chased, the one named Linfoot. And if Linfoot is alive, he's probably got Emmett's weapons.''

"You want these men brought back or killed?'' Winters asked.

"I want no more people to guard, no more mouths to feed. Rid us of them for good.''

Van Huss, making no effort to hide his unhappiness with the assignment, said, "Jordan, if all three of us go, that leaves only you, Lennis, Bert, and Conner to guard all these people.''

"We've got the guns; they don't. Besides, they're all too weary to cause any problems.''

"So am I,'' Van Huss muttered. "And I've almost been killed once today already.''

"Cheer up there, Reed. Things are about to take a better turn.''

"You have a new lead on that gold?''

"I do. The old man who died on us claimed at the end that he found the gold before we ever arrived here, and hid it. The one named Dillow claims to have been in on it with him. Me and him are going to make a journey out to fetch it.''

The three others exchanged glances. "You believe this ain't a bluff?'' Van Huss asked.

"The dying one had nothing to gain by bluffing. I believe it's the best possibility we've been handed so far.''

"What if Dillow tries to make a break from you out there?''

"I can handle him. Besides, I don't plan to still have him with me when I come back, if you follow me.''

They nodded. Good. It was time to reduce the numbers here a little. Even an unarmed and exhausted group of people posed a threat when they outnumbered their guards.

"Don't you think somebody should go with you? Just

you and that man alone . . . he might find a way to get a drop on you.''

"Don't worry about me. You three just go get rid of this Sam Underhill character, and anyone else straying around in this valley.''

"What if we can't find them?''

"Keep looking until you do.''

Mahaffery stood in the center of the lodge house and looked around at the sullen people.

"You'll be happy to hear that, for the moment, work up in the pass will cease,'' he announced. "You people will remain here, inside this building. You'll be closely guarded, and I do hope you've learned by now the sheer foolishness of trying to get away.''

"What are you going to do with us?'' asked Jack Gray, brother of Leora Winkle.

"What we do with you is entirely in your own hands,'' Mahaffery replied. "You cooperate and you'll be just fine.''

Young Arianna surprised them all with quite a bold question: "Did you kill Mr. Colfax?''

"No, young lady,'' Mahaffery answered. "Mr. Colfax up and died all on his own. I'm very sorry it happened. Now, if you'll excuse me, Mr. Dillow and I have some business to deal with. The rest of you, just be patient, stay where you are, and maybe this will be over soon.''

At the mention of business with Dillow, Conner Broadgrass, who had been half-napping where he leaned against the wall, the brim of his hat pulled low, looked up quickly and shifted his hat back.

"Where's the other three of your men?'' Art Bolton asked.

"Resting in another cabin. Close by and ready to give aid if any of you prove foolish enough to attempt anything rash in my absence.'' Mahaffery turned to Yeager. "Lennis, put some of these women to cooking. And be sure to save some of the food. Mr. Dillow and I are likely to be hungry when we get back.''

Without further discussion, Mahaffery ushered Dillow out of the lodge house. Broadgrass moved to a window and watched the pair trudge toward the pass, Dillow limping badly, yet staying slightly ahead of Mahaffery, who was armed with his rifle and two pistols, along with a knife and hatchet.

Some of the clouds had turned the color of indigo. A light snow, which looked fated to become heavier, was peppering down. Broadgrass looked at the sky speculatively, then back down at the departing pair again. After a few moments he went back to where he had been, leaned into the corner, and pulled the brim of his hat low once more.

"Mama," Arianna Winkle said to Leora, "that Mr. Mahaffery lied about the other guards resting."

"What do you mean?"

"I just looked out the back window, and saw them. They're walking back into the valley, with guns. Like they're going hunting."

Leora thought about that, and about Sam being out there. She pursed her lips tightly.

"Mama, what's wrong?"

"Nothing, dear. I'm just tired."

"Do you think they're going hunting, Mama?"

"Yes. I do."

"Then why would Mr. Mahaffery lie and say they were asleep in another cabin?"

"Because it's in his nature to be wicked, and tell lies, and do other bad things. And I suppose he'd rather all of us believe that there are more guards right here in the camp, than to know they're really gone off into the valley."

"Where do you think Mr. Dillow is going with Mr. Mahaffery?"

"I don't know, dear."

"Do you think he will be all right?"

Leora paused, then admitted, "I don't know."

"I hope he is." Arianna sat down beside her mother and nestled close. Although she was at an age when she had begun the process of pulling away from her mother, trying to be independent, she now was childish again, clinging. "Mama, I miss Daniel. I cry when I think about him."

"So do I."

"I wish he hadn't been killed. I wish this was over." The girl hesitated, then said something her mother had never allowed her to say about other human beings. "I hate these men, Mama."

"I hate them, too, Arianna. And I hope they all die, every one of them, very soon."

Arianna rested her head on her mother's shoulder for a few moments, then said, "Is it wrong to feel that way?"

"Maybe," Leora said. "But I find I can't help it."

"I wish Papa was still alive."

"Yes, sweetheart. Right now I miss him very much."

CHAPTER
TWENTY-TWO

"Is that the fastest you can move?" Mahaffery said. "This snow will worsen. I don't want to be trapped out in the mountains in the midst of a storm."

Ah, Dillow thought defiantly, *but that's the very idea, my friend.* "I can't move any faster. My ankle pains me. And I've never been able to move fast on snowshoes."

"How far to the gold?"

"Not far." But it would be far. He'd keep hiking, trudging, turning, moving from ridge to ridge, ever farther away, until by the time greedy, murderous Mr. Jordan Mahaffery realized that he'd been lied to and there was no gold to be had, he would have no idea where he was, or how to get back. This, at least, was Dillow's intention. He didn't plan for Jordan Mahaffery to ever set foot again in Texas Gulch.

Dillow knew it wasn't much of a scheme, and had the distinct disadvantage of likely costing him his own life right along with Mahaffery's, but maybe, God willing, it would work. What was the point of trying to save himself, anyway, when there was no hope of anything in the end but death at the hands of the outlaws? If Dillow was going to die, he intended to take at least one of these devils with him. Maybe, somehow, the others would then have a chance.

The pair trudged on, deeper into the mountains. The snow heightened some, but was still far short of the near-blizzard that had been under way the night the outlaws first came to Texas Gulch.

Travel was laborious, which began to worry Dillow. The point was to go as far as possible, as fast as possible. Otherwise Mahaffery would easily find his way back. Gritting his teeth because of the pain in his ankle, Dillow sped up. His breath was coming in great heaves.

"Stop," Mahaffery said at last. "Stop right here. I don't trust you."

Dillow, truth be told, was glad to stop, for he was exhausted. He turned and panted, his white breath mixing with Mahaffery's.

"Don't . . . trust me?"

"That's right." Mahaffery gasped a few times before going on. "I don't believe you and that old man carried that gold out this far."

"We did."

"No. No. Not that old fellow. I don't believe you."

"Believe what you want. We'll go back and you can keep us digging in that snow until the next century, and you'll find no gold, for it ain't there to be found."

"Then where is it?"

"I told you, I can't describe it. I just have to take you to it."

"Where, though? A hole in the ground? Up in a tree? Under a rock?"

Dillow glanced ahead and picked his spot nearly at random. "Up in those bluffs," he said, pointing at a high rock ridge ahead of them, its distance hard to determine because of the spitting snow.

Mahaffery looked at the bluffs unhappily. "How high?"

"Maybe halfway up."

Mahaffery frowned longer at the high ridge. "I don't believe you. You'd not have had reason to hide it so well. You didn't know we were coming to search for it."

Dillow's mind raced. He wasn't a habitual liar, so he

didn't contrive stories easily. But he managed to speak quickly enough to sound believable.

"We *did* know you might be coming," he said. "De-haven was still alive when me and Colfax found him. He talked."

"The hell!"

"He told us he'd taken gold, and that some men were after him for it. He said you were bad men who would search all creation, if you had to, for that gold. He said we'd get half the gold if we'd help him, but he died right after that. So we decided all the gold was for us, and hid it well, as far away as we could from Texas Gulch in the time we had."

"If you knew we were coming, why weren't you prepared?"

"We didn't really believe anybody would come this far, with the weather going bad. We hid the gold and figured that was precaution enough. Then we left the body to be found by someone else, and from then on played ignorant of it all . . . until Colfax spilled the truth with his chalk and slate."

Mahaffery looked at the sky. Snowing even harder now, but not intolerably. "We don't have much time. We need to get that gold quickly."

Thank God, Dillow thought. *He believes me.*

They headed for the bluffs, Dillow praying for the strength to make it that far, much less to climb.

Van Huss grew more angry the farther he advanced into the valley with the other two manhunters.

"I can't believe I'm here, doing this," he said. "Damn it, I should've taken my leave of Mahaffery long ago. And I sure shouldn't have let him set out alone just now with that Dillow."

"What are you thinking, Reed?" Winters asked.

"I'm thinking he has it in mind to get that gold and try

to make it out of the mountains with it, all alone. Keep every bit of it for himself.''

"You really think so?"

"I do. I do. I don't trust Mahaffery anymore. You wait and see. He has it in mind to cheat us out of that gold.''

Sam and Bushrod Underhill were perched high on a Sierra ridge, well hidden, watching the three armed men move through the valley below them.

"They've come hunting, I believe,'' Bushrod said. "Hunting us. Look . . . I believe one of them was one of the pair we fought with earlier.''

"Well, if hunting's their intent, let's give them a bit of sport, Pap.''

"Sport? No, no, son. Sport is for pleasure . . . and it's for the sportsman to bring it about, not the game. Besides, this ain't a sporting hunt those men are engaged in. This is war.''

"Meaning what?'' Sam asked.

"Meaning that we won't worry about sporting chances. In war, a man does what he has to do to kill his enemy.''

"I believe you may be thinking of doing some sniping at our friends down there,'' Sam said.

"So I am.'' He pointed at the three gunmen, now much closer. "See yonder tall fellow? Black coat, brown hat? He's my target.''

"I may as well pick one, too,'' Sam said.

"No. Save your shot to cover me while I reload afterward.''

This suited Sam, who wasn't the long-range rifleman his father was, anyway. Through the back of his mind flicked a thought he'd had many times over the years: *my father is indeed a remarkable man.* The old fellow had just traveled all the way from Texas and climbed the snowy Sierras, but to look at him and see him right now, even in such a tense and dangerous situation, he might be on a pleasure outing with one of his grandchildren no more than a mile or two from home.

Bushrod sat upright, taking a classic rifleman's stance. He

sighted down the long barrel, which did not waver at all, but held as rigidly as if it had been clamped in place. A steady hand, had Bushrod Underhill.

Sam watched the advancing men below, wondering if they had any clue they were about to be fired upon. He focused on the tall man—Perry Winters, though Sam could not know his name—and waited for his father to fire.

He saw Winters pause, look around . . . then up, right at them. Sam knew the moment had come.

"Good-bye, friend," he whispered, and half a second later, Bushrod Underhill's long rifle cracked and spit fire.

In the lodge house, Conner Broadgrass snapped up his head, listening.

"Did you hear it, too?" Mongold asked.

"I did," Broadgrass replied. "Gunfire in the valley."

Another shot followed, then a third.

"They've surely got a battle going," Yeager said. He shuddered, remembering his own fight with those two valley-roamers. It had scared him more than he wanted to admit.

"I'm going out there," Broadgrass announced.

"What?" Yeager said. "In direct violation to what Mahaffery told you to do?"

"He'd want one of us to go help them out. Sounds like they've found some real trouble." Another distant crack punctuated the statement. "See there? I'll be back soon." He headed for the door.

"You better not do it, Conner," Mongold said.

Broadgrass didn't reply. He reached the door and opened it.

"Conner, you're leaving only two of us here to guard all these people!"

The door closed behind Broadgrass and he was gone. He circled the lodge house, through the snow, and headed for the valley. Mongold went to the window and watched him a few moments.

"There he goes," Mongold said. "Mahaffery will nail his rump right to the wall for breaking his orders, just you wait."

"No, not Broadgrass, he won't," Yeager said with some evident bitterness. "Broadgrass never has been under Mahaffery's thumb. Broadgrass believes he's smarter and better than any one of us." He hesitated, then added, "He may be right. Maybe we ought to be following him instead of Mahaffery."

"You'd trust Broadgrass above Mahaffery?"

"Yes. I believe I would."

Outside, Broadgrass continued toward the valley as fast as the snow would allow, to all appearances an eager warrior intent on reaching the fight as soon as possible. But as soon as he was over a rise that blocked any possible view of him from the lodge house, he darted to the left and circled around, keeping behind cover, and headed for the pass.

It was impossible to make it all the way to the pass without coming into a potential line of view of the lodge house, so there was no choice but to take the risk. The battle in the valley was of no interest to him. What intrigued him was what was going on beyond the pass . . . Mahaffery and the man named Dillow. Going for that gold. Alone.

They'd not be as alone as they expected to be.

Whatever Mahaffery was up to, Broadgrass intended to know. And he wasn't about to accept on blind trust that Mahaffery, with that gold in hand, would ever come back to Texas Gulch at all.

Once he came into potential view of someone in the lodge house, he moved quickly. Sometimes a man could make up in speed what couldn't be had in stealth. But there was no good speed in this falling snow. He tried to run but could manage little more than a fast trudge. Still, he made the pass unchallenged from below, and when at last the lodge house passed behind him and out of sight, he was sure he'd succeeded. They hadn't seen him.

CHAPTER
TWENTY-THREE

Sam Underhill sighted down his rifle, squeezed the trigger, and felt the slam of the rifle butt against his shoulder. Being quite bruised and sore from his ordeal at the pit, the recoil hurt a lot. He pulled back behind the boulder that was his cover, waited for the gunsmoke to clear, then peered over. He ducked again, quickly, grimacing as a rifle ball struck the stone and threw chips and dust in all directions, stinging him badly.

Beginning to reload, he glanced over at Bushrod, who was taking new aim himself. He fired just as Sam was slipping the ramrod back into its thimbles.

"You hit him?" Sam asked.

"No," Bushrod snapped.

Sam shook his head, held his breath, and dared to peer over the stone again, hoping to find another, better target. Bushrod, meanwhile, was reloading with the kind of remarkable speed born of long experience.

"Pap, once again we ain't doing too well," Sam said.

"You think I don't know that?" Bush replied sharply. He finished loading, then mumbled, "At least I hit mine."

"You just wounded him, that's all."

This was true. Perry Winters, the tall fellow Bush had chosen to take the first rifle ball, had taken the wound in the side and fallen back with a yell. But he'd quickly scrambled away, leaving a trail of blood as he went, and found cover in a snow-filled gully. Since then he'd managed to fire off several shots. Every time Sam suspected the man had passed out from shock or maybe bled to death, he'd pop up again and shoot. It was he, in fact, who had almost taken off the top of Sam's head with that last rifle ball.

Sam raised his rifle and fired again. He drew back behind cover.

"Get one?" Bush asked.

"No," Sam said.

"Dang 'em. Harder to kill than a nest of ticks." Bushrod positioned himself, ready to take his turn at firing. "Maybe we took the wrong approach to this, Sam."

"Maybe so." Sam was half reloaded by now. But he was getting worried. Emmett Fish had not possessed a wealth of either powder or shot, and before long, Bushrod would be left to fight this battle alone, for Sam would have expended all his ammunition.

Bushrod raised up, took careful aim, then fired. He dropped again with a dour look on his face. Sam didn't even have to bother to ask how that shot had gone.

"Sam, there was three of them to begin with. Now, whenever I rise to fire, I only see two. What happened to the third man?" Bush wrapped a ball in patching and positioned it for a ram down the long, rifled barrel.

"I don't know. Maybe we killed him."

"No. We haven't killed anybody yet. He's out of view somewhere. And I don't feel very comfortable about it. What if he finds a way to sneak around on us? See them rocks there? If he came up there, he'd have us shot before we knew he was upon us." Bushrod finished reloading.

"Then maybe we should move. Try to get up there ourselves. Take the high ground," Sam said.

"Then lead the way, son."

They eyed one another, did a quick, silent three-count, and rose as one. For a few moments they were exposed, and in that moment the men below fired, one at a time. One ball struck a stone near Sam and spanged off to the left, singing into the snowing sky. Sam twisted away, a reflex action, and fell.

"Sam? You hit?" Bushrod said, ducking and turning.

"No, I just—"

There was no time to complete the answer. A second rifle below barked, and Bushrod jerked and pitched to the side, falling hard into the snow.

Sam stared at him, horrified. Bush lay on his side, eyes wide and suddenly quite glassy. The old frontiersman was staring at his son, unspeaking, mouth slightly open. He did not blink, did not breathe.

"Pap?"

Bushrod remained silent and unmoving.

"Pap . . . *Pap*!" Sam touched his father, shook him gently. "Oh, Pap, no . . . no . . ."

Sam opened his mouth and let out a scream that rebounded off the stones behind and above him, and out into the broad valley, the terrible echo of it coming back moments later, like mockery.

He heard one of the outlaws below give a hoot of triumph, and laugh aloud.

In the mountains beyond the pass, the wind began to whip up and the snow fell faster. Squinting against flakes that peppered his face, Mahaffery turned to Dillow and asked, "How much higher?"

They were halfway up a rugged slope, one they'd climbed with much strain. Here the wind was bitterly cold and the terrain so rugged that Mahaffery was growing even more skeptical about the claims of his companion. This seemed an unlikely place in which to have hurriedly stashed a cache of gold.

"Just a few more yards," Dillow said. He pointed. "See that bluff there, and the flat space above it? There's a little cave up there, just a small hole in the rocks. That's where the gold is."

Mahaffery looked hard. "Where? I don't see anything."

"You can't see the opening from down here," Dillow said. "Come on . . . you'll see it when we get up atop that bluff."

Mahaffery glowered. "You're a liar! What are you trying to do? Get me up here and get me lost? Maybe get me on that bluff and push me off?"

"You're way too suspicious, Mahaffery," Dillow replied. "You want your gold or not? We can turn back now and go back to Texas Gulch if you want to."

Mahaffery hesitated. "Hell, go on," he said. "We'll go as far as that ledge, but no farther. And if I find there's no cave and no gold there, I'm going to put a rifle ball through your brain on the spot. I swear I am."

Mahaffery shoved Dillow roughly. They continued to climb.

Bushrod Underhill's breath came back to him suddenly. He gasped and groaned, and Sam Underhill laughed aloud in pure, wonderful relief to hear it.

"Pap, I thought they'd killed you!" He knelt beside his father, rubbing snow on his face, trying to rouse him.

Bush breathed hard, blinking, making faces in protest of the cold snow being rubbed against his skin. Groaning again, he sat up. "Killed? No. Not me. I'm tenacious as a bad habit, son."

"Where are you hit?"

Bush made a face of pain and moved his right shoulder. "Here, I think."

But when Sam examined the shoulder, he found nothing but a crease cut through Bush's clothing, and to his surprise, the rifle ball itself lodged right against Bush's shoulder. He probed into the tear in Bush's clothing and popped the ball out. "Take a look at that, Pap! You'll probably never see that happen again! That ball hit at just the right angle to knock you over like a club, but not to penetrate."

"It sure knocked the wind out of my bellows when I

fell,'' Bush said, eyeing the ball that by all rights should be inside him now. ''Couldn't breathe for a few seconds.''

''You were staring like a dead man. I thought you *were* a dead man.''

Sam was looking into Bush's face, examining his eyes for evidence of concussion, when those eyes suddenly cut upward and widened. ''Sam, look out—''

The butt of a rifle pounded Sam's head from behind, very hard. Sam yelled and sprawled. Bushrod crabbed back for space, reaching for his pistol.

Reed Van Huss, who had so loathed entering this fray, had certainly risen bravely to the occasion now that he was in it. While Legarde and Winters had kept the Underhills occupied with gun battle from below, he had found a way up the slope toward their hiding place, creeping up and staying out of their view, managing to surprise them.

Van Huss stepped across Sam and swung his rifle up again, ready to club Bushrod. Sam, though, got a hand out and wrapped it around Van Huss's ankle, pulling hard and tripping the man before he could swing.

Ironically, the action saved Van Huss's life. Bush's pistol blasted just as Van Huss fell. The ball that would have passed through the center of Van Huss's forehead sailed off into the snowy sky instead.

Van Huss fell atop his rifle. Sam got up, intending to throw himself atop Van Huss and pin him, but the clout to the back of his head had staggered him pretty badly. He stumbled to the left and fell beside Van Huss rather than on him.

Bushrod, meanwhile, came to his feet, backing off and trying to bring his rifle into position to shoot.

Another shot fired from below, singing past the old frontiersman. Bushrod moved back, getting out of the line of fire from below, and raised his rifle.

Van Huss, however, had taken advantage of that extra moment of movement to get up again. He charged at Bushrod and was able to deflect the rifle muzzle before Bush had a chance to aim and fire. He wrenched at the rifle, trying to pull it free of Bushrod's hands, and was surprised at the iron grip of the old man. Swearing, he reached for Bushrod's throat with his left hand while still holding the rifle with his right.

Bush, who had been gripping the rifle in standard shooting position, let go of it with his right hand and drove a swift punch into Van Huss's face. The outlaw went down on his knees with a grunt, but didn't lose his grip on the rifle. Bushrod kicked him, then kicked again, but by sheer luck, Van Huss managed to grope out and wrap his hand around Bushrod's foot as it kicked at him the second time. With a heave he threw Bush off-balance, and back to the edge of the steep slope down which the Underhills had been firing.

Sam was on his feet again, and went for Van Huss, but not before Van Huss at last was able to wrench the rifle out of Bushrod's hands. At the same time, he shoved, and Bushrod teetered a terrible second, then toppled, rolling and sliding down the rocky slope, toward the very rocks behind which Winters and Legarde had taken cover.

Sam struck Van Huss from behind, but the blow mostly glanced off the outlaw's shoulders. Sam's head was spinning; he felt weak, and his skull ached where Van Huss's rifle butt had struck him. Van Huss wheeled, cursing. He'd tossed aside Bushrod's rifle, but there was a knife in his hands. He lunged at Sam with it, the blade aimed directly at Sam's heart.

Sam remembered the pistol he'd taken from the body of the man he'd killed with the pick. Reaching for it, he found only air. The pistol had come out of his belt and lay on the rocks behind him. There was no way to go for it, though, while he was occupied with dodging his enemy's blade.

Below, Bushrod came to a stop, battered and grimed and aching, at the base of the slope. He'd rolled as free as a stone, unable to stop himself, but he'd done the only thing a man could do in such a circumstance, and that was to relax his body as much as possible as he rolled, and to try to roll sideways, log-style, rather than head over heels. Thus, when he reached the bottom, he had to lie there only a couple of moments, moving fingers and toes and so on, to surmise that he was still in one piece.

Bushrod got up as quickly as he dared, and began looking around for a refuge.

He'd realized even as he fell that he was descending right into the snake pit, so to speak, and sure enough, the un-wounded gunman, Legarde, appeared almost as soon as Bush was upright, raising his rifle and shooting hurriedly at the prize that had all but rolled into his lap. Fortunately for Bushrod, the shot was too rushed, and missed him by at least two feet. Bush debated with himself only a moment—Run for cover? Attack while his foe's rifle was empty?—and opted for the former when he saw the fellow pulling out a pistol. Bush scrambled behind a big stone just as the pistol fired. The ball struck the stone and rebounded with a high, singing whine into the sky.

Bushrod saw his moment and seized it. Unless the man had a second pistol, something Bush was willing to bet against, he was at this moment unarmed. Bush reached to his belt and pulled out a bone-handled hunting knife that had been given to him many years before, back when Bushrod had lived in Missouri, by another old Missouri frontiersman then in his waning years: Daniel Boone. Locking the knife firmly in his hand, he came from behind the boulder and headed straight at the momentarily unnerved outlaw, who was fumbling about, trying hard to get his pistol reloaded in record time.

Meanwhile, atop the rise, Sam was engaged in a struggle for his life. Van Huss was a madman, slashing with his knife, cursing and shouting at Sam, trying to keep him off-balance. And Sam *was* off-balance, but not because of the noise. He was dizzy, too dizzy to see straight, and it took great effort to keep Van Huss in focus. For the moment Sam was engaged mostly in a dodging contest, trying to avoid the wild slashes of Van Huss's blade.

As he had earlier while trapped in that pit, Sam regretted deeply having failed to bring his own knife. He also regretted not having bothered to remove that pick from the skull of the fellow who had shot Hiram Linfoot. Right now any weapon would be welcome. He flicked his eyes away from Van Huss for a moment, looking for that pistol he'd lost. There it was, well out of reach, and blocked from him by the man who was doing his best to kill him.

Below, Legarde screamed. Bushrod had just stabbed him, not a deep wound, but right in his middle. A few inches up, and he could have been pierced through the heart. He danced back, bleeding. Bush came at him like a fighting dog, switching the blade in his hands so that now he could stab with a hammering motion. He knocked Legarde down with his body, making him lose his weapons, then rolled off and bounded up again. Legarde was deeply unsettled to see such agility in an obviously aging fellow. What kind of man was this?

He had little time to think it over further. Bushrod was upon him again, swinging the blade down, stabbing Legarde in the shoulder. The man screamed and twisted, turning his back unwittingly.

Bushrod buried the blade in Legarde's back.

Legarde hardly felt this one. Shock was beginning to set in. But he lurched away before Bush could pull his knife free, and staggered off toward the place he'd been hidden before with Winters. The knife was still lodged between his shoulder blades.

Again Bushrod was fortunate. Legarde had happened to position himself in a way that blocked Winters from getting a shot at Bush. Realizing the precariousness of the situation, Bushrod scrambled away, seeking cover.

On the top of the slope, Sam Underhill had just closed his hand around a stone. Not much of a weapon, but all he had. Summoning his strength, he heaved it at Van Huss, striking him on the nose. Van Huss yelled and staggered backward. Sam ran and leaped over him, hoping his dizziness wouldn't make him fall, and landed near the pistol he'd dropped. He grabbed it, cocked it, turned . . . and snapped the pistol without effect in the direction of Van Huss.

The percussion cap had come loose, at the worst possible moment. The pistol couldn't fire at all.

With nose bleeding, Van Huss came at Sam again, a wild, killing glitter in his eyes. Sam threw the useless pistol at him and hit him on the nose again. Van Huss howled, blood flying. Sam ducked low and dove at his knees, bringing Van Huss down.

They struggled there, rolling about, pounding one another, biting, head-pounding . . . men in primal, mortal battle, doing their best to kill one another. Van Huss, with his knife, held the distinct advantage.

But somehow Sam managed to strike Van Huss's head very hard against a stone on the ground, stunning him. He grabbed Van Huss's knife hand and tried to get the weapon free, but Van Huss managed to hang on. When it became evident that Sam was ultimately going to get the weapon, Van Huss brought up his other hand, hit Sam hard on the ear, then tried to shift the knife from one hand to the other. All he managed to do was drop the blade. It landed on its side on his chest. Sam groped for it, but Van Huss got his hand on the weapon first. Sam grabbed the wrist, and again there was a struggle for possession.

The men somehow came to their feet, fighting for the knife, hardly aware of where they were, dancing a lethal ballet together. Then, before either realized it, they were at the edge of the slope. Van Huss's foot slipped and he fell, dragging Sam with him. Together they rolled, still gripping one another, pounding down the very course that Bush had plunged along a little earlier.

When they hit the bottom, Sam found that Van Huss was struggling no more. His grip went weak, and Sam quickly pulled away from him.

The knife was sticking deep into Van Huss's chest, moving a little with each breath, blood gurgling around the place it entered the flesh.

Sam wondered if he had stabbed the man without really being aware of it. No, he hadn't, he realized, because he'd never really controlled the knife. Van Huss had simply rolled on the blade and stabbed himself.

"You . . . Underhill . . ." Van Huss muttered weakly, looking at him.

Sam knew right then that what Hiram Linfoot had told him in his last moments was no longer true: the outlaws holding Texas Gulch now *did* know that Sam Underhill existed and was alive in this valley. These manhunters had known exactly who they were searching for, at least in his case. Word had gotten out.

Bushrod appeared at Sam's side, looking down at Van Huss.

Van Huss's eyes shifted toward Bushrod. "You . . . old man . . . who are you?"

"I ain't *that* old, friend. Well, actually, I suppose I am."

"But who . . . ?"

"My name's Bushrod Underhill."

Reed Van Huss arched his brows, looked quite surprised, and died without ever speaking another word.

CHAPTER TWENTY-FOUR

"There's another one gone," Sam said. Only then did he remember the other two, whom Bush had been dealing with below. "Pap, where—"

"Don't worry," Bushrod interrupted. "They're gone. One dragging along with a bullet wound in his side, the other with my old Boone knife still sticking out of his back. Heading back for Texas Gulch, and no doubt hoping they make it before they die. They just up and gave up the fight on me." He paused and shook his head. "I surely do hate to lose that knife."

"Let's go after them, Pap. We can stop them before they get very far."

"Maybe we should just let them go. Let them tell stories about the two wild madmen who did that to them, and killed their partner besides. Maybe the whole gang will get scared and leave."

"You believe that?"

"No."

"Then let's go after them. If we succeed, there's three of them gone. Three! The odds would improve a lot."

"Son, you've got a mind about you. Maybe you're even smarter than your old Pap these days. Come on. Let's go catch them."

* * *

Broadgrass paused for breath and stared through the falling snow, looking for Mahaffery and Dillow. Their trail was clear in the white, though their tracks were filling remarkably fast. He wondered why they had come so far.

Something was wrong about all this, and he was beginning to suspect what it was. This Dillow fellow wasn't leading Mahaffery out here to retrieve hidden gold. Dillow—a clever man, Broadgrass had perceived from the moment he first saw him—was leading Mahaffery out here to try to kill him, or at least get him lost.

Broadgrass stood there, thinking. Much farther, and even he himself might become lost. And what was the point of going on, anyway, if there was no gold at the end of the trail?

Time to turn back to Texas Gulch.

As he turned, he wondered if Mahaffery really would become lost, or get himself killed. That would be an interesting scenario, to be sure. And not necessarily a bad one. Broadgrass had known for a long time, by instinct, that he was a better and more clever man than Mahaffery. He'd allowed Mahaffery to lord over him only because it had seemed prudent, and because Mahaffery's scheme to steal that gold had been so obviously a wise and workable one, the kind of plan Broadgrass would have come up with himself. But Broadgrass was sure he never would have lost the gold again, like Mahaffery had. No mindless fool like Dehaven would ever have gotten the best of Conner Broadgrass.

The snow began to obliterate the landscape in a vast bleakness. Broadgrass looked back and saw his own tracks rapidly filling. No more time to waste. He began trekking back toward Texas Gulch.

"Conner!"

Broadgrass wheeled, looking all around.

"Conner . . . is that you?"

Mahaffery's voice! Broadgrass peered through the snow and tried to find him. He sounded far away and muffled.

"Mahaffery! Where are you?"

"I can see you, Conner! Stay where you are! I'm coming to you!"

Broadgrass obeyed, though he didn't like being approached by someone he couldn't see. Years of living in a world governed by untrustworthiness and suspicion had left him edgy about such things. But this was Mahaffery, not a stranger, and from the tremor of Mahaffery's voice, it sounded like the man was in trouble.

He saw him then, a dark, faint figure struggling his way across the white mountain snowfield.

"I see you, Jordan. I'm coming to you now," Broadgrass said.

When he reached Mahaffery, he found the man panting, weak, and seemingly in pain. He was gripping his left wrist, his fingers hanging limply, looking bluish from cold.

"You're hurt, Jordan."

"My wrist. It's hurting bad. I don't know if it's broken. But it hurts."

"Your fingers are freezing. We need to get you to some warmth before they get frostbit. Here . . ." He pulled a rag handkerchief from his pocket and wrapped it around the hand, making Mahaffery grimace every time the hand moved.

"Where's Dillow?"

"Gone. The bastard tried to kill me, and almost did. Got me up on a bluff where he said the money was hidden, then tried to shove me off. It almost worked, but in the end, it was him who went over the edge, not me."

"And there was no gold."

"No. No gold. It was nothing but a ruse. He wanted to play the hero for his people. Get me out here on the pretext of finding that gold, and get me lost or dead. I should never have let him come so close to getting the best of me."

Broadgrass was thinking the same thing. "How'd you hurt the wrist?"

"Catching myself on the ground when he first knocked me over. Damn, it hurts!"

"Anything else injured?"

"Left ankle's a little painful, but nothing so bad I can't walk on it. Truthfully, I'm relieved to be able to feel it. If it was numb I'd be worried about keeping my toes. It's bitter cold out here."

"This ain't fit weather for a man to venture out in, Conner. The winter's here to stay, and I think we are, too. And I'll tell you something else: I'm beginning to think we'll not find that gold. That old Colfax fellow could have hidden it anywhere."

"There's one hope yet," Mahaffery said as they trudged along, following the ever-dimming backtrack through the snow toward the pass. "He might have told his wife or daughter."

"Something you should know, Jordan. There was gunfire out in the valley," Broadgrass said. "Our men must have run into this Sam Underhill and the old man, whoever he is."

"I hope it went well for them. I can't afford to have those two alive, either. No way to know how close they've been to us, and how much they may have seen or heard."

"Jordan, none of this is going to matter if we don't find that gold."

"I know. That's why I want to get right to work on those Colfax women." Mahaffery stumbled right then, almost fell, and swore.

"You all right?"

"I'll make it. But let's hurry. The snow's coming down even faster now. But there's something I want to know from you first: why are you here? I told you to stay with Mongold and Yeager and guard our prisoners."

It was a delicate situation. How did one explain direct disobedience? Broadgrass usually relied on his quick mind to see him through such situations, but just now inspiration was lacking, and the answer he gave sounded feeble and false even to himself. "I can't explain it, Jordan. It was just a feeling I had that you were in trouble. I knew I had to come after you.''

Mahaffery looked at him without expression for a few moments. ''So you've turned mystic on me, have you?''

''I told you I couldn't explain it. But it's a good thing I followed my instinct, don't you think?''

''I believe I could have made it in without you.''

Broadgrass had no more to say, and the silence was not comfortable for him.

''You said there was gunfire in the valley. If anything, it seems to me you would have gone there, to lend a hand,'' Mahaffery said.

''I set out to do just that, Jordan. It was after I was outside and heading their way that the feeling struck me that you needed help.''

Mahaffery's stare was almost as cold as the wind. ''You shouldn't have left that lodge house to help either me or the others. You should have done what I told you and stayed where you were.''

''I suppose you're right.''

''You wouldn't have had it in mind to try to desert us, would you? Were you trying to see if there was still a chance you could make it out of the mountains?'' Mahaffery paused, then added, ''Or might you have had it in mind to take the gold for yourself, like Dehaven did, if I'd managed to put my hand on it?''

''That's a serious accusation, Jordan.''

''So it is.''

Broadgrass, lacking any good reply, let a haughty look, and silence, do his talking for him.

Mahaffery studied him for several moments. ''I suppose we should get back,'' he said.

For a couple of seconds a distinct possibility materialized in Broadgrass's mind. They were alone here, and Mahaffery was already injured. He could kill the man with a deft blow, a slash of a blade, a clubbing from a rifle butt. Kill him and leave him to be buried in the snow until spring. He could return to the lodge house and assert his own authority in Mahaffery's stead. The weaker minds and wills of the others of the outlaw band would in the end acquiesce to his own. He could determine for himself whether the Colfax women knew where the old man had hidden the gold.

But this he would not do. As hard a man as he was, and as many wickednesses as he had done, he found he couldn't actually kill Jordan Mahaffery.

"You're right," Broadgrass said. "We do need to get back, before we lose the way."

They trudged on together, side by side, neither willing to let the other fall behind and out of view. *Interesting situation,* Broadgrass thought. *We've now entered a level of mistrust we've never had between us until now. The first dose of poison . . . and just how strong it will grow, it's too early to tell.*

Maybe he should have killed Mahaffery after all. A mistrustful Mahaffery was an enemy more potentially ruthless than any man would want to deal with.

CHAPTER
TWENTY-FIVE

There was blood in the snow, so much of it that the Underhills could have tracked Legarde and Winters even without the big tracks that the two hurt and stumbling men left behind them. It was their guess that the gun-shot one was leaving most of the blood. Legarde's knife wound was not as likely to bleed so profusely, especially if he still had the blade stuck in him. Bushrod had already commented to Sam on the man's wisdom in not instantly pulling the blade out of himself. A blade in a man's flesh is bad, but not nearly as bad as one stuck in and pulled out again. The man who pulls the blade out again is the one who bleeds to death inside himself.

Neither man was surprised when they soon encountered a dark, unmoving form lying facedown in the snow. One set of tracks continued on past the point where Legarde had abandoned his wounded and weakening companion. "One more of them dead, Pap," Sam said. "We're making some progress, anyway."

But when they reached the body, Bushrod rolled the man over, studied his face, put his head to his chest, and said, "This man's still alive."

Perry Winters's eyes fluttered open and he looked at the two Underhills. "You've killed me," he said.

"Not yet," Bushrod replied. "You're still among the breathing of this world."

"I'm shot . . . bad. The bleeding's going to kill me. Tell me your names . . . I want to know who's ended my life."

"My name's Bushrod Underhill. Don't believe half of what you've heard about me. The other half, do believe it. This here's Sam, one of my boys. And what's your name, young man?"

"Winters . . . Perry Winters."

"Son, listen: you are bleeding bad, and indeed you may die. I suggest you spend some time talking to Jesus before it comes time for him to talk to you. But let me take a look at your wound. Sometimes not every wound is as bad as it seems."

Winters closed his eyes, maybe on purpose, maybe because he'd just passed out. Bush opened the man's coat, studied the blood clotting in his clothing, then lifted the shirt.

The bullet had entered Winters from behind, passing deeply through flesh and lodging just below the skin on his lower left torso. Bushrod reached for his knife, and remembered that it was no longer with him, but still riding in the shoulder of an outlaw who was probably now almost back to Texas Gulch. He took Perry Winters's knife instead.

A small incision was sufficient to expose the ball, which literally rolled out of the wound into Bushrod's hand. He held it up for Sam to see, then pocketed it. He'd never been one to waste lead that could be remelted into new ammunition.

"That one was enough of a clean-through wound that this young man may prove lucky," Bushrod said. "Sam, you got a clean rag on you?"

"Mostly clean."

"Is it snotty?"

"No."

"Then we'll consider it clean enough."

Sam produced the linen handkerchief, which Bushrod

poked into the wound. With his finger he probed it in as deep as it would go, then with the knife blade he pushed it even deeper. Winters didn't budge; indeed he was passed out, and a good thing for him, for what Bushrod was doing would have been excruciatingly painful if he'd been conscious. Bush rolled Winters slightly to the side, and found the bloodied tip of the handkerchief poking out of the other end of the tunneling wound. He grasped it and slowly pulled the entire rag through. It came out richly red with blood, but also carrying some grit and fragments of Winters's coat and shirt that had entered the wound with the ball.

"If he's lucky, that ought to clean him out good enough to let him heal without much festering," Bush said. "Want your rag back, Sam?"

Sam eyed the gory cloth. "Don't believe so."

Bush tossed it aside. "Come on, Sam. Help me hoist him."

"What are we going to do?"

"The only decent thing a man can do. We're going to build this fellow a shelter and a fire and give him a chance to live."

"Why should we care what becomes of him?"

Bushrod looked sharply at his son. "Vengeance is the Lord's, boy, not ours. The moment we come to treat the hurt and captive like they were nothing but dogs, then we've turned into nothing better than that rabble that's holding your people hostage in the mining camp. So give me a hand with him. And consider this, Sam: if we can bring this fellow around enough, we might be able to persuade him to tell us a little about what's going on in the camp. We can get to know our enemy a little better, and like old Tuckaseh used to tell me, 'An enemy known is an enemy half defeated.' "

"What about the other half?"

"With the other half, you just have to do the best you can."

*   *   *

Arianna Winkle sat with the pieces of her broken slate in her lap, trying to piece them back together like the segments of a puzzle. She'd been heartbroken to find the slate shattered, for she'd always loved the schoolwork she did under her mother's tutelage, and prized the slate dearly. She wondered who had broken it, and why, and also what the chalk lines and markings visible on some of the pieces would say when the slate was put together again.

Sorry as she was about the shattering of the slate, she was grateful that trying to put it together again at least gave her something to do. Right now she longed to lose herself, to leave this terrible place mentally, even if she could not physically. But it was hard to keep her mind on her task while poor old widowed America Colfax continued to wail beside the corpse of her dead husband.

"Arianna?"

She looked up and was surprised to see Letitia Colfax before her, smiling sadly. Arianna didn't know what to think; Letitia had never paid her any heed before.

"Hello," Arianna mumbled.

"Can I sit down and talk to you, Arianna?"

Arianna, feeling shy under the attention of someone who had always seemed in a different world than she, mumbled an invitation for Letitia to join her.

Letitia sat down and looked sorrowfully at the broken slate.

"I just want you to know it wasn't Papa who broke your slate," Letitia said earnestly. "It was the bad man, Mahaffery. Poor Papa was trying so hard to write down where the gold is, so that the bad men would go get it and then leave us alone, but he couldn't write. That man Mahaffery threw the slate against the wall. I'm sorry."

Arianna looked at the pieces in her lap. She hadn't even known Herbert Colfax had used her slate. That must mean it was he who put those strange and intriguing scribblings on it. "That's all right," she said. "It wasn't your fault. And it's just a slate."

"I hope you don't hate Papa for having hidden that gold," Letitia went on in her soft, rather high voice, which she kept barely above a whisper. "I'm sure he didn't mean to do anything wrong. He never told Mama and me about it."

Not knowing what she should say, Arianna just nodded.

Letitia was in the mood to talk about the father she'd lost. "Papa was a good man. He could be harsh and mean sometimes, the way he talked to people, but he was a good man."

Arianna put another piece of the slate back into place and studied the chalk marks on it. "Letitia, did you say your father was trying to write something when the Mahaffery man broke the slate?"

"Yes. He was trying to write out how to find the gold, so that all our lives could be saved. He was an unselfish and good man, Papa was."

Arianna studied another fragment, then pieced it into its proper position. "I don't think he was trying to write words, Letitia. It looks to me like—"

The door burst open and Mahaffery stormed in, gripping his wrist. Broadgrass was right behind him. Their entrance was so swift, unexpected, and loud that every soul in the place started, and some came to their feet. Arianna lost a few pieces of the slate off her lap onto the floor, and quickly bent to retrieve them. Her mother, who had been standing on the other side of the room, fighting a sense of imminent emotional and mental breakdown, came over and joined her, putting an arm protectively around Arianna's shoulder. Arianna huddled against her, eyeing Mahaffery with hatred, then decided she didn't want to sully her vision with the sight of the wicked man and turned to peer around the edge of the shutter and across the snowy valley.

Yeager seemed revitalized by the reappearance of his leader. "Did you find the gold, Jordan?"

"Hell, no," Mahaffery said. Then loudly, to all: "Somebody give me a strip of cloth. I got a hurt wrist needs binding."

Marica Bolton, ever bold and levelheaded, moved to fulfill the command. Everyone else sat stock-still, staring fearfully at Mahaffery.

"You didn't get the gold?" Mongold asked.

"That liar never knew where the gold was. Or if he did, didn't lead me to it. His intent was to get me out there and try to kill me, or maybe get me lost in the mountains." Mahaffery raised his voice to make sure everyone in the place heard him. "None of it matters anymore. Mr. Dillow is now a very dead man."

Marica Bolton went white and looked like she was struggling not to faint. Letitia Colfax buried her face in her hands and sobbed loudly. Jack Spillane muttered something bitterly. The spirit of gloom well known to every captive of Texas Gulch deepened greatly. Old Man Skinner began to sing his Judgment Day hymn again, but Joe, his son, gently quieted him. Arianna, meanwhile, suddenly had trouble drawing her breath. Mr. Dillow . . . dead?

"Dillow died because he forced me to kill him. He died because he was fool enough to believe that he could outwit me," Mahaffery said. "Don't any of you make that same mistake." He looked around. "Where the hell is that cloth for my wrist?"

Marica stepped up with a strip of cloth torn from the same sheet that covered Colfax's corpse. "Here . . ."

Mahaffery yanked the cloth from her hands, and threw it on the floor. "I'll have no dead man's shroud cloth around my wrist. Get me a clean cloth, woman!"

Marica turned away, searching. Finding nothing handy, she sat down and began to tear away a long strip at the hem of her own dress. Mongold stared at her exposed ankles as she performed the task.

Mahaffery took a pull from his flask and glared hatefully around the room. "Maybe the time has come to show you people just how serious I am about finding my gold. *My* gold! It was taken from *me*! And this is no game we're playing here! I want my damned *gold*!"

Art Bolton found his courage and stood. "Mr. Mahaffery, if it was in the power of any of us to give you your gold, then we'd do so. And we'd do all we could to help you leave this place so that we could try to live our lives again . . . if our lives will ever be the same after witnessing such cruelty and wickedness as you've done. But we don't have your gold, sir. And if it's true that Herbert Colfax hid it, then none of us know where he did so."

"Maybe some of you do," Mahaffery said. "Maybe that fat, weeping daughter of his over there knows. Maybe his mindless widow over there, caressing his corpse, knows. Maybe we could find a way to jar her memory."

Bolton stepped forward impulsively, face reddening. "Mr. Mahaffery, there's not a man here who will stand by and see you do harm to two bereaved and innocent women! We'll die, to the last man, before we let that happen."

"Indeed you will." Mahaffery turned to Mongold. "Bert, lift your rifle and shoot Mr. Bolton through the head, if you please."

"What?" Mongold asked, not sure he'd heard rightly.

Just then Arianna jumped to her feet, spilling fragments of the slate from her lap onto the floor. She was staring out the window through the shutter crack. "It's Mr. Dillow!" she declared. "He's not dead!"

The timing of her shout was providential for Art Bolton, for it drew the attention of all and took the steam out of Mahaffery's execution order. Art Bolton sank back into his seat. His daughter, dress trailing the cloth strip still not quite fully torn from it, rushed to him, wrapped her arms around his shoulders, and wept.

"What'd you say, girl?" Mahaffery asked Arianna.

"It's Mr. Dillow! He's walking in from the valley! I can see him!"

"From the valley? Even if he was alive, he wouldn't come from that way."

Arianna, still peering out the window, seemed to deflate. She lowered her head. "It's not him," she said. "It's *not* him.'' She turned and sat down again, the broken slate pieces about her feet. She clung to her mother and cried.

The order to shoot Art Bolton forgotten in the distraction of this new development, Mongold had moved to the window and thrown the shutter open. His piggish eyes squinted hard. "It's Legarde," he said. "And he's staggering bad. I think he's hurt."

"What about Reed and Perry?"

"They ain't with him. He's alone."

CHAPTER
TWENTY-SIX

Two minutes later, after Lennis Yeager had gone outside and helped the weak and stumbling Legarde make it into the lodge house, the people inside, outlaw and hostage alike, stared in shock and fascination at the bone-handled knife that still was lodged deeply in Legarde's back. The half-frozen man lay facedown on the puncheon floor, pallid and very weak, staring glassily across the floor at nothing. His back rose up and down, making the knife move.

Mahaffery, still gripping his injured wrist, squatted and examined the knife, but did not touch it.

"Who did this to you?" he asked Legarde.

"The older one . . . older, but strong. He's killed me."

"You ain't dead yet. The younger one was there, too?"

"Yes."

"Describe them both to me."

Legarde, as best he could, fumbled out a description, and many glances were exchanged in the lodge house, hostage to hostage.

Mahaffery rose slowly and looked around at the people, settling on Copp Nolen. "The younger one he described: Sam Underhill?"

"It sounds like Sam, yes."

"And the older man? Bushrod, I suppose."

"Well, sir . . . impossible though it is, the description sounds exactly like him."

"Bushrod Underhill," Mahaffery repeated. "Bushrod Underhill, who you all say you left in Texas, has now magically reappeared in a mountain valley in California in the dead of winter. Am I really expected to believe that?"

"Sir, I ain't saying it is him. I'm saying it sounds like him."

"There's something else," Joe Skinner said. Mahaffery turned to face him. "That knife sticking into your man, there . . . that's Bush Underhill's knife. The Boone knife."

Every eye focused on the knife again. "My word!" Copp Nolen said. "It *is* at that!"

"What's this 'Boone knife' talk?" Mahaffery asked.

Nolen replied, "That knife there belongs to Bushrod Underhill. It was a gift to him from Daniel Boone, when the pair of them both lived in Missouri, in the Femme Osage country, during Boone's last years."

"So now we've not only got Bushrod Underhill roaming the valley, having appeared from nowhere to kill my men, but we're invoking the ghost of Daniel Boone," Mahaffery said coldly. "Do you people take me for a fool?"

Skinner said, "I'm just telling you the facts: that knife is familiar to us all, and it most definitely is the knife that Daniel Boone gave to Bushrod Underhill. Bushrod has carried and used it proudly ever since."

Mahaffery cursed, drank from his flask again, and in doing so generated a spasm in his hurt wrist. He turned to Marica. "Where's that binding cloth? How slow can you be, woman?"

"Please . . . tell your man not to kill my father!"

"Hell, I'd done forgotten that. Mongold, let him be."

Mongold grunted and looked a little disappointed.

Marica reluctantly let go of her father and rose. When she'd eyed the outlaws long enough to persuade herself they really weren't going to shoot her father, she stooped and finished tearing the cloth strip from her skirt hem. Rising, she held it up for Mahaffery. The outlaw held out his injured wrist, and she bound it silently.

"Very good," he said, wriggling his fingers. "Much better. You see, Miss Bolton, how much more smoothly things go when you people are cooperative?"

"Help me, Jordan!" Legarde begged pitifully from the floor. "I need a doctor."

Mahaffery knelt beside his subordinate. "I'm mighty sorry, but there is no doctor. The closest thing to one, as I understand it, was the late Mr. Dillow."

"Then get me a preacher . . . I don't want to die, Jordan. I ain't ready. I ain't ready!"

"I'm mighty sorry for you, my friend."

Suddenly Legarde was bitter. "It's your fault, Jordan! I should never have joined you! I never should have come into these mountains! All you've done in bringing us up here is get us killed . . . Searl, Emmett, Ross, Perry, Reed . . . now me."

"Yes," Mahaffery said softly, the gentle tone failing to disguise a quick-rising anger. "Now you." He reached over, grasped the knife, and jerked it out of Legarde's back. Joe Legarde screamed, then fainted.

"You shouldn't have done that," Fleenor said. "He'll bleed inside the wound now."

"I know," Mahaffery said. "But it doesn't matter. There's nothing I could do for him, anyway."

For almost a minute, silence lingered in the lodge house. Bert Mongold and Lennis Yeager stared at their dying companion on the floor, and at their leader, who paced around, drinking again.

It was Yeager who spoke up first.

"Jordan . . . I want a word with you." He glanced about. "Private."

Mahaffery swept his eyes over the people. "Private. Not much chance of that." But he came closer to Yeager and ducked his head toward him, waiting. Mahaffery's eyes were very bloodshot.

"Say what you got to say."

"Now that I think about it, maybe Bert and Conner should hear this, too."

On the floor, Legarde made a strange, wheezing sound. His breathing became more ragged.

Mahaffery sighed. "All right." He called the others over, and waited for Yeager to begin.

"Jordan, we have a problem situation here."

"Indeed we do. It's called missing gold."

"No. Beyond that. Look at us, Jordan. Four of us left. Ten to begin with, and now just four! Dear God, who could have imagined such a thing would happen?"

"All for the best, if we find our gold," Mahaffery replied. "Fewer ways to split it means a greater amount for us all."

"I don't believe we're going to find that gold. I don't believe anybody knows where it is, and even if they did, finding it in this snowfall would be all but impossible."

"So maybe you should just leave, Lennis."

"You're drunk, Jordan. You've stayed half drunk, or more, ever since you started pulling on that flask of yours. You've always been a smart man, a good leader . . . but all at once you don't seem to think things through. Look at us . . . four men left alive, once poor Joe dies on the floor there."

As if in reply, Legarde made a guttural sound, another wheeze, and his color went from pallid to gray. His head flopped to one side, and a trace of blood appeared at the corner of his mouth and trickled to the floor.

"Four of us to guard these people! We've got the weapons, sure, but they've got the numbers. And we can't stay awake twenty-four hours a day. It's only a matter of time before they find an advantage and turn on us."

"You'll notice there's not as many of them left, either," Mahaffery replied. "Seven men left to our four, and one of their seven is older than Adam. And none are armed."

"There's also four women and a girl."

"You're worried about women?"

"I'm worried about all of them, worried about everything. A woman can stab or shoot as easy as a man can. Hell, we've already seen your own brother killed by a little boy!"

"If a man takes care of himself, he needn't be shot either by man, woman, or boy."

"That's a weak answer, Jordan, and you know it. Face the facts! How long do you think we can go on this way? We're snowed in up here. The odds of making it out of these mountains now are slender. What are we going to do? Spend the entire blasted winter standing guard over these people?"

"That's not what I had in mind," Mahaffery said.

"All right, so we shoot them all. We've still got the two out in the valley to contend with, this Sam Underhill and whoever the hell the other one is. And maybe a third one out there, too, if the one who killed Emmett is still alive. And those men *are* armed! We're in a true predicament here, Jordan."

"I want my gold," Mahaffery replied flatly. "I'm willing to take some risk for it."

"It's my gold, too. It's all of ours. And all of us have *already* taken risks for it. But I, for one, am not willing to die for it. It was a goodly amount of gold, but not worth this."

The discussion, rising toward an argument, went on, but the outlaws kept their voices too low for anyone nearby to hear the conversation.

Arianna Winkle, meanwhile, had pieced the slate fragments together on her lap again, and was studying Colfax's final scribblings very closely.

Jordan Mahaffery just then swore loudly, looked at Yeager with disgust, and pulled out his flask for another swallow, never breaking his gaze from Yeager's. He was clearly growing angry, but still remembered to keep his voice low. "All right, Lennis. You've let us know how unhappy and worried you are. So what do you suggest we do about it? You say we can't leave. You say we can't stand guard over these folks all winter. So what does that leave?"

"I don't know the answer. Maybe we ought to go ahead and shoot these folks and be done with it."

"I believe you may be right. But there's a way to go about that by which we can solve more than one of our problems at a time."

"What do you mean?"

"I mean I got an idea brewing as to how we can draw them two out of the valley and to us . . . and then we can rid ourselves of all our problems here at once. It might get a little bloody, a little ugly . . . but we have to do what we have to do."

Yeager swiped a dry tongue over his lower lip. "Say what you mean, Jordan."

"Later. For now, I want to know you trust me, and that I can count on you to do what has to be done when the time comes."

Yeager's eyes swept across the faces of Broadgrass and Mongold, trying to read their thoughts. "Well . . . I reckon we may as well go on as we are for now."

"Good man, Lennis. I knew you could be relied on. Meanwhile, we still have a chance at finding where the old man hid the gold. I ain't convinced he didn't tell his fat womenfolk there."

Mongold said, "Want me to work on them for you, Conner?"

"I think we'll make better progress with a kinder approach to begin with," Mahaffery said.

"What should we do with Joe, and the other dead man?" Yeager asked.

"Pull Joe in the corner for now. As for old dead Colfax, leave him where he is. He's going to help us out a little later on, when it comes time to draw our unseen friends out of the valley."

CHAPTER
TWENTY-SEVEN

The shelter of poles and evergreen boughs had gone up quickly; both Bushrod and Sam had built hundreds much like it over the years, using whatever natural materials were at hand. With a fire blazing far enough away to ensure that the shelter didn't catch fire, but not so far away as to be useless for heat, they made Perry Winters as comfortable as possible.

"I'm dying," Winters said several times. "I can feel the dying going on inside me."

"You may yet live," Bushrod replied. "I truly believe you could go either way. But if you make up your mind you're going to die, you probably will."

"I don't understand why you're doing this for me," Winters said.

"Just because a man forces you to shoot him like a dog doesn't mean he *is* a dog," Bush said. "I'm sorry you chose to attack us, sorry I had to put a rifle ball through you. But what's done is done, and now we'll try to put you right again. And maybe, in return, you can tell us some things we need to know."

Winters, his voice wracked in pain, said, "About what's happening back in the mining camp, you mean."

"Precisely so," Bush said.

Winters thought it over only a moment or two. "Yes, I'll

tell you. Why the hell not? I owe Mahaffery nothing. I expect the bastard's already got the gold for himself and is trying to run off with it. I hope he freezes to death. He probably sent me out here to get killed. One less to share his gold with.''

"This gold, tell us about it."

Winters did so, describing to Bushrod and Sam his own road into the gang of Jordan and Searl Mahaffery, two worthless, criminal brothers who had only one advantage between them, that being Jordan's keen criminal mind. Winters proved a good and succinct storyteller, describing how the gang came together, how the elder Mahaffery concocted a scheme that would get into their hands enough stolen bank gold to keep them all in liquor and women for months, and how they'd managed to pull it off with hardly a hitch.

But Frank Dehaven, perceived by all to be Mahaffery's closest friend and ally in the gang—closer even than Mahaffery's own animalistic brother, Searl—had cheated them all by taking the gold for himself. He'd fled, but they'd found his trail and tracked him into the mountains, finally determining that he was bound for the old Dutch Camp. He described the encounter with the two children in the mountains, and from there on, the story became more familiar to Bushrod and Sam.

But Winters knew many things they didn't yet know, and told them freely, and with such an ease and fervor that both Underhills could see that he was telling the truth. He presented every event and told of every death, including the death of Colfax. That news shocked Sam. Colfax was older than most of the miners, indeed, but Sam had never perceived him as a candidate for sudden death. As far as Sam was concerned, Mahaffery was as responsible for Colfax's passing as for the death of Julius Setser. It was probably the mental distress of the ordeal that triggered Colfax's fatal attack of apoplexy.

More intriguing than the news of Colfax's death, though, was that of the deaths that had beset the Mahaffery gang itself. Sam ticked them off on his fingers, calculating. Assuming that the one who made it back to camp with Bushrod's knife in his shoulders was dead or soon would be, there were only four outlaws left in Texas Gulch out of the original ten. So astonished by this was Sam that he insisted that Winters himself name off the dead, which he did, from Emmett Fish on through Joe Legarde, who had abandoned him bleeding in the snow.

"I hate him," Winters said of Legarde. "He left me to die, and dead I would be even now if you two hadn't helped me. But I hate Jordan Mahaffery all the more. I was a fool to come out here just because he told me to."

Winters was tired when he finished his talking. He'd spoken with intensity, expending energy that best would have been kept. The Underhills held silence and waited for him to go to sleep, which happened in seconds.

"Pap," Sam said, "only four of them left! Maybe not even that, if Mahaffery really has gone on after that gold."

"Do you really think Ben Dillow knows where the gold is? Would he have been the kind to scheme with Colfax to hide it?"

Sam recognized the question for what it was: rhetorical. Both he and Bushrod had known Ben Dillow for years, and knew the kind of man he was. He'd never have taken part in a scheme to hoard gold at the expense of his peers and neighbors. Sam shook his head. "No. He'd never have done it. Which means he lied to Mahaffery."

"And why would he do a thing like that?"

Sam could see only one answer. "He was probably trying to lead Mahaffery away from the camp, so he could kill him, or lose him in the wilderness."

"A thing possibly to be achieved only at great risk to his own life," Bushrod said. "And that *does* sound like the Ben Dillow I know."

Sam figured that his father was right. He wondered where Ben Dillow was at this moment. Had his scheme worked?

"Pap, Mahaffery might be dead, or gone for good, if Ben's succeeded."

"Yes. But we can't know, sitting out here."

"Then maybe it's time for us to quit sitting out here," Sam said.

Back at the lodge house, Mahaffery was seated on a stool, leaning forward with elbows on knees and an earnest expression on his face. On a bench before him were the Colfax women, both wide-eyed and very afraid despite Mahaffery's best efforts to look friendly and harmless.

"I want you to know my sincere sorrow over the death of your husband. Of all the men here, he was the finest and best, and I thought highly of him. I see the doubt in your face, but it's true. I'd have not seen harm come to him, I honestly assure you."

The women simply stared, their disbelief of this obvious liar almost humorously palpable.

Mahaffery, who had been working hard to make his fulsomeness believable, paused and went on. "It's out of respect for Mr. Colfax that I'm asking . . . not demanding, but *asking* . . . that you tell me where he hid the gold. Because I'm sure he told you something . . . he obviously cared deeply about both of you. He loved you so much—he wouldn't have left you in the dark."

The women blinked and struggled against tears and remained silent.

"Mrs. Colfax . . . please." Mahaffery reached out and touched her hand, and she drew it back like it was snakebitten.

"He told me nothing."

Mahaffery swallowed again, harder. A vein made an appearance on his right temple.

"He must have told you."

"He didn't. I'm sorry. If he had, I'd tell you, so you'd take your cursed gold and go away!"

"I'm trying, ma'am, to be patient. To treat you as I know

Mr. Colfax would have wanted. I encourage you to co-operate with me. I promise, some of the gold will go to you—a very generous portion.'' He looked for a moment at the hostages. ''You might even save some lives through your cooperation.''

The Colfax women were none too keen mentally, but even they understood the subtle-yet-clear threat in Mahaffery's words.

''She's told you,'' Letitia spoke up, as loudly as her innate timidity would allow. ''He didn't tell us anything. If we knew, we'd tell you.''

Mahaffery's face lost its battle to remain tranquil-looking. He glared at Letitia. ''I don't have to continue to take such a kind approach, you know. I could have both of you telling me everything you've ever heard in your lives, in a matter of moments.'' He indicated Mongold with a toss of his head. ''I've got a man there who would be glad to help persuade you. He's already asked for the privilege.''

Letitia's eyes reddened, but she bravely held back tears. ''I really need to visit the outhouse,'' she murmured.

His hand shot out and closed around her wrist. ''You'll visit the outhouse when I tell you you can. You'll eat, you'll sleep, you'll sneeze and you'll cough when I tell you you can, and not before.''

''You're hurting me!''

''I haven't even *started* to hurt you, you ugly cow!'' He squeezed the wrist for a few seconds more, then relaxed, and when he did, his manner suddenly was gentle again. He patted Letitia's hand. Not as bold as her mother had been, she dared not pull it away.

''Now, let's begin again,'' he said. ''I want you both to tell me anything, anything at all that the late Mr. Colfax might have told you about where that gold might be.''

Over in the corner, while the interrogation of the Colfax women went on, Arianna stared at the slate, now fully pieced together on her lap. She studied the markings closely, frowning, her face an image of concentration.

Her mother, troubled by what was going on with the Colfax women and trying to block it out, sat down beside her. "What are you doing, darling?"

"Nothing," Arianna said. "I'm just looking at the slate."

"I heard that Mr. Colfax dropped that slate and broke it before he died," Leora said.

"No," Arianna replied, half distracted and now tracing the chalk markings on it with her finger. "No. It was the bad man who broke it. Letitia told me. He was mad because he couldn't read what Mr. Colfax had put on it."

Leora studied the seemingly random chalk marks. "Sad," she said. "He couldn't even make his letters. Apoplexy is a terrible thing."

"Yes," Arianna said. She brushed a finger across one of the slate shards, obliterating the mark on it. She repeated this action with the other pieces, until at last the slate fragments were erased, and the last attempted communication of Herbert Colfax to the world he was leaving disappeared for good.

Sam was sleeping deeply in the evergreen bough shelter, and what made him awaken he never knew. When he sat up, Bushrod was already awake, slumped over like a very weary man. Perry Winters lay on his back. Sam could barely make it all out by the tiny, faint beams of firelight that pierced through and danced in the gaps in the shelter walls.

"Pap?"

Bushrod lifted his head; his silhouetted form looked back at Sam. "Our friend here has died, son."

"What? But I thought the wound wasn't bad."

"I suppose it was worse than we thought."

"Pap . . . you sound like you're weeping."

Bush didn't answer at once. "I can't deny it, Sam."

"You're weeping for that dead outlaw?"

"No. Not for him. Though I suppose that every man has

something in him worth weeping for when it's forever gone.''

"If not him, then why?''

Again Bush paused. "I'll tell you soon enough. Not here. Not in the dark.''

"Why not?''

"Some things are easier said by daylight.''

Sam felt a cold terror inside him. He'd never seen his father this way, never heard him sound so irrational.

"Pap, I don't like you being this way.''

Bushrod sat up straighter, and when he spoke his voice was stronger. "You know, Sam, I've been thinking about what you said earlier. About how we can't just sit out here. The more this is allowed to drag on, the more dangerous it will become.''

"Pap, let's talk about what's bothering you.''

"Let's don't. Not now. Let's talk about what we need to do about our problem at Texas Gulch.''

"Pap, you listen to me. There's something that's been . . . *haunting* you. You're holding it back from me. You've been sitting up in the night, alone, weeping. Tell me what's wrong!''

"I'm going to lie down now, Sam. I'm weary. Tomorrow . . . we'll talk some more.''

"We'll talk now!''

"No. Not tonight. Tomorrow. I promise. We'll talk then.''

Sam swallowed his anger. Bushrod was not a man to be forced to do anything. "You'll tell me why you really came here?''

"I'll tell you whatever needs to be told. Now, pardon me while I drag our dead friend out of here.''

Sam watched as his father labored briefly, pulling the corpse of Perry Winters out into the snow. While he was outside, Bushrod replenished the fire, then reentered the shelter.

"Pap, I want to ask you something . . . do you think the

time's drawing near that they're going to commence killing hostages?''

"I do."

"So what can we do?"

"I really wish I knew, Sam."

CHAPTER
TWENTY-EIGHT

Nothing is private for those living under the gun. In the thin, cloud-filtered winter sunlight of the morning, the hostages were lined up outside and allowed, one by one, to use the privy nearest the lodge house, while a grumpy-looking Mongold and a nervous Lennis Yeager stood guard over them.

Among them were the two Colfax women, scared and weary, but unharmed. Their interrogation by Mahaffery the evening before had ended without violence done to either. Mahaffery had simply lost steam somewhere along the way while the effects of exhaustion came on, accompanied by a growing comprehension that these simple women really didn't know where the gold was hidden.

The line of hostages stretched all the way back past the corner of the lodge house. Though usually Leora Winkle kept Arianna close beside her, today they were apart, Arianna holding back toward the rear of the line as it advanced.

When at last the necessities of life had been dealt with, the sullen people moved back inside the lodge house. A minute after they were back inside, Leora was engaged in a quiet, desperate search. Where was Arianna? Leora dared not draw attention to her daughter's absence out of fear it would bring harm to Arianna when she was found, but with her heart in her throat she desperately looked about the lodge house, peering into corners and even under benches.

At last she saw the note, tucked under the pieces of broken slate, which lay on the floor near the bench where Arianna usually sat. Leora sat down and spread her skirt to cover the slate, then casually reached down a few moments later and took the note, which was scribbled on a torn scrap of foolscap.

MAMA, IT WASN'T WORDS ON THE SLATE, IT WAS A PICTURE MAP. I'VE GONE TO GET THE GOLD SO THEY'LL LET US GO. I LOVE YOU. ARIANNA.

By this point, searching the pass seemed futile and foolish, but on impulse Mahaffery had put them at it again. The men of Texas Gulch had once more trudged to the crest of the gap, there to labor anew, moving old snow and fresh snow, looking for gold that no one believed would be found. Hadn't Colfax admitted he'd hidden it somewhere? Yet dig they did, because Mahaffery, seeing his hope of finding the gold through the Colfax women now withered away, clung to the faintest hope that maybe Colfax had never really hidden the gold at all, and it really *was* still waiting for them out there in the snow, behind a stone or under a drift that nobody had happened to touch yet.

The circle the diggers made was quite wide by now, and the few remaining outlaws were challenged to keep their eyes on all the men at once. Kish Fleenor, who had gradually worked his way to the farthest edge of the snow clearing, suddenly made a break and darted toward the trees.

Lennis Yeager raised his rifle and fired. Fleenor grunted, threw his hands out to the side and pitched facedown into the snow. He did not move.

Yeager was already half reloaded before the other men fully comprehended that Fleenor was dead.

It was more than Jack Gray, the kindhearted and gentle uncle of Arianna, could bear. A great and unfamiliar fury aroused him to unplanned action. He lunged with his shovel at Bert Mongold, knocking Mongold's rifle out of his hands. But Mongold, though big, was quick when he had to be. He whipped out his knife and had it between Gray's ribs even before Gray could draw back the shovel for a second swing. Once, twice, three times Mongold stabbed. The shovel fell from Gray's fingers and he collapsed into the snow.

Mongold recovered his rifle and gazed down at Gray, then at Fleenor. After a moment he shook his head at Yeager. "Another couple of them gone," he said. "Oh, well. At least we've evened our numbers a little more."

Yeager wasn't listening. His attention was raptly turned to the west, his eyes looking at something out in the wilds of the mountains.

"Bert, there's a man out there. Maybe two."

"What?"

"I saw it, just now. Very clear. A man, and beyond him, I'm almost sure, another one. But they're gone now."

"Maybe that Dillow fellow's alive after all."

"Then who's the second man?"

"Could be the pair from the valley, gone out into the mountains. We didn't guard the pass last night. They could have gone out of the valley without us knowing."

"I don't think it was them. I've seen those two, remember? This was somebody different."

The outlaws gazed into the wilderness several moments in silence.

"It's the law," Joe Skinner said. "The law has followed you murderers up here, and they'll hang you when they get their hands on you."

"Shut up," Yeager muttered.

New snowfall began, light at first, quickly increasing. Yeager looked into the gloom and shrugged. "Well, I *think* I saw somebody, anyway.

"Let's go back down, Bert," Yeager said. "We need to let Mahaffery know what's happened. He'll have heard the shooting. Besides, we're gaining nothing digging in this snow. The gold ain't here."

Skinner asked, "Will you at least let us carry down these two men you've murdered?"

"Bring them on, or leave them to lie. It's all the same to me," Yeager replied.

The shooting had indeed been heard down in the lodge house, so the people were already braced to learn of more losses by the time Yeager and Mongold returned, herding the corpse-bearing prisoners before them. The sight of the bodies of Jack Gray and Kish Fleenor, carried down and laid out side by side in the snow outside the lodge house, lowered a pall of despair over all the hostages. Tears and wails rose among the women, and Old Man Skinner.

Leora Winkle shed no tears. She was too numb, too afraid. She looked sadly at the body of her valiant brother and couldn't even find a word to quite fit the odd emotions that she felt. As worried as she was about Arianna, she was actually glad at that moment that her child was not here to see her uncle lying dead in the snow.

They all wondered how and why the two had been killed, but no one asked. Reasons were beginning not to matter. This place had begun as a refuge of hope for new life and wealth that was no further away than the spring. Now it was hell, and nothing made sense.

Jordan Mahaffery fell to talking to his men—Yeager and Mongold nervous-looking; Conner Broadgrass still calm and seemingly unworried—and Copp Nolen approached Leora during those moments of distraction.

"I'm so sorry, Leora," he said.

"Mr. Nolen, Arianna is gone."

"Gone?"

"Yes . . . this morning, when we went to privy, she was there, and then she wasn't. Back inside the lodge house, I found a note from her." She described briefly the matter of the broken slate and Colfax's final markings, misinterpreted, apparently, by all except Arianna. "She's gone to find the gold, Mr. Nolen, and plans to bring it back and give it to Mahaffery, and bring all this to an end.''

Copp Nolen turned a little pale. "I hope she doesn't do that.''

"Why?''

"Ben Dillow believes . . . *believed* . . . that as soon as Mahaffery gets his gold, he'll have all of us shot. We've witnessed murders done. We could harm him and his men with what we know.''

"Oh, no.''

"Leora, do you have any memory of Colfax's map? If I could figure it out, like Arianna apparently did, I could go where she must be going. I could stop her from bringing back that gold. And maybe I could hide her somewhere where she could survive, where she would be safe.''

"Does any such place exist here?''

"I don't know. I wish I did.''

Leora wracked her brain, trying to remember the map, but all she could conjure up in her mind were general, shapeless, fluctuating markings that had meant nothing to her because she was persuaded at the time that they were nothing but scribbles. "I can't recall any of it. But Arianna studied it closely . . . then erased it all.''

"She memorized it, I'm sure. She's always been a clever girl that way.''

Leora smiled and nodded, but there was pain in her eyes and it was obvious she was wondering if she would ever be privileged to see that clever girl again.

Nolen thought hard. "That gold, if truly hidden by Colfax, can't be far from the pass. He wouldn't have had the time, strength, or need to have carried it far. He must have stashed it somewhere right at hand. So that map must indicate someplace within easy reach.''

"But you've dug up the entire pass, more than once, and there's nothing.''

"There's plenty of rocks and trees and so on around there that haven't been explored. I suppose Mahaffery will put us onto that next, unless he decides to just say the devil with it all, kill us, and be done with it.''

Those words, too casually spoken, brought tears to Leora. ''I've got to find my daughter, Mr. Nolen.''

''Consider this, Leora: she may be better off having gotten away. If the worst happens, they won't be able to get her along with the rest of us.''

Leora thought this over. ''Yes. Yes. Mr. Nolen . . . Copp, do you mean it when you say you'd find her and take her to safety?''

''Of course I do . . . if I can.''

''I want you to try. Please.''

''Well . . . I will. But how can I get away? They watch us every moment.''

''Arianna did it. You can, too. You *must*.''

He remembered the sight of Kish Fleenor lying freshly killed in the snow. He'd tried to get away, too. But what could he say to this pleading mother?

''Very well, Leora . . . I'll do my best.''

''It's all I can ask, Mr. Nolen.''

CHAPTER
TWENTY-NINE

Afternoon came, and the men of Texas Gulch dug again. Absurd, forced labor, slavishly done in driving snow, under the eyes and guns of increasingly desperate men. When they'd descended to the lodge house the last time, bearing the corpses of Gray and Fleenor, and the news—which Mahaffery had discounted as a trick of the snow—of Yeager's sighting of two distant figures out in the mountains, all had been sure the digging at the pass was finished for good.

Mahaffery had surprised them all by sending them back again. But the more perceptive of the exhausted laborers realized that this might be good. As long as they were digging, Mahaffery still saw them as useful. As long as they were useful, they had a chance to live.

Copp Nolen worked with greater energy than he had since the ordeal began, because he was powered by purpose. He'd worked his way to the edge of the cleared expanse, and was shoveling snow into a great, long mound, all the while keeping his eye on the guards and the others, looking for his chance. He'd told none of the other men what he planned to do. Only Leora Winkle knew.

The mound was high enough for his purposes now, and situated just so as to allow him to use its cover to reach a long, deep ravine that ran down one of the many slopes just beyond this place. Nolen felt a nervous terror, but also a sense of anticipation and the cooperation of fate. The snow was a heavy screen, cutting visibility. The mound he had made, seemingly an unplanned by-product of digging snow, was plenty big enough to hide the maneuver he had planned, and the guards seemed lost in their own thoughts.

The snow grew even heavier after a few more minutes had passed. Gray sky hung low, laden with freezing moisture. It might snow for hours yet.

"Hell with this!" Nolen heard Mongold say. "There's no point in going on, Lennis. Let's get them back down to the lodge house."

Lennis Yeager drew closer to his fellow guard. "I agree. And Bert . . . I don't believe we should come up here and dig anymore. It's a waste of time, and I'm tired of freezing my backside off."

Unseen by either guard through the veil of snow, and equally out of view of his fellow hostages, Copp Nolen cast himself over the mound he'd made and sat flat in the snow. With his shovel he began sweeping snow over his legs and feet, hiding them. Then he lay down on his back and pulled more of it across his torso, covering everything but his face. Across his face he laid his shovel, resting it so that its contours gave him breathing space.

He couldn't lie here long without freezing, but he could make it long enough.

He heard the guards rounding up the men. *Please, God,* he silently prayed, *don't let them count the men. Make them careless right now.*

There was no count. He heard the men moving away from the clearing, back into the pass. Now, if only his own friends didn't unwittingly betray him by noticing and pointing out his absence, he should be in the clear.

He rose, breaking out of the hiding snow like a resurrected corpse. Brushing himself off, he entered the cleared area again, which was rapidly refilling, and trotted across it.

He'd made it. He was free of them, for now. Free to search for Arianna Winkle, and, God willing, to stop her from finding and taking that gold back to Texas Gulch and thereby, with the best of intentions, sealing the doom of every hostage there.

The returning outlaws found Mahaffery staring out the back window of the lodge house, the shutters wide open and wind and snow blowing through. Mahaffery didn't seem to care that it was, nor that the diggers had given up.

"Why you letting in the snow and wind, Jordan?" Yeager asked.

Mahaffery continued to stare out into the whiteness. "They're out there," he said. "Watching this place. Can you feel them watching? I'm even pretty sure I saw one of them, creeping out there along one of those ridges. They're there, no doubt about it. Watching us."

"You've been drinking again, Jordan," Yeager said. "Maybe you just imagined what you saw. Maybe it was a 'trick of the snow' on your eyes." There was no small amount of contempt in the way he threw back at Mahaffery the same bland attitude of discounting that Mahaffery had given his own claim of seeing men out in the mountains . . . though by now, Yeager himself was secretly beginning to wonder if Mahaffery might be right. The falling snow, combined with perpetual weariness, could present all kinds of false visions to a man.

Mahaffery shook his head, produced his flask, unstoppered it, and turned it upside down. Not a drop remained in it. "No, Lennis. I'm not drunk. It's been empty since last night." Mahaffery pulled the shutters closed and turned to Mongold. "I'm glad you men came back; I was about to send Conner up to fetch you. Bert, when the snow clears, I want you to haul out the late Mr. Colfax. With our friends out there within eyeshot, the time has come to put him to use."

"What are you going to do?" America Colfax asked.

"Something that should bring Sam Underhill and his old companion, whoever he is, trotting right down here to give themselves up. You should be proud of your husband, ma'am. He's about to become a hero."

Arianna was sure she had waited too long. By now her absence was probably noted by the outlaws. Maybe they were tormenting her mother like that wicked man Mahaffery had tormented the poor Colfax women. Perhaps she'd made a mistake in escaping.

Hidden in the same broken-down old cabin from which Daniel Chase had taken the little pistol, she felt relatively safe and secure, though she was certainly cold. For several minutes she'd been weighing her options. She could return to the lodge house and hope she could sneak in without being noticed . . . something sly Daniel could have achieved, but not something she felt confident she could pull off. She could head back into the valley and try to find Sam Underhill, who she knew would protect and help her. But the weather was very bad, the valley piled deep in snow, and she was sure that Sam Underhill was probably deliberately making himself hard to find.

So she kept coming around to her original plan. She'd follow the map that Colfax had crudely drawn, and which she had memorized, find the gold, and bring it back. Then the bad men would have no reason to stay in Texas Gulch, and no one else would have to die.

Arianna didn't look forward to plunging out into the snow, but it made sense to do it now, before the accumulation grew much deeper. And with the snow cutting visibility, she could travel to the pass without fear of being seen from the lodge house.

Closing her eyes and saying a fast, sincere prayer, she slipped out of the cabin and headed for the pass.

Cold, tense, and uncertain, Bushrod and Sam Underhill crouched on the ridgetop, watching the silent tableau of Texas Gulch through the snowfall.

"What should we do, Pap?" Sam said at last. "Go down

there? Offer ourselves in place of the people they hold?"

"Don't think that would work," Bush said. "These people are held hostage mostly for what they know, and have seen. Mahaffery would have nothing to gain by letting them go whether he has us or not."

"Then what can we do?"

Bushrod said nothing.

"Pap?"

"Sam . . . listen to me. I need to tell you about something now. Something that happened back in Texas. Sam, Durham's sons are dead."

Sam turned to look at his father, puzzled. Bushrod would not look back at him, keeping his eyes fixed on Texas Gulch. "Dead, Pap?"

"Yes."

"Danny and Zeke?"

A silent nod.

"Dear Lord, Pap . . . how?"

"It's my fault, son. My fault."

Now it was coming, Sam realized. The truth at last about what was haunting his father, about what had driven him all the way here from Texas to the Sierras in the wintertime.

"Tell me what happened."

Bushrod sighed slowly and seemed to descend more deeply into sorrow before Sam's eyes. "It was . . . Danny. You know how the boy is . . . how he was. Always gentle, never much for hunting, roaming, fishing . . . all the things I had you fellows doing since you were small."

Sam nodded. Indeed the elder son of Durham and Chasida Underhill had been far from a typical young male Underhill: artistic, kind, prone to be solemn, deeply sympathetic to others and to animals, not prone to horseplay and rowdiness. Sam had watched the boy weep once over a string of fish his father had caught and brought home for supper. Weeping over fish, because he felt sorry for them! Sam had found it appalling, and worried about the lad. Danny's little brother Zeke, on the other hand, was more the typical Underhill always eager for some jaunt and adventure with his father or uncles or grandfather.

Bushrod went on. "I'd taken the boys hunting. Danny hadn't wanted to come . . . but I made him. Told him it would be good for him to come along, that he needed to become a better hunter. Make more of a man out of him. All that kind of thing. God. God forgive me. I wish I hadn't done that."

"How'd it happen, Pap?"

"Very simple, as such things often are. I didn't see the accident itself, so I've had to piece the facts of it together. As best we ever figured, it appears that Danny must have laid his rifle up against a tree, with the lock cocked back. Very, very foolish mistake if he did it, going against everything he'd been taught. But guns and so on were always alien things to Danny, you know. The lessons never took. Anyway, he must have bumped his own rifle, knocked it over. However it happened, it fired . . . little Zeke never even felt the ball hit him, I'm sure. It entered the back of his head and passed out through his forehead."

"Dear Lord." Sam lowered his head and blinked away tears.

"I was away from camp for a few minutes, down near the river with the horses. I heard the shot . . . then I heard Danny wailing. The most awful kind of sound . . . I ran. But by the time I'd gotten there, Danny had reloaded his rifle. No awkwardness about it this time. A perfect, fast job of it . . . and before I could reach him to stop him, he'd put the muzzle under his chin, tears streaming down his face . . . he triggered it with his toe. Punishing himself for having killed his own brother . . . punishing himself, maybe, for being different, and gentler, and disappointing to his old fool of a grandfather . . ." Bushrod stopped talking, lowered his head, and sobbed like a child.

Sam had nothing to say. He crouched there, numb and astonished and horrified.

"Pap . . . it wasn't your fault."

"Yes it was. Yes it was. Those boys were in my care. Those boys were mine to protect . . . and I protected neither of them. Poor Danny. Poor Zeke. Oh, God, if only I could go back. If only I'd not gone down to the river . . . if only I'd thought to make sure Danny hadn't left his rifle cocked like he was so prone to do . . . if only I hadn't forced him to come along to begin with.''

"Pap, none of this was planned. It was an accident."

"That's what Durham told me. And Chasida. As terrible as it was for them, they never blamed me." Bush paused, catching his breath. "And that almost makes it worse. I wish they would blame me. I wish they'd curse me and strike me and tell me what a sad and sorry old fool and failure I am, for letting such a thing happen to my own grandsons." Bush cried more, not speaking for a full minute. Then he regained his composure a little, wiping at his face with the heel of his right hand. "Sam, I wish I'd spent more time with Danny, just talking to him. Not about the things I thought he should be interested in, but about what *he* wanted to talk about. I wish I'd just let Danny be Danny. I wish I'd embraced him more, and harped on him less. I wish . . .''

"Hush, Pap. There's no going back, and nothing gained by horsewhipping yourself.''

"Maybe I've already lived too long, Sam. Maybe this hearty and hale old body of mine has done too good a job and kept me around longer than should be.''

"You've told me yourself many a time, Pap: there's no wisdom in questioning the ways and will of God. The things that happen that are beyond us are not for us to understand. We just have to accept what comes. You recall telling me that?''

"Yes." Bush actually grinned, feebly. "I'm surprised to hear that it stayed with you, though.''

"It did. But I don't think it's stayed with you. You've forgotten your own lesson.''

"I have, I guess." Bush swallowed, hard. "But don't think I haven't tried to persuade myself many a time that

I'm not at fault. I don't like bearing this weight of guilt. But I find I can't shrug it off. It just lingers, like a heavy stone on my shoulders."

"Why'd you come here, Pap?"

"Part of it was like I said. I'd pined to see you. But the deepest reason, I suppose, is that I was running away. I had to get away from Texas, and all the others . . . had to see if I could find a way to shed this guilt. But it's stayed with me. All the way here, all through the time I spent roaming and asking questions and tracking you down, that burden has stayed on my shoulders, and it stays there still."

There were things Sam could have said, predictable and wise and well-intentioned, even true, but he knew they would do no good. His father felt just as Sam himself would have felt had their circumstances been reversed. No amount of words would drive away the demon that tormented Bushrod Underhill right now. Sam could only reach over and pat his father's shoulder, silently, hurting for him, praying for him.

Bush dabbed away the last of his tears, took a long, slow breath, and gazed out across the white expanse at Texas Gulch.

"Sam, what did you say the name of that orphan boy was, the one our dead friend back there said was killed in the cave?"

"Daniel. Daniel Chase."

"Daniel. Just like Danny's name."

"That's right."

There was a long silence, then Sam spoke again. "Pap, let's don't let anyone else die. Let's end this thing . . . somehow."

"Yes," Bush said. "Let's do."

At that moment, a voice echoed from Texas Gulch out across the valley. "Underhill! Sam Underhill! I know you're there, for I've caught sight of you twice! Draw near, Mr. Underhill . . . my name's Mahaffery, and there's something going to happen that you'll want to see!"

CHAPTER
THIRTY

The Underhills looked at one another. This was an unexpected development.

"Should I reply to him?" Sam asked.

"Don't know," Bushrod said. "Obviously he knows we're here, and who you are. I suppose there's no way any of them can know about me . . . about who I am, anyhow."

"Come on, Pap. Let's get closer."

The two Underhills rose and scrambled down the ridge, sure they were being watched. Maybe watched over the sights of rifles . . . though at this range that wasn't much of a worry. They reached a ridge closer to the mining camp and dropped again to a crouch. Bushrod handed his spyglass to Sam, who opened it and put it against his eye.

"Well! Howdy, there!" Mahaffery's voice called. Sam looked for the man but couldn't see him . . . though there was one open window at the back of the lodge house, and a figure barely hidden in its interior shadow. Probably Mahaffery. "Good to know you a little better . . . that's the clearest view of you I've had!"

Sam called back. "What do you want?"

"Ah! Now I hear your voice. Good! No point in us playing foolish games with one another. What do I want? What I want, Sam—May I call you Sam?—is to show you and your old friend there what comes of interfering with our plans and killing our men. I hope you can see clearly what we're doing. Let me direct your attention to the clear area up past the north end of this building.''

Sam was already looking there. In that clearing stood Bert Mongold, holding up the slumping form of the late Herbert Colfax.

Sam could already guess what was coming.

''That's Mr. Bert Mongold you see there, with your own friend Colfax in his arms. Mr. Colfax has been knocked cold—we're merciful men, to a point. But only to a point. Please observe.''

Mongold let Colfax's body fall, drew a pistol, and fired a ball through Colfax's head.

Sam winced, but when he glanced over at his father, he rolled his eyes.

''That, Mr. Underhill, was to help even the score a little for what you and your old man friend there have done. And let me tell you that more of your friends will be shot, just as Colfax was, unless both of you turn yourselves over to me, right now.''

Sam cupped his hands around his mouth. ''Sorry, Mahaffery! Your partner Winters sang like a songbird before he died. We know Colfax was already dead!''

Bush made a face of pain. ''I sure wish you hadn't done that, Sam.''

Sam reddened as he realized his mistake. ''Oh, no,'' he said softly. ''I hope he doesn't . . .'' Sam trailed off.

What he hoped Mahaffery wouldn't do was in fact just what Mahaffery did.

''Ah, too wise for us to fool, are you?'' Mahaffery yelled. ''You want a fish still wiggling, we can provide that.''

With a growing feeling of dread, Sam and Bush watched in silence as Mongold disappeared back into the lodge house. A few moments passed, and he came out again, his rifle pressed into the small of the back of Leora Winkle.

''Oh, no . . .'' Sam murmured, and his stomach did a turn that made him fearful he'd heave on the spot.

"See her?" Mahaffery yelled from his place of hiding. "Think *this* one's already dead? Don't believe so! But she will be, in one minute, unless you show yourselves and commence to approach us . . . weapons above your heads."

Bush was evaluating the distance. "Sam, if we overload my rifle, and if I can aim high and calculate the drop of the ball just right, there's a chance I might be able to hit that brute. I recall a time when Boone told me about the big siege of Boonesboro, when there was an Indian fellow out waggling his rump at the fort, and one of the men there put an extra charge in his rifle, and aimed high, and—"

"No, Pap," Sam said. "No. We can't risk it. You might miss, or you might hit her instead of him. We've got to go in."

Bush paused. "I reckon we do."

"Time's wasting!" Mahaffery yelled. "Are you coming, or do we stain the snow with this woman's brains?"

Sam stood, rifle high. "Don't shoot her!" he yelled. "We're coming."

"Where's the other one?" Mahaffery yelled back.

Bush stood in silent answer.

"Well! Cooperation . . . that's what I like to see!" Mahaffery said. "Advance, gentlemen—and no tricks: The moment I see anything at all I don't like, that's the moment this woman dies."

Out beyond the pass, half frozen but still determined, Arianna Winkle heard the distant, thin sound of the shot that took off the top of Colfax's head, but she didn't know what to make of it. She prayed no one else had died. And she worried about her mother . . . unaccountably, she felt just then that something was wrong. The impulse to go back and investigate was strong.

But Arianna resisted it. It seemed to her that the quickest way to end this crisis was to find the gold and get it into Mahaffery's hands. Then it all would be over, and she and her mother could go about the business of living their lives.

The snow had lightened a little, and Arianna took advantage of the improved visibility to look around and coordinate the landscape she saw with her memory of Colfax's map. Once she'd comprehended what the man was trying to do, and had connected a few of his crude marks with certain landmarks in this area just beyond the pass, it had seemed fairly simple to get her bearings. With everything covered in heavy snow, however, it was harder to be sure. She felt a compulsion to hurry, but made herself work slowly, and think carefully.

After a few moments she nodded and made for the place the map—if she read it rightly—had indicated the gold would be found. There'd been an X mark on that area of Colfax's map, anyway, and in every story Arianna had read, an X on a map always marked a treasure or something else important.

She advanced, noticing with some alarm how numb her feet were. She wriggled her toes, or tried to, and was distressed to find she couldn't be sure whether she'd succeeded. For more reasons than one she needed to find that gold and get back to where it was warm and safe . . . well, warm, anyway.

She reached the base of a knoll. One not too steep, and easy to climb most times. But she'd never tackled it in the snow before. Still, she was sure she could make it up, and that even old Mr. Colfax could have made it up this slope that night he hid the gold. There hadn't been as much snow at that point. Besides, he'd have been very determined.

She began to climb, examining the ground in front of her before planting any steps. Her progress was slow, and she slipped when she was halfway up and tumbled back down again.

On the second try she was even more careful, with much respect for the course. She succeeded this time, making the top of the knoll, where she discovered a small, flat plateau, covered with snow, as she'd expected, but with an additional aspect that she hadn't.

The snow was heavily disturbed. Someone had dug here very recently. Arianna examined the plowed-up snow with a frown, then noticed the tracks.

Small tracks. A man's tracks, filled in somewhat by the falling snow? Maybe . . . but she didn't think so. Her impression was that these tracks had never been made by a man's foot.

She walked through the disturbed area of the snow, then began to follow the smallish tracks across the remainder of the knoll and down the other side. The slope there was more shallow, and probably, she realized, the route that Colfax had taken up, rather than the steeper one she had climbed. She watched the tracks, following closely, hurrying faster the farther she went.

Her heart was beating very fast, and she wasn't noticing the cold so much.

The slope grew even more shallow, the ground finally leveling entirely. The tracks became fresher, and Arianna moved even faster, the hope that was rising in her heightening.

The snow began to fall hard again, the terrain growing rougher. Arianna slowed, clambering over a few boulders, finding the tracks harder to follow now. The worsening weather made her feel compelled to rush, fearing the trail would be obliterated. Though she wore three layers of heavy trousers under her dress—a necessity in these wintry mountains—her legs were growing extremely cold, and the snow was drifting higher the farther she went. She climbed another stone, entered a small pass between two large, jagged stones . . .

He was in front of her all at once, pistol leveled in her face. She gasped and stepped back. The pistol lowered slowly, and he looked at her in utter surprise.

"Arianna . . . I didn't know it was—"

Before he could finish his sentence, Daniel Chase received the kiss he'd long dreamed of.

"You're alive!" she said. "They said you were dead, Daniel! They said you were killed!"

He shook his head solemnly, looking at her. "No. They didn't even get close to killing me. But I killed one of them. He came in the cave after me, and I shot him. He floated out again on the stream. The other one talked to me, and said he was going to leave me alone. He said he'd leave food . . . and he did."

Arianna was hardly paying attention. She was overwhelmed with joy. In this time of loss and dying, it was heartening indeed to see one who was thought dead actually alive, and seemingly well.

"Where have you lived, Daniel?"

"I have a place. Warm and dry and safe. And Arianna . . . I have the gold. I've been moving it."

"It was on the flat place, back there . . . on top of the hill?"

"Yes. How did you know?"

"Mr. Colfax put it there. He made a map, but nobody understood it but me. Oh, Daniel, I'm so glad you're alive! We can end it all now, Daniel. We can take the gold back and give it to the wicked men, and they'll leave!"

Daniel firmly shook his head. "No, Arianna. That's the last thing that we should do. If they get their gold, they'll kill everyone. I've been thinking about it. We could get them in trouble, all of us, just because of the things we've seen them do. The only reason they've left anyone alive at all so far is that they need someone to do their searching, and to use them as hostages and such if it comes down to it."

Arianna frowned, mulling Daniel's point and finding in it a grim kind of sense. "But what should we do, then?"

"Take the gold with us, like I've been doing. Hide it where they'll never find it. And then . . . I don't know. I don't know. We'll do . . . something."

"Daniel, my mother is still back there with them. She'll worry about me."

"You can't go back there, Arianna. You're lucky to have gotten away, and your mother wouldn't want you to go back. I can keep you safe. I can take you where they'll never find you."

Arianna was torn. She stood there, every kind of emotion coursing through her mind. "My mother, Daniel . . ."

"We'll think of something, Arianna. We'll find a way to help her."

Arianna hesitated.

"I need you to help me look for the rest of the gold, anyway. I think I may have even dropped some of it."

She considered only a few seconds more, then nodded. "All right," she said. "I'll help you."

CHAPTER
THIRTY-ONE

Copp Nolen followed the tracks he'd just found. He was bent almost double, squinting to see in the driving snowfall. Two sets of prints, both left by small-footed persons. One, he was sure, must be Arianna's. But who would have left the others?

One set of tracks was fresher than the other, and whoever left the more recent set certainly appeared to be following the first.

The wind howled and stung coldly against Nolen's face. His coat seemed very inadequate at the moment, and despite the outlaws, the danger, the misery of confinement, at the moment he longed for the warm lodge house. He decided he'd best find Arianna as quickly as possible.

Advancing several more yards, Nolen stopped suddenly and wheeled, facing the wilderness to the west. Squinting, he looked and listened, seeking whatever it was that had whispered at the edges of his awareness just now. Something out there . . . someone.

He saw them then. Two men, heavily bundled. Nearly shapeless figures trudging toward him through the snow. They were armed.

Nolen panicked. Had Mahaffery sent men after him? One of those advancing men was big—Mongold, maybe.

He knew they'd kill him if they caught him. Nolen turned and began to run, or to try to run.

He progressed a dozen yards far too slowly to suit him, and glanced behind him in a panic.

They were coming after him.

Mahaffery strode back and forth, looking with great interest at his two newest prisoners, who stood side by side in the very middle of the lodge house. The outlaw chief wore a half grin, and looked the pair up and down, circling them completely, then stopping to stare Sam Underhill in the face.

"Well, Mr. Underhill, pleased to meet you in person at last. You've been a thorn in my side, sir."

Sam stared at him, silent, then turned his eyes and stared past him, refusing even to acknowledge the outlaw. Mahaffery gave a small, disdainful chuckle, and took a step over to face Bushrod.

"And you, sir . . . judging from the name I heard called by these people when you entered just now, I dare to say that I'm actually facing the famous Bushrod Underhill. Is it true?"

"Back up, mister, if you would. Your breath has a stench worthy of a privy hole."

The hostages laughed, softly, and Mahaffery's left cheek twitched. "Well, Mr. Underhill, I'm sorry about that. I'm afraid you'll just have to endure it."

"Adversity breeds strength," Bushrod said. His eyes remained locked with Mahaffery's.

"You really are Bushrod Underhill?"

"The same."

"I've been told you were still in Texas. How'd you come to be in this valley?"

"Ever heard of something called traveling?"

"But how'd you get in? We had that pass guarded at the start, then all at once, there you were, already in the valley."

"I rode the lightning in from the Brazos country. It's how I travel when I'm in no hurry."

"Believe your own legends, do you, Bushrod?"

"Believe them? Son, I live them."

Mahaffery didn't seem to know what to make of this man. "How old are you, anyhow?"

"Old as the mountains, son. Old as the sky."

"I doubt that. But you're up there in years. Got to be. Yet you're spry and strong."

"My good health comes from the thinking of only pure thoughts and the frequent killing of outlaw rubbish."

Mahaffery laughed. "Your killing days are through, old man."

"You never know."

Mahaffery stuck his face close to Bushrod's. "Oh, I know. I know. You're in *my* hands now, Underhill, and all that sharp-tongue talk of yours will do you no good."

"Your breath, son. Your breath."

Mahaffery pulled back his fist and struck Bushrod hard on the side of the face. But the old man pulled back and turned his head just in time to make the blow glance, and it did much less damage than it would have otherwise. Though Bushrod was rocked on his feet, he didn't fall.

Still, Mahaffery seemed pleased by what he'd done. "You see that, Bert? I just hit Bushrod Underhill himself!" He laughed.

Lennis Yeager stepped forward. "Hell with this!" he said. "What's the point of all this, Jordan? So now we've got two more hostages. Now we've got our phantoms out of the valley. So what? We're still here, still don't have our gold, and the snow's still falling! We're still deep in trouble, still poor as before we started, and you're crowing about having hit Bushrod Underhill! What the hell does it matter?"

Mahaffery, for once, had no answer. He glared at Yeager, lips moving vaguely but no words coming out.

Mongold cleared his throat. "I think he's right, Jordan. We're not going to find that gold. I say let's line these people up and shoot them dead, then get out of these mountains the first time the weather breaks.''

The Colfax women sobbed aloud. The other hostages glanced in terror at one another. The Underhills stood as before, no change in their expressions.

"Think about it, Jordan,'' Mongold went on. "If that old man made it up these mountains, we can surely make it down again.''

"Shut up!'' Mahaffery said. "We'll do what has to be done when the right time comes. For now, I've got some more questions for this pair.''

"Hell, they won't answer you,'' Yeager muttered.

Mahaffery ignored him. "Tell me, Underhills, is that fellow—What's his name? Linfoot, I think—is he still alive?''

"Alive and kicking, and raising an army of savages out there to come in here and scalp you alive,'' Bushrod replied.

Mahaffery drew back to strike the frontiersman again. Sam said sharply, "Don't do that! I'll answer your questions even if my father won't.''

"Well! Smart man. What about Linfoot, then?''

"Hiram Linfoot is dead. He was killed by one of your men who shot him dead with a rifle. I killed the rifleman with a prospector's pick through the skull. Your other man, fat boy over yonder, didn't linger around long after he found the body. Got a little nervous, I guess.''

"But Linfoot *is* dead.''

"Yes. I hid his corpse with my own hands.''

Mahaffery seemed pleased to hear that. One less potential witness against him to worry about. It wasn't hard for Sam to read the direction of Mahaffery's thoughts. He was seeing before him an opportunity to end every threat against him and his men with a few quick blasts of powder and shot.

"Jordan.'' The speaker was Broadgrass, who had been standing silent for so long that the sound of his voice was mildly startling. "Where's the little girl? And the man named Nolen?''

Mahaffery looked around, frowning. "What the hell . . . ?"

Mongold and Yeager, equally surprised, swore in unison. Mahaffery wheeled to face Broadgrass. "How long have you been noticing them gone?"

"Just now noticed it." The bland way he said it made the truth of the statement seem doubtful.

"We've got to find them," Mahaffery said. "Bert, you and Lennis, get out there and—"

"No!" Yeager shouted. "Hell, no! I'm sick of this, Jordan! You strut around here like some little piece of royalty, sending us out to do this and that, to get shot and froze and every other kind of thing . . . I'll not do it anymore! This has to stop!"

Mahaffery yanked out his pistol and shoved it into Yeager's face. "Lennis, you're mighty nigh to making yourself useless."

Mongold stepped up. "Don't shoot him, Jordan. Please don't. I'll go look for them. At the very least I can see if there's tracks up toward the pass."

"The way this snow is falling, tracks may already be gone," Broadgrass said.

Mahaffery ignored Broadgrass, and looked at Mongold like a man admiring a faithful dog. "Good man, Bert. I need more like you."

"Don't go, Bert," Yeager said. "This man has gotten too many of us killed. It's time we start directing ourselves instead of letting him shove us around."

"Lennis," Mongold replied, "the reason we can't do that is the very thing you said: There's too few of us left. We can't go dividing up amongst ourselves now."

Yeager glowered and said no more. Broadgrass seemed privately amused, a man to the side of it all, watching but not acting as if he were really a part of it all. It was almost always that way with Conner Broadgrass.

*　　*　　*

Mahaffery wouldn't allow the Underhills to sit. They were forced to stand as they were, side by side, trophies on display in the center of the room, while Mahaffery paced about, clearly missing his liquor, and cursed and muttered under his breath. Broadgrass was smoking and looking bored, and Lennis Yeager looked like he could either explode or wilt away at any moment.

The sound of relatively distant rifle fire made everyone in the place snap to attention. Mahaffery swore softly and cocked his head, listening. The gunfire came from the vicinity of the pass.

He stomped over and shoved his face almost against Bushrod's. "Who'd you bring with you, old man? Who's up there?"

"I didn't bring a living soul with me. And your breath, son . . . smells to me like you ought to check for a rotten tooth or two."

Mahaffery hit Bushrod again, but once more the old man was able to deflect the worst of it with a deft turn of the head.

"I'm going to kill you, old man. Kill you with my own hands, and enjoy it immensely," Mahaffery said. "Maybe they'll put me in one of those almanacs. 'The Man Who Killed Bushrod Underhill.' I wouldn't mind that at all."

"Somebody's drawing near," Yeager said abruptly.

Broadgrass was looking out a window. "It's Mongold. Running back down."

"Anybody on his tail?"

"No. He's alone. Looks scared to death."

When the hefty outlaw burst into the room he was gasping like his heart and lungs were racing to see which would explode first. He turned a pallid face to Mahaffery. "Men . . . up there . . . tried to . . . take me . . ."

"Men? How many?"

"Two, maybe . . . three . . . got to catch . . . my breath . . ."

"Tried to take you—you mean they tried to kill you?"

"I believe they . . . wanted me hostage . . . but I fired at them . . . got away."

Mahaffery aimed a finger at Bushrod. "You're a lying old devil, and you'll die for it. I don't expect you're going to be sensible and tell me who you've brought with you."

"I believe maybe it was Jesus and the Twelve Disciples."

While Bushrod was busy being difficult, Sam was wondering quite seriously who *was* up at the pass. Maybe whoever it was hadn't followed Bushrod here, but had trailed the outlaws themselves. He had visions of bands of armed officers of the law closing in on that snowy pass, ready to move in and rescue the entrapped citizens of Texas Gulch.

Mahaffery had had enough of Bushrod's sarcastic tongue. He pulled his pistol out. For a terrible moment Sam was sure his father was about to be shot. But Mahaffery pulled back the pistol to club him instead. The first swing hit Bush in the temple and knocked him down on one knee, half stunned. The pistol rose again, the second blow aimed at Bushrod's forehead.

"No!" Sam bellowed, and threw himself between Mahaffery and his father. He groped for Mahaffery's arm, but the outlaw was fast, and diverted the direction of his swing. The pistol struck Sam on the jaw. He grunted in pain. Mahaffery struck him on the head with the follow-up blow, and Sam collapsed. As Bushrod, disoriented, reached out and tried to save the son who moments before had been trying to save him, the third blow hit Sam squarely on the top of the head, breaking the scalp to the bone. Sam pitched to one side, bleeding and unconscious.

Bushrod came to his feet, roaring in fury, and reached for Mahaffery's neck. Mahaffery dodged to the side. Bush would have caught him easily on a better day, but the blow to the temple still had him reeling. He staggered to the side, and Mahaffery managed to hit him a second time, on the back of the head. Bushrod fell to his hands and knees, his head hurt and spinning.

Conner Broadgrass strode up quickly, reached across

Bushrod, and grabbed the arm in which Mahaffery held the pistol.

"Jordan, I'm sorry, but you've just grown too darned aggravating." And with a skillful twist of the hand, he made Mahaffery howl in pain and let go of the pistol. Broadgrass caught it with his free left hand, let go of Mahaffery, and flipped the pistol through the air, catching it again with his right hand. He cocked it, stuck the pistol against the confused Mahaffery's chest, and shot him at point-blank range.

Mahaffery jerked and grunted, though the sound of the roar masked the sound he made. He staggered back, looking in shock at Broadgrass, then down at the bleeding hole in his chest.

"You've shot me!" he said, sounding meek and a lot like his late brother, Searl, in the latter's more childish moments.

"Yes, and I'm going to do it again," Broadgrass said. He dropped the expended pistol, drew his own from his belt, aimed at Mahaffery again, and put a second hole in the already dying outlaw's chest.

Mahaffery sighed slowly and sank to the floor, dying on nearly the same spot where Colfax had breathed his last.

Broadgrass calmly began reloading his pistol. "Sorry I had to do that, folks," he said to the group. "But I swear, I was beginning to grow mighty tired of that man."

CHAPTER THIRTY-TWO

Mongold and Yeager walked slowly, like dead men who'd been not quite fully reanimated, and gaped at the body of their former leader. Yeager lifted his face slowly and stared at Broadgrass, who calmly finished loading his pistol, stuck it back in his belt, then began reloading Mahaffery's.

Old Man Skinner began singing about Judgment Day again.

"You killed him!" Yeager said. "You killed Jordan!"

"Yep. And ain't it just so quiet and peaceful now?"

"Why the hell did you do it?"

"He deserved it. That man was going to do a Dehaven on us, Lennis. From the moment he left with that Dillow fellow, alone, I knew he wasn't to be trusted. He planned to take that gold for himself, and leave us up here. He'd have gotten back down that mountain again even if he'd had to roll in a snowball."

It took Yeager a moment to digest all that. As for Mongold, he was still staring at the corpse, rather stupidly. "But why'd you choose right now to kill him?"

"Because I'd put up with him as long as I could. And because we couldn't afford to have him get the rest of us killed like he's gotten all our companions killed. And he'd have done it, no doubt. There's somebody out there now, somebody we don't know. Somebody hostile, who's already tried to capture Bert and to kill him when they couldn't catch him. Facing that, men, it's time for a change of leadership and a change of tactics.''

Mongold shook his head. ''I can't believe he's dead. But he is. Look at him. Dead as a stone. Never got his gold back, neither.''

''No, he didn't, and neither will we,'' Broadgrass said. ''That gold is gone, gentlemen. We'd best forget about it and concentrate on getting out of this valley alive.''

Bushrod, meanwhile, was leaning over Sam, who remained unconscious. Examining the broken flesh on Sam's head, Bushrod winced, tore a strip from Sam's shirt, and began pressing on the wound, not too hard, but enough to begin to staunch the flow of blood.

The rest of the people of Texas Gulch were utterly silent, too taken aback and scared to speak. The only exception was Old Man Skinner, still in the midst of his brittle-sounding song.

Yeager gave Broadgrass a cold stare. ''So you were concerned that Mahaffery was willing to cheat us. What about you? You ran out of here, going to the battle, you said, running to help our men fighting out in the valley . . . but once you're out of sight, you turn and go after Mahaffery and Dillow, all by yourself. If you'd found Mahaffery with the gold, would you have brought it back here? Or would it have been *you* trying to make it out of the mountains with all the gold for yourself?''

''I don't believe you trust me, Lennis.''

''I don't.''

''Then you're a wise man, for the wise man doesn't trust anyone without proof. But this time I'm afraid you'll just have to. I would have brought back that gold, Lennis. I swear it. But don't ask me to prove it, for there's no way I can.''

''I think you're looking out for yourself and yourself alone.''

''Then I advise you to cooperate with me, and stay close.

For if I can save myself, maybe I can save you, too."

That seemed to make sense to Yeager, because his antagonistic tone faded a little. "Very well. I don't see much choice, now that you've made the choice for us. But what about these people?"

"Ah, yes. These people. What to do with these people?"

Art Bolton stood. "You've treated us like slaves, like animals. You've talked about us as things and not people. But by heaven, if you seek to murder us, you'll find me, at least, fighting you to the end."

"And me," Joe Skinner said.

"And me." This came, surprisingly to all, from Letitia Colfax.

"Shut up, all of you," Broadgrass said. "I have no desire nor plan to kill any of you."

The looks of surprise that came onto every face were instantly followed by irrepressible expressions of relief.

"What are we going to do, then?" Mongold asked.

"We need these people alive. Whoever is out there will be more restrained with innocent folks to be considered."

"So we're still just pawns to you," Bolton said.

"My friend, in this life every one of us are pawns, trying not to get knocked off the board. But suffice it to say I'm not Jordan Mahaffery. I'm Conner Broadgrass, and though I'll kill when I must, I do try to avoid it."

Bushrod left Sam's side, came to his feet, and faced Broadgrass. "Sir, even though you shot to death the man who would have likely beat myself and my son to death, if he could have, I do want to tell you that I regard you and your ilk there as nothing more than worthless, murdering, thieving, godless, damnable, becursed pieces of dung not fit to breathe the air of this world. I have no regard for you at all. But I have a bargain to offer you."

"Coming from the famous Bushrod Underhill, a bargain is no doubt worth hearing," Broadgrass said, apparently not at all offended by Bushrod's words. "Speak on."

"Whoever is out there is not going to let you leave this

valley by the pass. That's evidenced by the fact that they've already shot at fat boy over there. But there's another way out of this valley, the way by which I came in. I can lead you out again, safely. But I'll not do so unless you pledge to me to leave these people here behind, unharmed.''

"I may need some of these people for hostages, Mr. Underhill, in case we're pursued."

"You'll have me. I'll be your hostage."

"You will be, that's true. But you'll also be our guide, and I'll want to make sure you have the right kind of incentive not to lead us astray. But your bargain interests me, and I'm inclined to take it, or a high percentage of it. Tell you what, sir: I'll take you for my hostage, and Mr. Mongold and Mr. Yeager will take one hostage each, of their own choice. The rest of these people may remain here, in this building, tightly tied up. They'll not be tied long; whoever's out there will free them.''

"I'll not have you take hostages other than me. No bargain," Bushrod replied.

"Mr. Underhill, you have no choice," Broadgrass said firmly.

Bushrod stared at him. "I suppose I don't," he admitted.

"So when do we leave?" Yeager asked.

"Shortly before first light," Bushrod replied.

"But what if whoever's up there comes down tonight?"

"Then I suppose you'll have a battle on your hands."

"Then I say we leave now," Mongold said. "Don't give them a chance at us at all. Let them find us long gone when they come down here."

"Going to be getting dark . . . and cold," Bushrod said.

"How long to get us out of this valley?" Broadgrass asked. "Could you have us out before dark?"

Bush thought it over a few moments, calculating. "I could. It would cut it close."

"I agree with Bert," Broadgrass said. "We don't wait. We don't know how many are up there in that pass, or what

they have in mind. I have no desire to find this place sur-
rounded come morning."

"Then we'll leave now," Bush said.

"You took quite a blow to the head. Can you do it?"

"I've had worse. I can do whatever needs doing."

Broadgrass turned to Mongold. "Bert, find some rope.
We've got a whole gang of folks here who need tying up."

"You really have to do that?" Bushrod asked.

"Indeed we do," Broadgrass replied.

They'd made Bushrod tie up his own son. He hated them
while he did it, but he did it all the same. Few times in his
life had Bushrod Underhill found situations where he felt
almost no sense of control, so this one sat quite uncomfortably with him.

Sam had looked awfully pitiful to Bush while they left
the lodge house. He lay on the floor, semiconscious, his
head raw and bloody. Sam's face had already been bruised
from his ordeal in that pit the first night of this terrible
adventure. All in all, Sam looked almost like a fit candidate
for a coffin.

Broadgrass had had them sneak out of the lodge house,
using the same window that Daniel Chase had crawled
through a time or two. By careful maneuvering and use of
landscape cover, they'd managed to keep the lodge house
between them and the pass, hiding their escape from whoever was up there. Once far enough into the valley, they no
longer had to worry about being seen. Broadgrass relaxed
and turned the guidance over to Bushrod.

Bushrod wasn't inclined to betray Broadgrass, not with
Marica Bolton and Leora Winkle also along as hostages,
being prodded and threatened by Yeager.

After a time of mostly silent, concentrated travel, Broadgrass asked Bushrod, "How long will it take us to climb
out of this second pass?"

"It's high and difficult. I can't assure you we'll make it
out before dark, especially with the clouds as heavy as they

are. It'll get dark quicker with the clouds. We'd best press on.''

"We will," Broadgrass said. "But I'm afraid there has to be one delay.''

"Why?"

"I'm surprised your sharp eye hasn't noticed that Mr. Mongold left us momentarily a little while back. We need to wait here to give him time to catch back up with us.''

Indeed Mongold was gone. Bushrod was ashamed of himself for not having noticed. But a departure of one of the outlaws wasn't something he'd anticipated. "Where did he go?" Bushrod asked.

Broadgrass smiled. "A little something was forgotten at the lodge house. He had to run back to take care of it.''

A wave of dread rolled through Bushrod. He looked back the way they'd come.

The first trails of dark smoke were beginning to stream into the gray and white sky.

Bushrod stared. He couldn't even find words, and was too numb with shock for tears.

Broadgrass looked at him with an expression of sympathy that wasn't entirely fake. "I am sorry it had to come to that," he said. "But given all the crimes those people have witnessed, we had no choice but to minimize our risks. They had to be disposed of.''

Bushrod watched the rising smoke, fury growing inside him.

"Don't worry . . . there was no suffering. Bert had clear directions. Slip back in, make a few deft blows to their heads, enough to knock them out or kill them, then set the fire and flee. If any of them happen to still be alive, Mr. Underhill, they're not feeling a thing. Meanwhile, the fire is a distraction to keep the attention of whoever has come after us.''

"I'll see you pay for this, Broadgrass," Bushrod said, voice choking. *Sam, have I let you die, too? Just like*

Danny? Just like Zeke? "I'll see you pay ten-score for the wickedness you've done."

"Now, don't get dramatic on me, sir. You've lived a long time. You know that a man's success or failure doesn't hang on his morality, but on his cleverness. That was Mahaffery's failing. Clever in planning robberies, clever in general as a leader and strategist . . . just not quite clever enough. If I play my hand properly, there's no reason I should have to pay for anything."

"I'll kill you."

"Now, Mr. Underhill, no threats! Would you want to have to watch me put a pistol ball through the pretty head of one of these women? You know I'd do it."

The smoke was rising higher and faster, and now Mongold appeared, loping back toward them at as fast a jog as his weight and the snow accumulation would allow.

Marica and Leora, just now coming to understand what had occurred back at the lodge house, bowed their heads and cried. Bushrod had to struggle not to do the same.

Mongold was red-faced and out of breath. Bushrod eyed him hatefully, hoping the big man's heart would burst here and now. But after some panting, Mongold was able to converse. He actually seemed reinvigorated.

"Didn't take you long, Bert," Broadgrass said. "Did it all go as we'd planned?"

"Indeed it did."

"Are you sure? I'd expected you to be gone longer."

"I'm quick with killing work."

"You clubbed them before you lit the fire, like I told you to do?"

"Every one of them. Blow to the back of the head with the flat of a hatchet." He looked at Bushrod. "Except for Sam Underhill. Him I used my knife on. I'm afraid he died a little slower and harder than the others."

Bushrod lunged at Mongold, knocked him down, and had his hands around the fat neck in an instant. Broadgrass grabbed Marica, pulled his knife, and put it to her throat. "Underhill! Let him go, or she dies!"

Bushrod, with a great groan of suffering that went deep as his soul, let go of Mongold and rolled off. He came to his feet, breathing hard, and stared through wet eyes at the rising billows of smoke back at Texas Gulch.

Mongold got up, rubbing his neck. "You'll die for that, Underhill. I'll make you squeal like your boy did."

"Enough, Bert," Broadgrass said. "We've wasted more time than we could really afford. Underhill, move us on. I'm ready to get out of this valley."

CHAPTER THIRTY-THREE

Sam Underhill, coughing and choking and very much alive, gritted his teeth, steeled himself against the pain to come, and with a great effort wrenched his right hand free of the ropes that tied it. He'd tensed his wrists while Bushrod tied him up—as loosely as he could get away with—and that had given Sam a slight amount of slack, though not enough to save a good part of his hide when he actually had to pull his hand free.

The bloodied, abraded right hand cleared the rope, and he pushed up, pulling his left hand around and making quick work of the knot. The ropes around his ankles were harder to deal with, and he struggled to keep himself focused on the task amid the rising screams of panic around him.

The fire had come as a surprise, though Sam would later realize he should have expected something like this. The only thing he couldn't figure was why they hadn't killed everyone in the lodge house before they set the blaze, just to make sure nobody got out alive. Maybe whoever had been assigned to the task had simply turned coward and taken the shorter, safer route, figuring that smoke and fire would do the dirty task for him without requiring him to linger under possible endangerment from whoever was up beyond the pass.

While the lodge house filled with smoke and panic, Sam

finished untying his feet, and rose. He went first to Art Bolton and freed him, then the pair of them hurried to untie the terrified, screaming Colfax women, both of whom bolted straight for the door, only to find it blocked closed from outside. New howls of terror escaped them.

Fire licked through the floor on the far end of the lodge house. Sam and Art hurried to free others, who in turn helped their neighbors, and soon all were free. Sam turned to the nearest window, which had also been closed and blocked from the outside, but whoever had done it had worked hurriedly, and it was easy to ram the shutter open. Fresh air spilled in while smoke spilled out, but the inrush of oxygen made the fire rise faster, too.

"Out! Get us *out*!" America Colfax screamed, pounding the door with her fists.

"Out the window, then!" Sam said.

But just as he spoke, something scraped and bumped loudly on the outside of the door. America Colfax screeched harshly and jumped back. "They've come back again! Oh, Lord, they've come back again to kill us all!"

Sam had his doubts that the outlaws would return, but just in case, he picked up a big stick of firewood and held it ready to use as a club.

The door swung open, letting in light and cold and snow and fresh air. Sam gazed at the figures in the doorway, dropped the firewood, and said, "I'll be! Who'd have figured it would be you?"

The newcomers were instantly knocked to the ground outside. America Colfax had bolted out of the lodge house like a panicked cow tearing out of a burning barn, and she was not a small woman.

As the snowfall intensified, the going got harder. The clouds were thick as old syrup, spitting their frozen contents toward the earth but seemingly growing no lighter for shedding the burden. The threat of coming darkness pushed them harder, and Broadgrass, for the first time since he'd come here, was beginning to show signs of strain.

"We need to move faster," he said. "How much farther, old man?"

"Not far. But tell me why I should even cooperate with a man who had my own son murdered, and a houseful of other good people besides?"

"Because if you don't, there'll be three other people murdered: these two women and yourself."

"And if I do lead you out? What happens to us then?"

"Then you live. You have my word."

"I had your word that you'd spare the lives of those back in the big cabin."

"So what do you propose? Die for a certainty here, along with these lovely ladies, or risk trusting me and maybe living once we're past this valley?"

Bushrod stared at him for several moments. "Come on," he said. "I'll show you the way out."

"Are we almost there?"

Bushrod's eye scanned the high bluffs and ridges around them, then stopped for a moment. He was sure he saw someone up on a ledge, in the snow, huddled back against the bluff . . . but a closer look convinced him otherwise. This was just a bit of colored stone, blown free of snow by the hard wind . . .

. . . And he remembered. Sam's story, told in detail. A hunt for the two missing children, a ledge with a colored stone that fooled his eye and led him into a time-wasting climb, and then a fall from that bluff into a pit where there was a cavern entrance, and the corpse of a dead Forty-niner . . .

All these things passed through Bush's mind in no more than three seconds, and by the time a fourth had passed, he knew what he would do. Glancing quickly down, he scanned the base of the bluff, and saw the mouth of the pit that had been Sam's temporary prison.

Another glance up, a taking of measure and bearings . . . yes. Yes, it should work.

"Up there," he said. "There's a cavern up there, impossible to see from below but big enough to walk through. It leads through the ridge and out into a hidden pass on the far side, and that pass leads all the way through the wall of the basin out into the mountains."

"We'll have to climb all the way up there?" Broadgrass said.

"'Fraid so."

Broadgrass swore loudly.

"You'll have to leave your rifles here below," Bushrod said. "You'll never make that climb with them in hand. Nothing but pistols for you from here on."

Broadgrass clearly hadn't thought of that. He frowned, pursed his lips, then said, "Pistols will have to be enough."

"Conner," Mongold said in a rather small-sounding voice, "I can't make that kind of climb. I'm too big. Too fat."

Broadgrass turned on him. "Is that right, Bert? You sure you can't make it?"

Mongold looked up at the ledge with sorrowful eyes, and nodded. "I'm sure."

"I suppose that makes you useless baggage, then," Broadgrass said. He pulled out his pistol and shot Mongold in the head. The outlaw died without ever having had time to realize what was happening.

The echo of the shot was swallowed by silence that lingered a few moments.

"If I was a murderous, worthless scoundrel like you, I wouldn't have been averse to doing that myself," Bush said quietly, eyeing the corpulent corpse. "That man murdered my son."

"In other circumstances, I might have allowed you the privilege," Broadgrass replied.

Bushrod snapped his head up and showed Broadgrass two piercing eyes. "I hold you as responsible as he was. He may have lit the flame, but you gave the direction.''

Broadgrass gave Bush no more than a brief, flickering smile. He went to Mongold and removed the fat man's pistol, which he raised and pointed at Yeager.

''What about you, Lennis?'' Broadgrass asked. ''Are you a climber?''

Yeager nodded firmly. ''A good climber, Conner. Believe me, I'll not slow us down.''

Broadgrass seemed satisfied with that answer. He wheeled to face Bushrod.

''Underhill, hear me: if at any point along the way I begin to suspect you've lied to me, or that you're leading me toward anything but a way out of this valley, then you'll be a dead man. No matter what happens to me or to anyone else, you'll be a dead man.''

There was a pain in Bushrod Underhill's soul that would have allowed him to reply with full honesty that he didn't think it made much difference to him whether he lived or died. There were two dead grandsons back in Texas whose memories tormented him. And now his own son, hardly found before he was lost, lay inside a burning cabin back in the mining camp. What did it matter whether Bushrod Underhill went on?

Bush said none of this. He merely nodded.

''Let's continue,'' Broadgrass said.

The lodge house was fully engulfed now, but devoid of human inhabitants. Bert Mongold, anything but a perfectionist, having only half done his assigned task, thus had failed to really do it at all. Every surviving inhabitant of Texas Gulch had gotten out of the lodge house well before the worst of the flames took it over.

The heat was actually pleasant, and given that everyone there had come to perceive the big cabin as no more than a prison, no one mourned the loss of the building.

Sam Underhill, with a blood-crusted, broken scalp and a very bad headache, paused beside Durham and Cordell Underhill, his brothers, watching the flames licking at the logs. Their reunion had been joyous, but there was no time for standing about a moment longer. These brothers had tracked their despondent father all the way from Underhill, Texas, to Texas Gulch, California, and were not about to lose his trail now.

"It'll be dangerous," Sam was saying. "There's three armed men, all desperate, and they have two women hostages along with Pap. They'd kill any one of them at the slightest provocation, if they felt it would help them. The leader for now is a man named Broadgrass, and he's cold and pure mean."

"They can't be out of the valley yet," Cordell said. "The snow's too heavy. Durham and I thought we'd not make it up these mountains, and it's worsened since then."

"No, I doubt they're out of the valley. I also doubt whether Pap will ever take them out. He's bound to have seen the fire at the lodge house. He probably believes right now that I'm dead. Given his state of mind—and Lord, Durham, you don't know how sorry to my soul I am over what happened with your sons—he might decide to bring it all to an end, even if it brings him to an end right along with it."

"He's that bad off?" Durham asked.

"Yes. I've never seen him like he is now."

Durham, with rising urgency, said, "Come on, Cordell. Let's find their trail."

"I'll come, too," said Joe Skinner.

"Have you weapons?" Cordell asked him.

"No," Skinner replied. "They gathered all our weapons when they took us hostage. What ones they didn't take with them, they took the caps from, and emptied the powder in the snow."

"That's no good. I don't know there's much to be gained by your following, if you're unarmed."

"I for one, *will* come along, weapons or not," Art Bolton said. "They have my daughter."

"Then indeed you must come," Durham said. "Sam, are you clear-headed enough after that blow to keep up with us?"

"I am. If I prove not to be, I'll drop behind and let you go on."

"Fine. Let's go get them. Night will fall before we know it."

CHAPTER THIRTY-FOUR

They crept along the rocky and uneven ledge, which varied in width from two feet to five or more. Bushrod was in the lead, followed by the women, then Yeager, with Broadgrass at the rear. Interesting positioning, Bush thought. Broadgrass had insisted on being last, and Bushrod suspected it was so he could keep Yeager in view at all times. Broadgrass had shot Yeager's partner, after all, and had reason to be wary of Yeager.

"Not too far ahead!" Broadgrass yelled at Bushrod as they edged around a hump on the bluff that made it quite difficult to hang on. "I want you where I can see you!"

"What's the matter, Broadgrass?" Bushrod returned. "You afraid I'll skip right through the mountain and get away from you?"

"Just shut up and lead us on . . . and when you get to that cave mouth, stop before you go in. Let us all catch up together."

Bush's eyes scanned the terrain at the base of the slope. The depths of snow piled there made it hard to make out details, but with that distinctive colored stone ahead as his landmark, Bush was able to know he was near what he was looking for . . . and yes, there it was below. A black, upturned opening at the base of the cliff, encircled by snow like the open mouth of a hoary-bearded old man. Bush studied its location, the bluff above it, locating the spot on the ledge—the place was mere feet ahead at this point—just above the opening.

He had plans for that spot, but it all depended on positioning himself and Broadgrass right above it, something that wouldn't happen the way they were all aligned right now.

He had to think of something, quickly. In moments he'd be past the right point on the ledge. What he had in mind might work elsewhere on the ledge, without benefit of that pit down there, but on the other hand it might not. The snow was drifted so deeply at the base of the bluff that it would cushion a falling man, perhaps enough to protect a man from death or even serious injury.

When Broadgrass went over, Bush wanted him to hit hard. Fatally hard. And in case he didn't hit fatally hard, to be in a place from which he could not easily exit. And if the same happened to Bush himself, well, so be it. Death would be an escape from grief and ghosts and the pain he'd tried to run from, but which seemed always to catch him anyway.

But with three people between himself and Broadgrass on this narrow ledge, how could he hope to get Broadgrass where he needed him?

At that moment, fate lent a hand, though not in a way that Bushrod would have desired. Beneath the feet of Marica Bolton, a stone moved. Her legs went out from beneath her; her feet went over the rim of the ledge and she fell, clawing at the frozen, rocky ground.

"Marica!" Leora Winkle cried out. "Hold on . . . I'll reach you!"

Marica *was* holding on, her face twisted in fright, her nails digging into the dirty, trampled snow, finding a claw-grip in the gritty, graveled surface of the ledge. The ledge was narrow where she'd fallen, and the entire lower half of her body extended into empty space.

Bushrod turned and began working his way back toward

her, planning to reach down and give her his hand. But
Leora was quicker, putting her own hand out before Bush
could get there.

Marica reached gratefully for Leora's hand, holding herself for those few moments with only her left hand gripping
the ledge . . .

Her grip gave way. What had felt like the rough surface
of the ledge itself had been only loose stones frozen in place.
Her weight and grip were greater in strength than the feeble
cement of ice that held the stones in place, and with a
scream Marica was pulled back from the ledge by the weight
of her hips and legs, and she fell.

"Marica!" Leora yelled, her cry mixing with that of the
plunging woman.

Bushrod winced and felt his heart skip a beat. No. No.
He craned his neck, looking over the edge.

Marica was down there, in a drift of snow, lying still.
From what he'd heard and seen, he didn't think she'd struck
the ledge itself on the way down, but he couldn't be sure.

Leora was in a panic. "Oh, dear Lord! Oh, Marica . . . is
she alive?"

"Careful, there," Bushrod warned her. "Don't go falling
after her."

"Can you see her?"

"I can," Bushrod said. "She hit in the snow, a heavy
drift. She's not moving, but she can't have struck as hard
as she would have if there was naught to cushion her."

"What if she's dead?"

"She may be. And if she is, as far as I'm concerned, we
can credit our gun-toting friends with another murder."

Yeager turned slowly, hugging the wall, and asked Broadgrass, "What do you want to do? Leave her?"

"Can you tell if she's dead?"

Yeager looked over, cautiously. "She ain't moving."

Broadgrass swore, frowning and thinking. "Can you get
in position to put a bullet through her, to make sure she's
gone?"

Leora turned so fast she almost fell off herself. "You'd shoot an injured woman in cold blood?"

"I'd shoot my own sister in cold blood if it was necessary."

Yeager said, "Conner, I don't think I want to shoot her."

"You're developing a conscience suddenly, Lennis?"

"I'm tired of all this. I just want out of this valley. I want to go as far away from here as I can."

"These people have seen too much, Lennis. You want to leave them to trouble us with the law later on?"

"We'll never see these people again if we run far enough," Yeager said. "I've been thinking . . . we could leave California. Then none of it would matter. We'd never be caught away from California."

"I have no ambition to leave California," Broadgrass replied. "I've been here too long." He looked down over the ledge. "But I suppose we needn't shoot her. If she's not dead now, she will be soon. Too bad, really. I had plans for that young beauty."

Leora exploded. "You're a beast! You're not even a man! Is that all a human being is to you? Something to use, or to abandon?"

"Ma'am, I grew up in a home where I knew only being used and being abandoned. It's the way of life that I learned, and the way I accept."

"Let me go down to her. I want to make sure she's alive." Tears came. "And I want to find my daughter again."

"Sorry, ma'am. But I need you. You provide protection . . . and perhaps some needed warmth on cold nights."

Leora looked down at Marica, whose body was already being covered by snow. "She moved! I saw her move! She's alive . . . please, let me go to her and help her. We're never going to be a threat to you! We'll never see each other again . . . and besides, I've already decided: if God allows me to live through this, and if He allows me to find my daughter again, I'm taking her back to Texas. There's been nothing here for me but sorrow.''

"Listen to her, Broadgrass," Bushrod said. "Do something decent. For the sake of that poor woman down there, and for the sake of Leora's little girl, let her go. You still have me for a hostage."

"She could cause me trouble later on."

Lennis Yeager said, "Well, Conner, you got to consider that the little girl has gotten away, and also that Nolen fellow. So even if we killed both these women, there's still those around who could identify us. So what difference does it make if we spare them? Let her go down and help that woman if she can. They're both likely to die up here before the springtime, anyway, once we're gone.''

"I don't know what's gotten into you, Lennis. This softening is a dangerous change."

Yeager glared. "So what will you do? Shoot me, like you did poor old Mongold?"

"Would you force me to?"

Yeager pulled out his pistol and aimed it at Broadgrass. "I say this woman goes down to help the other below, if she can. We go on and leave them behind. I say there's been enough bad done in this valley, and that we do no more."

"Why don't you preach us a sermon, Reverend Yeager?"

Yeager ignored Broadgrass. "Come on," he said to Leora. "You can work your way past me and go back down."

"Thank you, sir," she said. "God bless you for this."

"And, Conner, you let her go past you, too. And if you shove her off, I'll shoot you dead."

Broadgrass was looking at Yeager not with anger, but amusement. "What is this, Lennis? A mutiny?"

"No. Just something that ought to be done. All I want is to get out of this valley alive, forget that gold, and go on."

Leora was moving back toward Yeager, who kept his eye on Broadgrass and his pistol leveled. When she reached Yeager, he pulled in close to the wall, allowing her to move around him. It seemed a likely time for Broadgrass to act if he planned to do so, yet he did nothing but stand there with a bemused half-smile on his face, as if he were a patient schoolmaster secretly laughing at the silly rebellion of some petty schoolboy.

She got past Yeager safely, and now crept toward Broadgrass, who smiled at her. This was a highly dangerous moment, because her positioning blocked Yeager's potential line of fire at Broadgrass. Just now she was at Broadgrass's mercy; he could shoot her dead with ease.

But for some reason, he did not. She came closer, closer, and finally reached him.

"You'll let me around you?" she asked.

"Of course I will."

Leora drew in a deep breath, went to him, stepped toward the edge of the ledge just enough to clear him, and passed by him as quickly as she safely could, her face inches from his. He smiled and winked, made a kissing sound, then a little false lunge as if to push her off.

He didn't push her, though, and she went on, back down the way they'd come up.

Bush, relieved, prayed for her and for Marica Bolton below. Then he turned his concentration on the situation as it was.

Nobody between him and Broadgrass now except for Yeager.

"Gentlemen, it appears it's just us," Broadgrass said. "Lennis, please put that pistol away. I'm not going to try to hurt you, and God knows there's no longer any gang to lead. Just you, me, and our hostage."

Bushrod was watching Marica below. He could no longer see Leora. He hoped she would get to the base of the bluff and down to where Marica lay in time to help the injured young woman.

"Guess we should move on," Yeager said.

Bush looked down at the gaping hole below and slightly ahead, then calculated once more the place on the ledge where he would need to make his move if it was to work. Somehow he had to bring Broadgrass within his reach at that exact point. But there was still the problem of Yeager, inconveniently positioned between him and Broadgrass.

What the devil. Perhaps he'd be forced to take both of them down with him. Both deserved it. Yeager's turn toward mercy where Leora Winkle and Marica Bolton were concerned wasn't nearly enough to atone for his part in the sins already committed by him and his ilk at Texas Gulch.

An idea came.

"I wouldn't go on with him behind you," Bushrod said to Yeager.

"Why?"

"If I was you, I'd want him in front for the same reason he wants you in front. So he can keep an eye on you."

Yeager made strange expressions as the snow and cold wind battered his face. "Underhill's right," he said to Broadgrass. "I don't trust you back there. We've gone this far with me before you. Now let's got the rest of the way with me behind."

Broadgrass didn't look quite as poised as usual. "If you think I'm going to pass you on this ledge, you're a fool."

"He aims to shoot you like he shot Mongold," Bushrod said.

Yeager brandished his pistol at Broadgrass. "Move on up here. Get in front of me."

"Lennis, I'm not going to shoot you. You have my word."

"And you have mine that I won't shove you down off this ledge when you go past."

Broadgrass flared his nostrils and narrowed one eye, revealing an anger that he was trying to keep hidden. "I'll not pass you."

"I'll kill you! Underhill can lead me out of this valley without you!"

Bushrod looked below. Marica moved again, but the cold snow would quickly rob her of warmth and life. Still no sign of Leora. He supposed she was still making her way down the bluff.

"You'd best shoot him, Yeager," Bushrod said. "You've crossed the line now. He shot Mongold just because he couldn't climb a bluff."

Yeager was trembling, partly from the cold, partly from anger . . . and fear. Broadgrass had always been an intimidating man, like Mahaffery, but in a different fashion. As much as he wanted to kill him right now, Broadgrass was somehow keeping him from it with no more than the coldness of his gaze.

Bush had seen this kind of failure in men before, and knew it would be the end of Yeager. Sure enough, Broadgrass drew back suddenly, letting the curve of the bluff come between him and Yeager. Yeager, panicking, fired. The shot ricocheted off the stone into the emptiness. Yeager dropped his pistol, one of two he'd carried away from Texas Gulch, and scrambled for the second one.

Bushrod dropped to minimize the size of the target he made in case the inevitable answering shot from Broadgrass also missed and hurtled his way.

Broadgrass did not miss. He appeared again, pistol drawn, and shot Yeager through the stomach. Yeager had freed his second pistol and cocked back the lock hammer, but hadn't aimed the weapon yet by the time that Broadgrass's pistol ball tore through him. Reflexively he squeezed the trigger and fired upward.

The ball tore through a great, overhanging mass of heavy snow that had collected on the sloping stone face above the ledge.

The equivalent of a few barrow-loads of snow poured down around Bushrod. He glanced up just as Yeager was pitching over the ledge to fall, dead, mere yards from where Marica lay.

Bushrod might have found a chance to attack an unarmed Broadgrass right then, had not Broadgrass, like Yeager, had the foresight to arm himself with a backup pistol. He put

away the emptied one quickly and drew the loaded one in
its place, grinning at Bushrod through the smoke of his pistol shot, the echo of which was only now coming back,
snow-muffled, from across the wide valley.

"Just me and you now, old man," he said.

A little more snow dumped down on Bushrod, and he
heard a strange, ominous noise . . . a kind of heavy, deep,
groaning that was quite different from anything he'd heard
before.

He comprehended quickly what it was, and the opportunity it gave him.

Bush drew in a deep, groaning breath, clapped a hand
dramatically over his chest, and sank back onto the ledge,
gasping wildly.

"What's the matter with you, old fellow?"

Bush, still clinging to his chest, began dragging himself
farther along the ledge, seemingly trying to come to his feet,
then falling down again.

"What the hell are you doing?" Broadgrass yelled, coming after him. "Are you sick?"

"Sick . . ." Bushrod said. "Hurting . . . my chest . . ."

More snow slid off the slope above. Bush hurried. There
it was, below . . . the open hole. Days ago a prison for Sam
Underhill . . . now to be a burial place for Bushrod Underhill
and Conner Broadgrass.

Bush looked toward where Marica lay. To his delight he
saw Marica actually rising, and Leora reaching her. The
snow into which Marica had fallen had cushioned her suf-
ficiently, it seemed, to let her escape crippling injury. He
breathed a prayer of thanks as he watched the two women
join and begin a clumsy scramble back down through the
drifting snow toward the safer levels away from the bluff.

Good. Maybe they'd get far enough away before the snow
avalanched down.

Broadgrass reached Bushrod. "Old man, what's happening here?"

Bushrod looked up at him. "We're going to die, me and you, together."

"Die? Maybe you, old man. Not me."

A loud, low-level rumbling from high above made Bush look skyward and smile.

"It's the end, Mr. Broadgrass. Judgment Day. May Jesus pardon our sins and have mercy on our souls at this, the moment of our death."

Broadgrass seemed to comprehend, but it was far too late. He looked up as the great wall of white came down upon them. At the same moment, Bushrod, still half-lying on the very brink of the ledge, grabbed Broadgrass around the knees and heaved both of them over the side just as the snow hit them.

They rode the crest of the avalanche downward, the open mouth of the pit growing bigger and closer. Then everything was whiteness and darkness all together, and the snow descended and filled the pit and the two men who had plunged into it were seen no more.

Leora Winkle and Marica Bolton reached the edge of the great snowdrift into which Marica had fallen. It had almost proven too great a barrier to allow Leora to reach her, but effort and stubbornness had availed and the pair had gotten just far enough away from the bluff to miss being swept under the snow mass as it fell. Lennis Yeager—still alive after his gunshot and plunge, groping and bleeding and hurting, hadn't been so lucky. The snow had buried him deep.

Battered, frightened, and weeping, the women moved through the snow, looking back to see the ledge along which they'd moved before now devoid of humans.

"Poor Mr. Bushrod!" Leora said. "Poor man!"

"Take me back, Leora," Marica said. "Maybe some of them are still alive."

"Poor Mr. Bushrod," Leora said again. "What a good, good man. God rest him."

"Yes," Marica said. "And God help us."

CHAPTER THIRTY-FIVE

Bushrod opened his eyes, but it made no difference. All was as utterly black as before. He was lying on his belly, face turned to the side, grit and gravel and very cold rock beneath him.

He lay there for at least a minute before he managed to believe that he was really still alive. How could it be? He'd fallen far, with a world of heavy snow piling down after him.

But here he was. And the most amazing thing was that he could breathe.

Whether he could move, though, was another question, and the truth was he was afraid to try. He'd seen a man once who had been paralyzed from the middle of his back to his feet, and had prayed that such a fate would never be his. And what scared him right now was that he didn't think he felt his lower body at all. Just a general, numb pressure, incredibly heavy.

His arms. That's what he'd start with. He shrugged his right shoulder, successfully, then tried his right hand. That worked, too, and to his joy, he felt his fingers scratching against his thigh while he did so. So there was feeling in his lower body after all . . . the numbness, he surmised, came from incredible cold in which his legs were encased.

His left arm worked, too; he found it was stretched out

beside him, but pulled in closer to his body when he asked
it to. He felt his own face, detecting no major cuts, no pits
or holes in his skull.

His ability to breathe remained the greatest mystery. The
amount of snow that had fallen in atop him and Broadgrass
by all rights should have crushed them flat. Yet he wasn't
crushed, and even had open space around him. He tried to
make sense of it.

As he lay there, thinking, details of what Sam had told
him of his own entrapment in this pit began to come to
mind. Sam had mentioned a cavern entrance in the pit, with
a shielding overcrop of stone above it. As best Bushrod
could guess, he must have fallen in such a way that he was
rolled by the incoming snow beneath that outcrop of stone.
It was a theory that fit the facts. The stone above would
keep snow off him, and allow him an air space. It would
explain why the upper portion of his body was not buried
in snow while his hips and legs were.

It was all surmise, of course, for he was blind in this utter
darkness and could verify nothing by sight.

But there might be one way to tell. He recalled how Sam
had told him of moving that corpse he'd found. He'd
dragged it away from its original place and laid it out in the
entrance of the cave at the base of the pit.

If Bush was where he thought he was, he ought to be able
to locate that corpse by feel, even if he couldn't see it.

He extended his right arm slowly, feeling around him. All
he found was snow and cold rock and gravel. Extending his
arm up relative to his head, he groped in the area ahead of
him . . . and his hand touched something that felt like old
fabric. A bit more exploration, and he closed his hand
around something brittle and sticklike, and encased in loose
cloth.

A bone. A human bone, probably part of a leg, still
clothed. Bush felt like crying in relief. Merely to have some
sense of where he was, and why he was alive, was remarkably moving.

Die he yet might in this place, but at least he would know where he was, and that a son he had loved from birth had been in this same place, too. To know this mattered very deeply to Bushrod Underhill.

He closed his hand around the bone and held on. To touch something that he could identify, even something as lifeless and morbid as the bony leg of a leathery corpse, was a connection to the world he'd left behind when he plunged into this dark hole. In its own odd way, it was a comfort.

For a long time Bushrod remained in this posture, unmoving, his eyes open and gazing into a darkness blacker than ink. Against that black screen his mind began to play images of importance to him. His wife, as she had been when she was young. His first children, small and pink and crying, then older, growing strong and making him proud. Old friends, long gone, such as Cephas Frank, and Becker Israel, and the old man Daniel Boone.

And again, his wife. Lorry, the strong, the beautiful, the faithful and loving. Lorry, not as the young girl she had been, but the woman she was now, the wonderful and grand person whom Bush loved more than any other, and who loved him in turn more than she loved herself.

Lying there in that darkness, waiting for death, Bushrod found his mind turning again toward life. He thought of Durham's sons, one dead by the most terrible of accidents, the other by his own hand. Sorrowful, horrific, saddening . . . but unchangeable. What had happened had happened. Bush could cry over it, regret it, blame himself for it . . . but that changed nothing. Healed nothing. It only brought more sorrow to others he loved.

Lorry. Dear Lorry. How could he think of dying while she yet lived? How could he turn away from the greatest treasure he had ever possessed, or ever could?

A cave, opening before him. Sometimes caves went nowhere. Sometimes they led to exits. Ways out to the world beyond.

It was a world that Bushrod realized still mattered to him.

"Lorry, I'll try," he said. "I'll do my best to live."

He put his hands before him and tried to scoot himself forward. The effort was excruciating, and he realized how heavy the weight upon his lower body was, and also how cold and numb his lower extremities were. He gave up his first attempt without being sure whether he'd moved at all.

After a few moments' rest, he tried again. Slowly he went forward, feeling his legs moving under the dead weight of the snow. He dragged twice more, and advanced more than a foot.

A little more rest, and he tried again. This time he got his legs fully out from under the snow. He reached up and determined that he did have room to sit upright beneath the protective stone overhang. Making the attempt, he was rewarded with success. It was odd, sitting on legs he couldn't feel, but at least those legs moved and lived, and the longer he sat, the more feeling began to return. He bowed his head and said a prayer of thanks.

Light. He needed light. Reaching into his pocket, he found phosphorus matches. Hard to tell by feel how dry they were, so he tried one. Nothing. The second match, however, struck fire.

So black was it, and so accustomed had his eyes grown to seeing nothing, that the mere flare of the match made him wince and blink. The brief light bathed the interior of his little chamber with illumination. He saw the snowy wall that blocked him in, the stone above him, the dead man laid flat on the gravelly floor, the dark hole of the cavern opening.

Then the match blew out.

Blew out. Bush realized that the flame had been pulling toward the cavern opening. Drawn by a breeze, obviously. And a breeze had to mean that the cavern was connected to some kind of opening.

By feel he counted the matches remaining on the block. Most of a block. Good. He lit a second one and scooted himself a little farther into the passage, nearer the corpse. He looked into the opening, extending the match in. Hard to tell how deeply it penetrated, but the match flame was definitely drawn toward the opening.

He might try crawling back there in the darkness, feeling his way along and, if lucky, finding a guiding breeze to lead him toward the outside, but he'd much rather have a source of light. His matches wouldn't last long, however, if he used them in continuing succession. He needed a torch of some kind.

His own clothing was cold and sodden. But his long-deceased companion was dressed in dried, nearly crisp rags, and thanks to Sam's placement of the body in the protection of the cavern opening, very little of the snow that had fallen into the pit had gotten onto the corpse's rags.

Bush tore strips of cloth from the dead man's garments and tied these loosely around his wrist. Striking one more match, Bushrod examined the now-exposed legs and discovered that the right was devoid of flesh, nothing but brownish bone remaining. Bushrod shook out the match, reached down, and wrenched loose the thighbone of the left leg.

He wrapped a strip of cloth loosely around one end, leaving the ends of the cloth dangling. He struck fire to this and held the bone by its opposite end. The cloth burned readily and illuminated the cavern much more brightly than had the matches alone.

Bushrod crawled back into the passage, fearing that at any point it might narrow so much it wouldn't accommodate him. At places it did grow small, but on the whole it actually seemed to be enlarging the farther it went.

The first cloth strip was about burned out, so Bush paused to supplement it with a new one, wrapping it around. The flame rose again, and pulled hard in a forward direction. Bush grew encouraged. Even without the visual evidence of the flame, Bush could now faintly feel the draft. A cross-draft actually, indicating at least two openings other than the now-snowblocked one through which he'd entered.

Bush was dismayed for a few moments when he saw a

stone mass at the end of the passage, then realized when he got closer that it was merely a bend in the natural tunnel. The stone mass was the wall of the passage, curving around to face him.

Replenishing his torch as he went along, Bush discovered that the passage grew quite large, and the draft stronger. He experienced overwhelming relief and happiness. He would indeed find a way out. Life would go on. There would be grief and loss and pain, but there would be good, too. His wife, his children, grandchildren . . . himself.

The torch gusted and went out. An unusually strong burst of air, quite cold, had found it. Bush knelt and wrapped a new cloth around the end of the bone, but paused before striking another match.

It seemed he could catch a glint of light in the corner of his eye. Extremely dim, and maybe a trick of vision left from the flicker of the torch in his vision . . . but maybe authentic. When he looked directly at its seeming source, he couldn't see it, but when he gazed to the side of it, the light seemed to return, very faint and moving, rippling.

He lit the match and renewed his torch. Lifting it, he prepared to advance, the tunnel now so large as to allow him to stand nearly straight.

He stopped. The torch's light had caught a reflection on the floor. Stooping, Bushrod examined what he'd found, then picked it up.

A tinderbox, made of battered pewter. Bushrod turned it over. On the back were the initials "C.B." scratched into the metal, roughly, maybe by the head of a nail.

C.B. Conner Broadgrass.

Bush's happiness drained away in an instant.

He advanced, very cautious. The draft grew stronger, and the passage bigger. Before long, that vague flicker of light he'd seen revealed itself more strongly, now there beyond any doubt.

Bush's torch went out again, and this time he didn't even bother to relight it. It wasn't necessary. The passage turned again ahead of him, and reflecting back to him from its walls was firelight.

Bush halted and stared at the light flickering on the stone wall.

"Underhill!"

Bush closed his eyes and shook his head. The voice was that of Broadgrass, and came from the lighted area ahead.

"Underhill, is that you? I'm sure it is . . . who else could it be?"

"So you survived the fall, did you?" Bush answered.

"Indeed. But I didn't think *you* did! If I'd had an inkling, I'd have paused long enough to make sure you never wiggled a toe again. But I had some things on my mind at the time . . . like surviving. Getting out of that hole in the ground. You and me both were lucky not to be crushed alive, Underhill! If not for a fortuitous tumble under that rock, we would have been, you know."

"I suppose we should give thanks for our lives."

"Maybe I'll get around to that someday. But come on around. A couple of things here I want you to take a look at."

Bushrod, the expired thighbone torch still in hand, walked slowly toward the bend in the passage. When he rounded the turn, he was looking into the midst of a large natural chamber in which a big fire blazed, filling the space with light, the smoke rising and being pulled into a crack in the roof, obviously some sort of natural chimney.

Bruised, filthy, wet, clothing torn, face cut and bleeding, left arm hanging broken, Conner Broadgrass sat on a boulder in the middle of the chamber. At his feet were Arianna Winkle and a boy Bushrod didn't know, but whom he guessed at once to be Daniel Chase.

Bushrod's eyes locked with Arianna's. "Hello, young miss," he said. "You've grown a lot since I saw you last in Texas."

He could read her questions. His appearance here was surely an astounding mystery to her. But she asked nothing.

"Where'd you get the pistol?" Bushrod asked.

"The boy had it. Tried to use it, but it misfired on him. Loose flint. But I tightened it after I got it away from him. It'll fire next time."

"Your arm's broken."

"Believe me, that's not news to me. But I don't care that much. I'm very excited, really. Take a look."

Bush just then noticed the strongbox. It sat nearby, atop a leather bag with bank markings on it.

"I have to give these children credit," Broadgrass said. "They found the gold when all the rest of us couldn't. And they had the wisdom to hide it rather than turn it over, because Daniel here knew that when Mahaffery got the gold, he'd have everyone killed. Clever boy. He's even trapped rabbits and such for food."

"So what's your plan now?" Bushrod asked.

"I plan to keep my gold! All mine, now. As soon as possible, I'll take it down the mountain and very much enjoy spending it."

"And the rest of us?"

"I haven't quite decided."

"Don't play games, Broadgrass. You know you plan to kill us."

"Well, now that you mention it . . ."

"You coward. Let these children go and face me."

"Face you? What do you mean, face you?"

"I mean just that! Aim that pistol at me and shoot it, if you have the courage! Go ahead! Shoot me dead right here!"

Broadgrass laughed. "You're insane, old man. I told you I retightened the flint. It'll fire this time. I've seen this pistol fire before. It's the one the boy here used to kill Searl Mahaffery. Ross Romine, too. I have much admiration for this young fellow. Tough and clever, like I was."

Bushrod stepped toward Broadgrass, who started a little and began to rise. Broadgrass brandished the pistol at Arianna. "I'll kill her!"

"If you do, you'll be dead. You've got one shot, Broad-grass. If you use it, it had best be used on me. And it had best be effective."

Broadgrass was on his feet now, raising the pistol, his face going white.

"Move to the side, young ones," Bushrod directed, walk-ing toward Broadgrass.

Daniel and Arianna scrambled away. Broadgrass raised the pistol and thumbed back the lock. "Stop where you are!" he demanded.

Bushrod broke the thigh bone he carried, leaving in his grip a long, sharp splinter. He kept advancing.

Broadgrass fired the pistol. The crack of the shot was intolerably loud in the cave. Bushrod grunted and fell back a step. He looked down and saw blood running down his chest.

"Got me," he said, then began advancing again.

Broadgrass put out a hand to stop him, but Bushrod ducked him. Broadgrass cursed and was about to say some-thing, but Bushrod moved too fast for him. He jammed the sharp end of the splintered thighbone into Broadgrass's right eye, and shoved hard, penetrating deep into the brain.

Broadgrass shuddered and died, falling at Bushrod's feet.

Bushrod looked at the children. "Are you all right?"

"Yes," Daniel Chase replied, staring at Broadgrass's body.

"Good," Bushrod said. He closed his eyes and fell atop the man he'd just killed.

CHAPTER
THIRTY-SIX

Sam Underhill looked down at his father's face, tension building within him until he realized he'd been holding his breath. He let it out in a gust.

"Are you sure, Leora? He opened his eyes?"

"Yes," she said. "Just a flicker, but he did. Keep watch on him. I think he'll be waking up soon."

Sam held his breath again.

Bushrod Underhill awakened slowly. Sam grinned and wanted to weep all at the same time. When at last his father's eyes focused on his, Sam said, "Hello, Pap."

Bushrod's dry lips bent into a smile. "Gone to heaven together, me and my son. Good to see you here, Sam." He grew intense suddenly. "What about Zeke and Danny?"

"Pap, I'm afraid this ain't heaven, and you ain't dead. This is Texas Gulch."

Bushrod looked around, blinking fast. Tears appeared in his eyes. "Sam, I thought you'd burned up."

"We got out, Pap. With the help of somebody you'll want to see. Somebody that followed you all the way from Texas because they were worried about you."

"You mean—"

Cordell was there before Bushrod could finish. He bent over and gently embraced the old man, mindful of the wound in his upper left chest. Broadgrass's rifle ball had entered just enough to avoid striking Bush's heart, and had missed major blood vessels as well.

"Hello, Pap. I'm glad you're alive. Durham's here, too."

Bushrod greeted Durham differently than he had his other sons. "Hello, Durham," he said. "Son, I don't know what to say to you."

"Why wouldn't you?"

"You know why."

"It wasn't your fault, Pap. What happened with Zeke and Danny just . . . happened. I've never blamed you."

Bushrod looked away.

"It'll take you some time, maybe, to see things as they are," Durham said. "But take the time, Pap. Because I want you to stop holding yourself responsible for what was never your responsibility to start with."

"That's right, Pap," Cordell said. "No more running across the country in the dead of winter. You've worried Ma sick."

"Sick? Truly sick?"

"No. But she is mighty worried about you."

Bushrod closed his eyes and wept. "I suppose she must be."

"We're going to take you back to her as soon as you're well enough, Pap. And as soon as the weather clears."

"Sam . . ."

"Right here, Pap."

"How bad hurt am I?"

"I'm afraid it's going to take a lot more than that one little pistol ball to end the days of Bushrod Underhill. The ball's been dug out, by the way. That's one advantage of having a man as senseless as you were. You can dig on him without him feeling it."

"Arianna and the orphan boy . . . ?"

"Both alive. Both fine. Scared, cold, and with things to remember that will probably have them going through nightmares until long after they're grown . . . but they're alive. They credit you. If you hadn't killed Conner Broadgrass, they believe he would have killed them. And I think they're surely right.''

''So maybe I've atoned some for Danny and Zeke.''

''There's nothing to atone for there, but if you want to see it that way, then see it that way. By the way, if Daniel and Arianna owe you for their lives, you may owe them for yours. Arianna stayed with you in that cave, stopping the bleeding, while Daniel left, came all the way around to the pass, and down into Texas Gulch to take help to you.''

''So Daniel had found a third way in and out of the valley . . . through the cave.''

''That's right. And he had the good sense to hide the gold in that cave, knowing that if the outlaws got it, it would be the end for all of us.''

''The fire . . . how'd you get out?''

''Durham and Cordell arrived in time. They'd run across Copp Nolen out in the mountains . . . he'd sneaked away, at Leora's bidding, to try to find Arianna when she'd gone missing, looking for the gold. We'd have gotten out of the lodge house even if they hadn't shown up, though. Fat boy Mongold didn't do his job right. I suppose he was in a hurry to get away from the phantoms up in the pass who'd shot at him.''

''Cordell and Durham.''

''That's right. They'd talked to Copp Nolen by then, and knew what was happening here. They were determined not to let any of those outlaws have free passage out of this valley.''

Bush looked around. ''Where am I?''

''In my cabin,'' Sam said. ''Me and Ben Dillow's, God rest him. He gave up his life trying to save us. In the spring, when the snow melts, we'll seek his bones out there and try to give him a decent burial.''

''The woman who fell . . .''

''Marica. She's alive. Leora got her away in time to avoid being crushed in the snowfall. She has a broken ankle and a couple of cracked ribs, but other than that, she's fine.''

"What now, Sam?"

"What now? You rest, heal. All of us, I guess, have some resting and healing to do. And in the spring, we go back to Texas."

"We?"

"That's right. I'll not stay here any longer, Pap. I've somehow lost all the desire for gold."

"Gold . . . I know where there's plenty to be had."

"It's gone, Pap."

"Gone?"

"That's right. When nobody was paying attention, Daniel Chase threw it deep into a hole in that cave. Or so he says. It fell a long way, and there was a splash when it hit."

"Why did he do that?"

"He said it was blood gold. It had cost too many lives. He declared it wicked and decided to rid the world of it."

"Imagine that. A boy thinking so deep as that."

"He's a clever lad." Sam paused. "Maybe clever enough to think to hide that gold somewhere for himself."

"It's bank gold. It should be returned."

"Well, it's gone gold now. Whether Daniel tossed it down a hole or hid it, it's out of reach for us or the bank that lost it."

Bush closed his eyes. "I think I'll sleep now."

"Pap, is everything well with you?"

Bush smiled without opening his eyes. "I've found a son I thought dead, to be alive. I've found two other sons willing to follow a foolish old man all the way to California from Texas just because they were worried about him. I've been privileged to help bring an end to a hellish ordeal that never should have befallen a group of innocent people. And I've lived through it, when I was ready, truly ready, to die. I figure there must be a reason . . . more yet to come for Bushrod Underhill. So, yes . . . I think everything is well. Or will be. In time."

"Time, right now, is about all we've got," Sam said.

"It's all we need," Bushrod said. "I think I'm going to sleep now."

"You do that, Pap. I'm going to go build up the fire a little more. The snow's coming in again, harder than ever."

CAMERON JUDD
THE NEW VOICE OF THE OLD WEST

"Judd is a keen observer of the human heart as well as a fine action writer."
—Publishers Weekly

THE GLORY RIVER
Raised by a French-born Indian trader among the Cherokees and Creeks, Bushrod Underhill left the dark mountains of the American Southeast for the promise of the open frontier. But across the mighty Mississippi, a storm of violence awaited young Bushrod—and it would put his survival skills to the ultimate test...
0-312-96499-4___$5.99 U.S.___$7.99 Can.

SNOW SKY
Tudor Cochran has come to Snow Sky to find some answers about the suspicious young mining town. And what he finds is a gathering of enemies, strangers and conspirators who have all come together around one man's violent past—and deadly future.
0-312-96647-4___$5.99 U.S.___$7.99 Can.

CORRIGAN
He was young and green when he rode out from his family's Wyoming ranch, a boy sent to bring his wayward brother home to a dying father. Now, Tucker Corrigan was entering a range war. A beleaguered family, a powerful landowner, and Tucker's brother, Jack—a man seven years on the run—were all at the center of a deadly storm.
0-312-96615-6___$4.99 U.S.___$6.50 Can.